The
Country Doctor's Choice

MAGGIE BENNETT

Allison & Busby Limited
12 Fitzroy Mews
London W1T 6DW
www.allisonandbusby.com

First published in Great Britain by Allison & Busby in 2014.

A CIP catalogue record for this book is available from
the British Library.

First Edition

ISBN 978-0-7490-1601-2

Typeset in 12/17.2 pt Sabon by
Allison & Busby Ltd.

The paper used for this Allison & Busby publication
has been produced from trees that have been legally sourced
from well-managed and credibly certified forests.

Printed and bound by
CPI Group (UK) Ltd, Croydon, CR0 4YY

To my dear granddaughter
Scarlet Anne Margaret Bees

CHAPTER ONE

Autumn 1962

Dr Shelagh Hammond looked at her watch: three-fifteen. Councillor Ben Maynard's funeral was over, and the congregation was streaming out of St Matthew's church and crossing the road to the church hall where a substantial buffet was laid out on long tables.

'A good turnout,' commented Paul Sykes at her side, 'and quite a few from the hospital – look, there's that mousey little Sister Oates from Outpatients. What's *she* doing here?'

'Iris Oates sings in the choir at St Matthew's – and she's here for the same reason as we are. Ben was chairman of the hospital's League of Friends, and did a lot for us. I see Mr Fielding who operated on Ben is here.'

'Too bad it was unsuccessful. So, are we going over to the bunfight, darling?'

'I'm not, because I want to pop home and see Mother before going back to Maternity. But don't let that stop you from going, Paul. Actually, I'd better say a word or two to Phyllis Maynard first. Coming?'

'Righto, but I don't know the lady. I'll stand beside you looking suitably grave.'

Outside in the mellow October sunlight, Ben Maynard's widow was pale but composed, unlike her younger daughter, Marion, who was weeping silently while her husband kept an eye on their little boy and girl; the elder daughter, Jennifer, stood beside her mother, her husband at a discreet distance. As Shelagh opened her mouth to offer sympathy, the organist came forward, kissed Phyllis and offered his condolences.

'We'll *all* miss him, Phyllis, he was a remarkable man. Everham won't be the same without him. We're all thinking and praying for you and – Mrs Gifford and Mrs – er—' He nodded towards the daughters; he knew Jenny Gifford as a teacher at Everham Primary.

'Thank you, Mr North, and for taking time off to play the organ for us,' Phyllis responded with automatic politeness. 'Will you have to go back to school now?'

'No rush, I've left my deputy head in charge.' He caught sight of Shelagh waiting to speak. 'Good afternoon, Dr Hammond – I'm sorry for barging in. Ah, I see his reverence Mr Bolt over there, and I need a word with him, so I'll catch him now.'

He kissed Mrs Maynard again, and moved away.

'I can only echo what Mr North has just said, Phyllis, and – and so does Dr Sykes,' she said rather awkwardly, beckoning to Paul who came forward to shake the lady's hand. She nodded in acknowledgement.

'I remember seeing you at the hospital, doctor, when my Ben was in Male Surgical.'

'Yes, I'm Mr Fielding's registrar, Mrs Maynard.'

'Thank you for coming this afternoon. I know you all did what you could for him.'

'There must be many here who want to offer their condolences, Phyllis, so we'll make room for them,' said Shelagh, tactfully moving away.

'Shall I see you at the weekend, darling?' Paul asked in a low tone.

'I'm not sure, Paul, I'm rather worried about Mother. I may need to stay with her over the weekend.'

'Well, do try, because we'll soon have to close the caravan – it's getting chillier.'

'I'll let you know, Paul. I want to be with you just as much as ever, but – well, it depends. Bye for now.' She held up her face for his brief kiss – which did not go unnoticed by some eyes in the crowd – and made her way to the car park.

* * *

9

Shelagh and her mother lived in a neat mid-terrace house on Alexandra Road in the older part of Everham. Shelagh had grown up there, leaving to go to London University, from where she had returned, a qualified doctor, and had not left again. At Everham Park Hospital, greatly enlarged since its foundation as a war memorial after the First World War, and now a teaching hospital for nurses and midwives, she had completed six months as a house officer on both the surgical and medical wards, and had by now completed six months as houseman on the obstetrics and gynaecology team, which she enjoyed.

'Is that yeself, Shelagh?'

'Hallo, Mother!' She no longer used the name of Mum or Mummy. 'I'm on call tonight, so thought I'd pop in to see you. Shall I put the kettle on? No, don't get up, I'll do it, and you sit down!'

'Can ye not stay for half an hour, girl?'

''Fraid not. I went to Ben Maynard's funeral this afternoon, and can't take any more time off today.' In fact Shelagh's real reason for the quick visit was to check on her mother, who had been looking tired and pale lately.

Bridget Hammond crossed herself automatically at the mention of a funeral. She was an Irish immigrant who had come over to Liverpool before the war to train as a nurse, but having given birth to Shelagh, she had never gone back to her family in Donegal. Deserted by Jim Hammond, she had remained a strict Roman Catholic, and had supported herself and her daughter by working as a hospital domestic during the war and later as an auxiliary nurse at Everham Park. Arthritis had forced her to give up work early, and now at fifty she looked older, and treated Shelagh as if she were a schoolgirl instead of a professional woman of twenty-six, refusing to take any medical advice from her, on the grounds that she was in charge of her own health, and when necessary consulted old Dr McGuinness, the semi-retired senior partner of four general practitioners, her only authority on medical matters. He prescribed iron tablets and painkillers, and Bridget said that she needed no other treatment. Shelagh had tried and failed to get her mother to see an orthopaedic surgeon.

'So did they give Mr Maynard a good send-off, girl?'

'Yes, St Matthew's was packed. His wife looked strained, and the two daughters took part in the service, one reading the lesson and the other giving the eulogy.'

'God help the poor woman,' Bridget sighed. 'If it had been at Our Lady of Pity, now, I'd have asked ye to take me.'

Shelagh did not reply. It was an unresolved issue between them, that Shelagh no longer attended church regularly, and would only drive her mother the six miles to the Convent if she happened to be free on a Sunday – and for most of her free weekends during the summer, she had stayed with friends in the caravan at Netheredge on the other side of the Blackwater river. Bridget did not know that there was in fact only one friend, Paul Sykes, to whom Shelagh had been unofficially engaged since the spring. It plagued Shelagh's conscience from time to time, this telling of a downright lie to her mother, but she considered it the lesser of two evils; if she ever told Bridget the truth, there would be endless trouble, and their relationship perhaps permanently harmed. When she and Paul were free to announce their engagement and name a wedding day, that would be time enough to introduce him to her mother; meanwhile, she reasoned, she spared Bridget deep distress, and was immensely grateful to a kind Catholic couple who were willing to drive her mother to the 10 a.m. Mass every Sunday.

'You still look pale, Mother,' she said, pouring out tea for them both. 'I hope you're remembering to take your iron tablets.'

'I'll take anything Dr McGuinness orders for me, though they don't agree wid me, I'll take 'em for sure.'

'How do they disagree with you?'

'Nothin' you need know about, girl.'

'No, please, Mother, I've a right to know. Are you getting any sort of discharge? There was a bloodstain on the side of the toilet seat the other day.'

'I didn't mention anythin' to yeself, Shelagh, and I'll be seein' Dr McGuinness next week.' Her voice rose indignantly. 'And if ye think I'm goin' to take down my drawers for *you* to interfere wid me, ye can think again, me girl.'

Shelagh did not answer, but her heart gave a sudden lurch. She cursed herself for not being more alert to her mother's pallor and loss of weight – and the bloodstain in the lavatory. She would have to get her mother to attend Mr Kydd's gynae clinic as soon as possible. But *how*?

The insistent peep-peep-peep of Shelagh's bleeper could not be ignored, and she picked up the receiver of the nearest phone to dial the switchboard.

'Dr Hammond here.'

'Oh, Dr Hammond, there's a call for you from Antenatal,' said the switchboard operator. 'They sound urgent. I'll say you're on your way, shall I?'

'Thanks.' In less than a minute she had climbed the stairs two at a time rather than wait for the lift, and hurried along the upper corridor to the antenatal ward of the maternity department. Her eyes swept the twelve-bedded unit: a few patients were sitting in their beds or in armchairs. There was no sign of any emergency.

'They're down in the day room, doctor,' they chorused. 'We've been chucked out!'

She turned and sped along the corridor, past

the office, treatment room and kitchen, making for the day room where the new black-and-white television set was now switched off. A woman lay on the carpeted floor, and Shelagh recognised Mrs Jane Blake, a known epileptic. She appeared to be unconscious, and the rigidity of her face and staring eyes, plus the convulsive jerking of her limbs indicated that she was having an epileptic fit of the grand mal severity. Sister Dickenson and Staff Midwife Moffatt were kneeling on each side of her, and looked up when Shelagh hurried in.

'We've been bleeping you for ages, Dr Hammond,' said Tanya Dickenson. 'I've bleeped Dr McDowall.'

Shelagh's heart sank. Jane Blake's epilepsy was usually controlled by daily medication, but the complex hormonal changes of pregnancy had disrupted her equilibrium, and she had been brought into hospital where she could be closely observed. Brief petit mal fits were occurring almost daily, lasting only a few seconds; but this was a full-blown grand mal, a threat to both mother and unborn child.

'When did this one start, Sister?' asked Shelagh.

'Five or six minutes ago, she was watching the news and the other patients called out to us,' answered the efficient, newly appointed Sister Dickenson. 'I've managed to get a padded metal spatula between her teeth.'

'Can we get her over on to her side?' ventured Shelagh, and kneeling beside the patient's head, she placed her fingers firmly behind Jane's jaws in an attempt to open her mouth wider, but there was no response, and Jane's face and lips were turning unpleasantly blue.

'Be careful, Dr Hammond!' cried Staff Nurse Laurie Moffatt as the patient ground her teeth, and Shelagh involuntarily withdrew her hand in a moment of panic.

At that moment a firm, hurrying step was heard in the corridor, and into the room swept the tall figure of the medical registrar, Dr Leigh McDowall, his white coat flapping. Shelagh had met him on other occasions when pregnant mothers had medical conditions such as epilepsy, diabetes or asthma. She respected his skill, though his over-familiar manner was irritating.

'Hey, buck up, girls, don't just kneel there saying your prayers! What she needs is oxygen – send somebody to lug a cylinder up here *now*!'

'I've already sent for one,' said Tanya, and he nodded.

'Good girl.'

'Ought we to use tongue forceps?' asked Shelagh.

'No, we oughtn't, barbarous things. Let's get an airway in.' He produced a rubber airway from his pocket, and manoeuvring the metal spatula between Jane's teeth, he inserted it into her mouth and throat, then removed the spatula. As soon as the oxygen cylinder arrived, he placed a black rubber mask over her nose and mouth, sending a stream of pure oxygen into her lungs and thence to her blood vessels. Within thirty seconds the convulsions began to subside, her body relaxed, her eyelids fluttered and her skin began to turn a healthy pink. They all looked at each other with sighs of relief, and McDowall listened to the baby's heartbeat with his stethoscope.

'Hi, Jane,' he murmured softly as her eyes opened, though with no sign of awareness of her surroundings. 'Don't worry, m'dear, you're all right. We're going to take you back to your bed for a nice long sleep, OK?'

The auxiliary nurse who had brought the oxygen cylinder now appeared with a stretcher trolley, and McDowall lifted Jane bodily on to it, while Tanya and Laurie held her legs. She smiled at them in a bemused way, like someone waking up from a deep sleep, and when she was gently laid on her bed, Tanya put up the cot sides, clicking them into position.

McDowall turned to the midwives. 'Always keep the O_2 at hand, girls, wherever she goes – to the bathroom, the TV lounge or kissing her husband behind a screen, she needs to have it at hand, and the nipper needs it even more.'

Back in the ward office he picked up Jane's treatment chart. 'Give her a stat dose of phenytoin, a hundred milligrams, and up the daily dose to four hundred milligrams in all. We can't go any higher than that because of junior – and carry on with the phenobarbitone at night. I'll write it all up. Heigh-ho! Time for a reviving cup of tea all round, I'd say, don't you agree, Tanya?'

The auxiliary was sent to the kitchen to prepare a tray of tea, while McDowall continued, 'You know, girls, the old man had better get that girl delivered sooner rather than later.'

'That's just what we've been saying,' said Tanya, a slim ash-blonde, and Shelagh saw her cool, light-blue eyes appraising McDowall who returned her look, also taking in the attractions of Laurie Moffatt, plump and giggly. Nobody had addressed her, the doctor, and she stood a little way apart from them, her heart still thudding after the incident, and annoyed at herself for not showing as much initiative as Sister Dickenson in dealing with a serious epileptic fit, and being late to answer her bleep. Thankful as she was that McDowall had been summoned, and for his prompt action, she felt that she had appeared to be incompetent; she also disliked hearing the consultant obstetrician and gynaecologist, Mr Kydd, referred to as 'the old man', though she silently agreed that an early delivery for Mrs Blake was indicated.

McDowall suddenly turned round in his chair and addressed her over a mug of tea.

'Don't you agree, Dr Hammond? The poor little nipper won't take kindly to his mum flaking out and cutting off his oxygen supply – no fun for either of them.'

'Mr Kydd will take everything into consideration,' she said coolly, 'though the baby's not very big, even for thirty-six weeks.'

'And won't get any bigger if he's going to have *this* caper day after day, plus all this dope we're pumping into her – the little chap'll be stoned out of his mind.'

Tanya and Laurie giggled, but Shelagh felt her face flaming, cross with herself because this medical man was right, and had made her look silly in front of the midwives.

After the funeral Mrs Maynard's daughter Marion left with her husband and the children, and Jenny offered to stay overnight with her mother, but Phyllis Maynard told her to go back with Tim to their Everham home, and she would call them if she had any problems. She was at last able to discard the iron self-control that had kept her stony-faced and dry-eyed all day. Unutterably weary, she climbed the stairs to her bedroom, where she found Pumpkin, the old, long-haired grey cat curled up on Ben's side of the bed; she laid down beside him, and he began to purr a welcome. She buried her face in his thick, soft fur, her tears at last flowing unrestrained, wetting his fur; he made no attempt to move away, but regarded her with his wise feline eyes in the mysterious way that animals can show in times of trouble.

'Oh, Pumpkin, Pumpkin, you know, don't you,

poor old boy? He's gone away, and we'll never see him again.'

It was the only comforting moment in this dreadful day.

The Reverend Derek Bolt opened the door to Jeremy North, and showed him into his study.

'So what are your plans for expanding the choir, Jeremy?'

'I'd just like to do more with it, recruit more members, and maybe even sing at local venues, especially at Christmas – maybe a special choir I could train up, teach them a few new pieces, part-songs, soloists with a chorus backing, something a little more adventurous than the regular Sunday choir, though that would continue, of course, and hopefully improve.'

'Where would you rehearse – the church or the hall? And you'd need more than one rehearsal a week, surely, in addition to Thursday evenings?' Derek Bolt sounded doubtful.

'That and another evening – I'm pretty sure there'd be a good response, we've got some good voices to start with, and the word would be passed round.'

'There's Rebecca Coulter, she's a fine contralto,' said Derek, 'and that Miss Oates, she's got a sweet soprano voice, hasn't she? But she's a sister at Everham Park, so she wouldn't be able to attend all the evening rehearsals—'

'Actually, she's on Outpatients, so her hours are more regular than ward staff, and she'd be able to attend most of them,' said Jeremy casually. 'There's old Mr Wetherby, he doesn't always hit the right note, but he's loud, so useful *pour encourager les autres*.'

'And that chap who cycles here from North Camp, bit of a loner, and – er – likes to mingle with any boys – is he any good? And could he keep his hands to himself? I don't want to hear of any parental complaints!'

'Poor old Cyril, fancies himself as a tenor, but a bit whistly. No need to worry, there won't be many boys under the age of forty-five. What about that quiet little woman who attends just about every service held here, could she add a bit of a joyful noise if asked?'

Derek Bolt frowned. 'I dare say she would if you asked her, but be careful. She's a bit – er, neurotic, and inclined to get overemotional.'

'Really? She always seems as if butter wouldn't melt in her mouth.'

Ah, but you don't know her as I do, thought the vicar, and continued, 'There are those two stalwarts, Mrs Maynard and her friend Mrs Whittaker – and Phyllis's daughter Jennifer, what's her name, Gifford. She'd probably join with her mother, and if her husband's interested—'

'Poor Phyllis Maynard won't be up to it yet, though it might be good for her.'

'Give her time,' said the vicar. 'What about the music? Will you use the organ?'

'No, the Sunday-school piano will do fine.'

'It seems like a lot of extra work for you, Jeremy, you'll have to give up two evenings a week. Won't the family object?'

'Shouldn't imagine so. I'm not that necessary at home these days.'

'How are they all? Didn't your son get a job at the printworks?'

'Yes, and daughter Denise got a job at the coal merchant's, and they've both got their P45 cards.'

'Oh.' Derek heard the warning note not to enquire further. 'Well, you have my blessing to go ahead with your search for singers. You can put a bit in the newsletter and on the noticeboard. I'll say a bit from the pulpit if you like.'

'Thanks a lot, Derek, that'd be great.'

Driving home, Jeremy North smiled to himself. Hooray! Two evenings a week away from the chaos, teaching willing amateurs to sing, not that Iris will need much teaching, she's a natural. Nice little thing, must be thirty-something, wonder where she lives and with whom?

He turned into the drive of the large detached house with lighted windows gleaming through the October dusk: a house that had once been a happy family home.

* * *

21

'Ah, Shelagh my dear, how are you? Sit down, sit down,' invited Mr Kydd, who usually addressed her as Dr Hammond, but this was an informal interview. He waved her towards a comfortable armchair in his office, and smiled in a fatherly way.

'It's good of you to see me, sir—' she began, conscious of his sharp though kindly eyes peering over the top of his gold-rimmed half-moons.

'Not at all, my dear. I've thinking that we ought to have a little chat. Your work for the past six months has been quite splendid. I've been impressed by the way you have developed your skills, and I'd like to keep you on the team – but your next step should be to find a registrarship for a couple of years. I haven't in fact got a vacancy until next year, but in any case you should go somewhere else now, to widen your experience – see how they do things in Birmingham or Liverpool!' He beamed at her. 'I'd be delighted to give you an excellent reference, you know that.'

Shelagh hesitated. 'Thank you, sir, I appreciate that, but I have a particular reason for wanting to stay in Everham just now.'

The consultant frowned. 'Oh, you women! People accuse me of male chauvinism, but it's not my fault that so few women reach the top of our profession – you throw your careers away! Time enough to settle yourself in one place when you've got a husband and family to look after! I'm a firm believer that motherhood should take precedence over all other careers, and that rearing the next generation is of top priority – but you're young, intelligent and *free*, my dear girl. You've plenty of opportunity to advance yourself before you get tied down with a family. Why on earth should you stagnate in Everham just because some wretched man has decided to dig himself in and study for a fellowship, no doubt with an eye to stepping into Mr Fielding's shoes!'

Shelagh squirmed with embarrassment at his bluntness and accuracy.

'I have to advise you to move on, Shelagh,' he continued. 'Of course you're welcome to stay here if you really wish it, but you should go and find out some of these new ideas, like electric foetal monitoring with a sensor connected to the woman's abdomen – they're trying them out in some of the bigger medical training hospitals. Let your man wait a year or two, and he might appreciate you more!'

Furious with herself for blushing crimson, Shelagh said, 'It isn't only because of – of Dr Sykes, sir. There is another consideration.'

'Yes?'

'It's my mother, sir. I'm not too happy about her. She's a widow and we live in Everham so that I can keep an eye on her, which is convenient.'

'Go on. Why aren't you happy about her?'

'I suspect it's your – our department, sir. She's had a slight prolapse for years, and a tiresome discharge.

I noticed by chance a smear of blood in the toilet the other day—'

'Good God, woman! – and you call yourself a doctor?' he said with untypical vehemence. 'You've let your mother suffer for years, when all you had to do was bring her to my gynae clinic. I find it hard to believe, Shelagh.'

She closed her eyes momentarily, and put a hand up to cover her face. 'It's not that simple, Mr Kydd. You don't know her. She comes from an old-fashioned backwater in Donegal, I'm her only child, and we've never spoken of – of intimate matters. She can be very stubborn, and won't consult anybody but her old GP, and I suspect she doesn't even tell *him* everything. I think she might have a cervical erosion, in which case—'

'How old is your mother?' he interrupted.

'Nearly fifty-one, sir.'

'Now, listen to me, Shelagh. You are to bring Mrs Hammond to my gynae clinic at nine on Monday morning without fail – no, make it a quarter to, before we start – is that quite clear?'

'Yes, sir. Thank you.' Her eyes filled with helpless, shameful tears at his confirmation of her own suspicions; post-menopausal bleeding could mean uterine cancer.

'Whatever must you think of me?' she faltered.

'Oh, my dear, I understand, perhaps better than you think,' he said with a sigh of regret for some private memory. 'We don't always want to face facts when dealing with our own families, though we're quick to make pronouncements on strangers. I'll see her on Monday, and we'll get to the root of the trouble, whatever it is.'

'I'm very grateful to you, Mr Kydd,' she said simply.

'Glad to be of help, my dear. Now, as you want to stay on as houseman on obs and gynae, I'll get another contract drawn up for you with the management committee for a further six months. There's just one thing I should point out to you, Shelagh.' Was that a gleam of mischief behind the half-moons? 'You'll be senior houseman this time, and your junior will be Dr McDowall, who's senior to you in all other respects. An unusual situation, as you'll agree.'

'Dr McDowall?' Shelagh exclaimed in astonishment. 'But how – I mean he's a medical registrar!'

'Not permanently. He plans to go into general practice eventually, and feels he needs to recap on obs and gynae – so he's taking demotion for six months as a houseman. Very good man in his field, and will be an asset on the team, to deal with our diabetics and asthmas and epileptics – oh, and that reminds me, I intend to do a caesarean section on our Mrs Blake next week. It's one of those difficult questions, a choice of two evils. Would the baby stand a better chance inside its mother, or in the Special Care Baby

Unit? After a discussion with McDowall, I've come down on the side of the latter. Do you agree?'

'Yes, sir, I most certainly do,' she said, getting up from her chair and shaking the hand he held out to her.

'Good luck, my dear. Actually, I think our friend McDowall could learn a lot from you. And I'll see you in Outpatients with Mrs Hammond on Monday.'

CHAPTER TWO

'It's early days as yet, Phyllis,' said Mary Whittaker. 'Up to about six months you're allowed to break down and weep in the supermarket, but after that you have to buck up, or you become a bit of a bore. I know, I've been through it.'

Phyllis Maynard, who remembered when Tom Whittaker, a friend of Ben's on the town council, had died, appreciated her friend's frankness, but did not yet feel ready to face the world.

'People are very kind, Mary, and I get asked to coffee mornings and bring-and-buy sales, but to be quite honest I'm always tired, and I find company even lonelier than solitude.'

'Ah, you poor dear, take it from me, you *will* find that it starts to get better,' said Mary. 'Look, have you heard about this new Christmas choir that Jeremy North's getting together? He's such a nice, humorous man, isn't he, and so full of enthusiasm – why don't we both join, it will be good for us, and brighten up the winter evenings.'

'I'm dreading Christmas, Mary.'

'Oh, my dear, Christmas will come and go like it always does, and in the New Year you'll start to look ahead again. Come on, let's go and have a coffee at Edward's.'

Getting her mother to the clinic was not easy, and Shelagh needed all her forbearance. Bridget refused to hurry over breakfast, having resisted her daughter's help in producing an early morning specimen of urine into a plastic jug which Shelagh then poured into a small sterile labelled container. She then refused help in getting dressed in her clean, lavender-scented underwear – Directoire knickers and lisle stockings held up by suspenders dangling from a belt beneath her long woollen vest, and a petticoat. She must be the only woman in Everham who still wears such outdated undies, thought Shelagh; whoever would know that we're into the 1960s? She wondered where Bridget would shop when the old-fashioned ladies' outfitters in North Camp finally closed its Edwardian doors. When at last she helped her mother into the car, the two were scarcely on speaking terms, although Shelagh did her best to be patient.

The outpatients department was at the front of the building, and consisted of a series of examination rooms with a large waiting area in the middle. Shelagh was thankful for Bridget's early appointment, but Mr Kydd had not yet arrived. Sister Oates was there beside his consulting room, and invited them to sit down in the front row, though Shelagh felt self-conscious among the other early patients attending the gynae clinic.

'Dr Hammond!' said a voice close to them, 'and waiting to see Mr Kydd? Nothing serious, I hope?'

Dr McDowall in a pristine white coat stood before them, and Shelagh burnt with embarrassment.

'My mother is waiting to see Mr Kydd,' she said shortly, and before he could reply, Bridget Hammond broke in with, 'Who's this one, then? Is he the one who's goin' to meddle wid me?'

'No, Mother, this is somebody quite different. Mr Kydd will be here in a minute.'

'Pleased to meet you, Mrs Hammond,' said McDowall politely, holding out his hand which Bridget pointedly refused to shake. 'You'll like Mr Kydd, he's—'

'Ye can save the blarney, Dr Whoever-ye-are, I'm here against me own wishes entirely,' she interrupted. 'All I want is to get out o' this place!'

He glanced at Shelagh. 'Look, let me get you both a cup of tea from the WRVS stand over there.'

To Shelagh's relief she saw Mr Kydd arrive and go

into his examination room. Sister Oates beckoned to them.

'Come on, Mother, we're going in to see Mr Kydd now, so if you'll excuse us, Dr McDowall—'

But Bridget objected strongly to Shelagh's presence at the consultation. 'Holy Mother o' God, I won't have *you* standin' there watchin' me – your own mother, it's not decent! *This* tidy little body can come in,' she added, indicating Sister Oates who gave Shelagh an apologetic look.

'Perhaps you'd care to wait, Dr Hammond.'

McDowall turned down the corners of his mouth in a sympathetic grimace. 'Let's have that cup of tea now, shall we?'

'No, thank you, Dr McDowall, I'll wait for my mother. I'm sorry for the way she spoke to you, but I'm sure you have other duties to attend to. Good morning.'

He raised his eyebrows, shrugged and walked away.

It was dark when the Reverend Derek Bolt drove into his garage, not sorry to be done with the day's business. The meeting of the diocesan clergy had been dominated by the church's dire financial straits, and the best that they could hope for was that their Christmas Fairs or Fayres would bring in a thousand or two from the stalls, raffles, tombola, various competitions and for the children a visit to Santa in his grotto; Derek hoped that a better volunteer than old Mr Wetherby would come forward, willing to put on the red coat, white moustache and beard. With Daphne being a little temperamental at present with menopausal moods, he could not rely on her to bake and decorate the usual large Christmas cake for the raffle; perhaps Mrs Coulter would oblige, or Miss Oates – he couldn't ask Mrs Maynard, though in fact it might be good for her, give her something to do . . .

The light in the kitchen window beckoned invitingly. He pulled down the overhead garage door, and was about to lock it when – oh, *heck*. There was a tug at his arm and a breathless, urgent voice in his ear.

'Mr Bolt – Derek – will you listen, just for a minute, for the love of God!'

It was Beryl Johnson, again. He swung round, but her hand still clutched his arm. He took a sharp intake of breath. 'Now, Miss Johnson, you really must not – er – waylay me in this way.'

'You showed me kindness, you showed me pity at my mother's funeral. Can't you please show it to me again? Don't send me away, *please!*' Her voice rose, and he feared they might be overheard in the kitchen. He shook her hand off his arm.

'Stop this, Miss Johnson, stop it at once, do you hear? I only meant to comfort you at Mrs Johnson's funeral, nothing more. I'm a happily married man, and you must stop this *now*.'

'Only if you promise to come and see me, listen to me—'

'Of course I can't come to your house, you know that.'

'But you visited Mrs Maynard yesterday, I saw you. You stayed there half an hour.'

'You've been following me again. It's got to *stop*, I tell you.'

'Then let me meet you in the church, just for ten minutes, just to talk, only for a few minutes, it's not asking much, Derek!'

'Pull yourself together, Miss Johnson,' he said firmly. 'Look, I know you've suffered at losing your mother, but that was some weeks ago, and it's time to move on. Rejoin the land of the living, for heaven's sake.'

She stood there beside him in the dark, crying quietly, and he felt at a loss. She lived alone in the semi she had shared with old Mrs Johnson, and her only near relative, a brother, lived in Canada. He had come over for the funeral and to help Beryl sort out the various formalities that surround a death in the family, and had returned to Ontario. At the funeral Derek Bolt had put an arm around her and held her head against his chest for a moment, a public gesture seen by all present; and this is where that spontaneous moment of sympathy had led. He admitted to himself that he had a certain responsibility towards Beryl Johnson who was, after all, in his spiritual care by the nature of his office. And Christ would have been gentle with her. Poor woman, he thought. Poor, unhappy woman.

'I do feel for you, my dear—'

She stopped crying, and held her breath. He had called her his dear. His *dear*.

'Oh, thank you, Derek, thank you, God bless you, bless you!'

'Sssh! You must go home now.'

There was a pause, and she whispered, 'All right, as long as I know that you feel for me just a little, I'll do as you say.'

'Good girl.' It seemed the right thing to say, though she was over fifty. She was also in an emotional state, it was dark, and she had about a mile to walk, and two main roads to cross. Suppose a car or bus . . .

'I'll get the car out again and run you home. Only you must *never* do this again, do you understand?'

'Yes, I'll try. Thank you, Der—Mr Bolt,' she whispered.

He opened the garage, backed the car out, and she got in. He reminded her to fasten her safety belt, then drove her across Everham, pulling up outside the unlit semi in Angel Close. He reminded her to unfasten the belt, and leant across to open the passenger door. He did not get out to help her, but stayed where he was, with the engine running. Before she got out, she faced him.

'Let me kiss you.'

He let her kiss his cheek while he sat still as a statue, looking straight ahead.

'Good night, Miss Johnson.'

She got out of the car and walked slowly to her front door. He watched her unlock it and disappear inside. A light went on in the hall. He reproached himself for not once mentioning prayer; he should have told her to pray about her situation. And so should he.

'What was going on out there, Derek?' asked Daphne when he went in through the kitchen door. 'I heard you arrive and put the car away, but then you took it out again, said something to somebody and drove off. What happened?'

'Yes. Remembered I was out of—out of—'

'You don't have to tell me if you don't want me to know. I'm used to being the vicar's wife, the last person to be told anything.'

Poor Daphne, he thought guiltily. There were so many confidential matters that people told him, which he was not free to tell her or anybody. He should have just said that he'd had an urgent call and dealt with it as well as he could, as had happened on previous occasions. So why try to lie to her? He felt uneasily ashamed, and tried to apologise.

'You're wonderful, Daphne, being married to a "man of the cloth", and having to put up with his round-the-clock duties!' he said, kissing her and patting her bottom. She made no reply except to say that his supper was in the oven, and she hoped it was not too dry.

Shelagh managed to keep her emotion under control when Mr Kydd invited her into his office, indicated a chair and offered her coffee and biscuits. Such largesse warned her of unwelcome news.

'I see what you mean, Shelagh, your mother's quite a character, isn't she? Not the easiest patient to deal with! It must have been difficult to persuade her to come to my clinic, and I have to congratulate you on achieving it!'

He smiled, and Shelagh waited with bated breath for his verdict.

'I've told her that she needs an operation as soon as possible,' he said. 'I shall need to do a radical hysterectomy without delay – uterus, ovaries, tubes and any lymph glands in the area, a complete pelvic clearance.'

Shelagh gasped and put her hand to her mouth. She stared at the consultant, eyes wide.

'Yes, Mr Kydd,' she whispered.

'So, my dear, I'd like to admit her on Monday next, for surgery on Wednesday. We'll need to do the usual tests, and cross-match a couple of pints of blood. You know as well as I do what the prognosis is likely to be. I've left Mrs Hammond – she doesn't approve of first names! – a glimmer of hope, and I offer that glimmer to you, Shelagh. We'll follow the operation with a course of chemotherapy, and possible radium, depending on how she responds. It's going to be difficult for you, Shelagh, and we'll arrange for social services to visit and give some daily help when she's discharged. She says she doesn't want it, and I didn't waste my time arguing with her, because I feel pretty sure that she will change her mind after the op.' He drew a long breath and added, 'I'm so sorry, my dear. We'll all rally round on obs and gynae, you know that you are highly valued.'

She gave a wintry smile. 'Thank you, Mr Kydd, I appreciate your frankness.' She rose from her chair. 'I'll get my mother admitted on Monday.'

'Good. I'll speak to Sister Kelly on Gynae about a single room. We must provide the very best care for Dr Hammond's mother!'

'I'll encourage her as much as I can, Mr Kydd.'

'And I'll do my best for her, Shelagh,' he said as they shook hands.

'Mum! Oh, Mum, I've been dying to tell you for weeks, such wonderful news, but I had to wait to be really sure!' Jenny Gifford's excited voice came across the phone, and Phyllis Maynard immediately knew what she was about to hear.

'Go on, dear, what is it?' she asked, allowing Jenny the pleasure of breaking good news.

'It's *fifty-seven days*, Mum! I realised at Dad's

funeral that I'd missed a period, and put it down to the shock, but now I've missed *another*! Fifty-seven days since the first day of my last period – that's over eight weeks – I'm into the third month!'

'Jenny dear, that's wonderful news,' said Phyllis, tears springing to her eyes at hearing the joy in her daughter's voice. Jenny was now thirty-two and after four years of marriage there had been no news of a baby. All sorts of measures had been tried: the keeping of a daily temperature chart which was supposed to show a slight rise at the time of ovulation, in the middle of the monthly cycle. A lady gynaecologist had suggested that Jenny should obtain a specimen of her vaginal secretion at this time, and examine it for its elasticity, pulling it between two spoons and noting if it stretched into a long, jelly-like strand; if so, that was the right time to have intercourse. Tim had undergone many sperm counts, all of which had been normal.

'But it was that suggestion the science master made that's done the trick,' Jenny went on. 'The fact that elephants' testicles are within their bodies until the mating season, when they descend and can be seen, suggesting that they need a cooler environment to produce sperm – and it's worked!'

Phyllis suppressed a smile, remembering how Tim had sat in a cold bath with ice cubes floating around him to ensure coolness before intercourse. Poor Tim! She had been sceptical, but now it had appeared to have the desired results. A baby at last!

'It'll make all the difference to Christmas, Mum, our first without Dad – you'll be coming to us this year, and I'll come to church with you and belt out "Silent Night"!'

What a comfort she was, this elder daughter of hers, thought Phyllis gratefully. Living near each other as they did, a baby would be the centre of their world.

'Let's go shopping on Saturday, Mum – we'll have a look in Mothercare and see what they've got. Marion dressed her two in cosy little sleeping suits.'

'It's *much* too early to go shopping, dear, we'll have to be really sure,' warned Phyllis cautiously.

'But I *am* sure, Mum, I can feel it down here in my pelvis, it's *there*!'

Lord, let it be true, Phyllis prayed silently. Let them have their wish, *please*, let it be!

Saturday was chilly but fine, and Jenny appeared at the door early, ready to go 'window shopping' in Mothercare. There she and her mother looked at cots, clothes and little toys to dangle from the top of the cot or pram. In the maternity-wear section Jenny noticed a beautiful dress in midnight-blue velvet.

'Isn't it exquisite, Mum? I'm tempted to buy it now, before it gets sold. Yes, that's what I'll do.'

'I'll get it for you, dear,' said Phyllis, though the dress was quite expensive, and as she paid for it, she told herself silently that with the addition of a soft leather belt it would be a good dress for formal occasions if by any sad chance . . .

That was when Jenny caught sight of the bear.

'Mum! Just look at that gorgeous teddy bear, up on the shelf, see, the one with the red bow tie!'

Phyllis agreed that he was a handsome fellow with a smiley face, but—

Jenny was asking to see the bear, and took him from the assistant's hand. 'Feel him, Mum, he's so soft and cuddly – mmm!'

Like the dress, the bear was expensive, but Phyllis could not deny her daughter. The salesgirl put him into a Mothercare bag, which Jenny put into her own shopping bag, leaving his head sticking out above it.

'Definitely a case of love at first sight,' smiled the assistant as they turned to leave the store with their purchases. They ran straight into a notorious gossip as she was emerging from the hairdresser's.

'Oho!' she said at the sight of the bear. 'Isn't he *adorable*? Now I wonder who *he's* going to belong to!'

Phyllis started to say that it was early days yet, but Jenny's shining eyes were answer enough for the interested lady. 'So you've managed it at last – well done! Congratulations!'

'We're not saying anything yet,' said Phyllis hastily, but it was too late. Jenny Gifford's news would soon be all over Everham, and by Monday morning it had reached Everham Primary School.

'We're all so happy for you, Jenny,' chorused her colleagues in the staff room, and even the headmaster came to her classroom.

'Glad to hear your news, Mrs Gifford,' he said quietly, using the formal address in front of the children. 'And it will give your mother something to look forward to – good timing!'

'Thank you, Mr North,' she said, blushing happily, and he left the room with his unspoken thoughts: *trouble is, the little buggers grow up. I wish them better luck than we've had.*

Sister Kelly, buxom and bustling, showed Bridget Hammond into the single room on the gynaecological ward which was to be hers during her stay in hospital, with its en suite bathroom and toilet, moveable bed-table, locker and call-bell.

'All you have to do is press that, and a nurse will come to answer it, Mrs Hammond. Would you like a cup of tea or coffee now?'

When Shelagh went to see her mother at lunchtime, she was relieved to find Bridget clearly impressed.

'It's better than I expected, girl. Ye never told me it was like one o' them four-star hotels where grand folks go for their holidays!'

Shelagh smiled affectionately, looking down on the worn, blue-veined hands clasped together over her prayer book; her mother was very different from the suspicious, defiant woman of a week ago.

'Is there anything you'd like me to bring in for you, Mother? Lemon squash? A magazine? More tissues?'

'I'm fine, I've got me rosary and me missal, that's all I need. Ye're a good girl, Shelagh, and aren't you the fine lady doctor, in your white coat and your what's-it-called hangin' round your neck? It's like seein' ye for the first time.'

Shelagh had seldom heard such praise since childhood. She kissed the pale, papery cheek, and then went straight to the hospital chapel where she knelt and prayed earnestly for her mother – and for herself, that she might have sufficient courage and stamina to face the critical days following the operation.

Paul Sykes caught up with her in the doctors' mess. The dining room adjoined a smaller one called the smoking room, though smoking was beginning to be discouraged in the hospital. They were alone here, and he drew her towards him.

'Shelagh, you poor darling, I'm so sorry about your mother. Harry Kydd's not wasting any time, is he? She's in good hands – he's the best gynaecologist in the county.'

'I'm trying to be calm and sensible, Paul, but I won't have a minute's peace until the op's over. She's first on the list for Wednesday morning – oh, *Paul*!' She clung to him, unable to stop the tears from falling. He held her close against him, stroking her hair and whispering reassurances.

'I've got an idea, darling – we're both free tomorrow evening, aren't we?'

'Yes, it's the night before her operation, and I'll spend it with her.'

'Why not let me take you out to dinner?'

'Oh, no, Paul, my place will be beside my mother. It's terribly kind of you, but I couldn't. I'm sorry, but—' She wiped her eyes with the back of her hand.

'Actually, darling, it would be best for both of you. She needs the rest and you deserve a little treat, rather than sitting with her and going over the details of the op again. Trust me, it would be a good idea.'

Shelagh reluctantly but firmly repeated that she could not leave her mother, but thanked him for his kindness, and they kissed hastily as they heard the door open on medical staff arriving for lunch.

When Shelagh went to Bridget's room on the following morning, she found her full of praise for the staff.

'That nice Sister Kelly makes Irish lace the same as me mother used to,' she said, 'and I'll try me hand at it when I get out o' here. And that cheeky young feller who came to see me last night, talk about daft Mick, he was so funny!'

'What, a doctor?' asked Shelagh.

'Sure, what else could he have been, him with the white coat an' all? He was talkin' about me goin' for me op tomorrow.'

Shelagh supposed he had been the anaesthetist, visiting his pre-op patients, but she was grateful to him.

'This time tomorrow, Mother, it will all be over, and you'll be back here in your own room,' she said, smiling. 'I'll come in this evening to—'

'No, girl, don't come this evenin', Father Orlando's comin' over from Our Lady o' Pity to give me the Last Rites, so I want to be left in peace, before and after.'

'Oh, *Mother*! That won't be necessary, you'll get over the operation, and feel a new woman!' Shelagh remonstrated. 'Let me ask the Catholic chaplain to come and see you.'

'No, Shelagh, Father Orlando knows me, and he's bringin' me the Holy Sacrament, in case I don't come round,' Bridget insisted. 'Sister Kelly's fixed it up wid him for me. Besides, there's no sense in you and me sittin' and goin' over it again and again, is there?'

Shelagh noticed her unconscious repetition of Paul's words, and agreed that she would come to visit *after* the operation, on the following day. As she kissed her mother, she decided to phone Paul straight away and gladly accept his invitation.

'That's great news, darling,' he said. 'Your dear mum sounds a very sensible lady. I'll pick you up from home at half past six, all right? We'll go to the Mitre, that's a good way off, away from this place and all the tittle-tattlers, OK?'

'That sounds wonderful, Paul, I'll expect you at six-thirty,' she said, adding to herself, ready and waiting for you, my love. The anxiety over her mother had made her feel more strongly her need for Paul Sykes' love; she revelled in the comfort of it, even though the secrecy from her mother bothered her.

What to wear? She looked through her skirts, long and short, and decided on a soft wool dress in a paisley pattern. She swept her hair back into an elegant coil, secured with a silver clip. With long earrings and a necklace of semi-precious stones, she would look at her best, or nearly her best, she thought, applying a hint of blusher to her pale cheeks. A spray of the perfume Paul had given her completed her preparation and gave her confidence, even at this testing time, and although she longed for her mother's operation to be over, the thought of the Last Rites no longer seemed a matter of life or death, but rather a somewhat extreme caution on Bridget's part.

Seeing her standing at the door, Paul could only murmur, 'You look stunning, Shelagh, absolutely stunning,' and all her efforts seemed worthwhile.

On the drive through the dark Hampshire countryside, he enquired about her mother, and she longed to lay her head on his shoulder and confide her deepest fears to him, but this was to be his treat for her, and she merely replied that her mother seemed more relaxed and rested; closing her eyes momentarily, she saw again Bridget's calm face on

44

the pillows, her hands folded over her prayer book.

A few tables were already occupied at the Mitre when they arrived; Paul had booked a table near a curtained window, and helped her off with her navy fleece-lined jacket before pulling out a chair for her to sit down at the candlelit table. It was a perfect romantic setting, a handsome couple dining together.

'What will you drink, darling? We'd better order now while we're waiting to be served. Look, here's the menu – we must decide what we're having. I'm ready for my dinner, aren't you?'

Shelagh smiled, but to her dismay felt the beginnings of a headache which she would have to conceal. She realised how tired she was, how the events of this week had told on her, and secretly thought it would have been better for them to have spent the evening at her home, enjoying a light salad supper.

The waiter took orders for wine, white for Shelagh, red for Paul who put his hand over hers on the table. 'To tell you the truth, I almost called off this evening, darling, and settled for baked beans on toast at your place, only it seemed a cheek – and I know how much you want to get away from things, so I left it as we arranged.'

She could only smile to hide her disappointment at losing a quiet evening in, but only said, 'It's so good of you, Paul,' and raised her glass to clink against his.

'Here's to your mum, Shelagh – a happy outcome!'

When the waiter brought the halibut steak for

her and rump steak for him, they heard a woman's peal of laughter in the middle of the room. When Shelagh looked, she saw to her immense chagrin that the sound came from two girls and a man – Tanya Dickenson, Laurie Moffatt and Leigh McDowall. Paul saw them too.

'My God, that chap knows how to enjoy himself! He's bagged the two best-looking midwives – d'you think he's carrying on with them both?'

'I neither know nor care,' she answered, averting her gaze. What on earth would the trio think, to see her out with Paul on the evening before her mother's serious operation?

'Well, as long as they don't see us and come over,' she said, trying to speak lightly.

Paul rolled his eyes. 'Knowing him, he probably will, all nudge, nudge, wink, wink—'

Oh, no, I just couldn't bear it, thought Shelagh, hardly able to cut into the fish with parsley sauce, for which she had lost all appetite. And in front of that supercilious Sister Dickenson, it was just too awful.

'Please don't look in their direction, Paul.'

A roar of welcome went up from the threesome as a latecomer joined them, sitting down beside Laurie and kissing her apologetically. She smiled up at him, and Shelagh caught herself staring at them. So they were a foursome, with McDowall partnering Tanya who seemed to be returning his teasing banter with much amusement.

'Roger, old sport, so you've come to join us after all!' said McDowall. 'It's been hard work for me, keeping Laurie satisfied as well as Tanya!' More laughter.

'Do you recognise the late arrival?' asked Paul. 'I don't. Is he at Everham Park?'

'Sometimes,' muttered Shelagh. 'He's Roger Stedman, a freelance photographer, and comes to Maternity to take photos of the newborns. They're quite good, actually.'

Suddenly a sensation of utter weariness descended on her, and she could eat no more. She declined the dessert, and only accepted coffee because Paul ordered it. Her head swam, and the jolly foursome and all the other diners receded into a grey mist: she could not follow what Paul was saying, and longed only for the peace and privacy of her home and bed.

'Let's go, Paul. Please, let's go.'

'Darling, what's the matter? You've gone as white as a sheet.'

'I'm all right, except that I'm so tired, and it's going to be a long day tomorrow.'

'All right, I'll take you straight home. Here's your jacket, and I'll go and pay the bill. Wait for just a minute.'

She sat there taking deep breaths to clear her head and ward off nausea until he returned and took her arm to lead her out of the restaurant and to his red Saab in the car park. Little was said on the journey home, and when they reached Alexandra Road, he helped her out and escorted her to the front door.

'I'm so sorry, Paul. I shouldn't have come. I'll say goodnight here.'

'Goodnight, darling. I'm sorry too, but never mind. We should have settled for baked beans on toast after all! Get a good night's sleep, and you'll be better after your mum's had her op.'

They kissed briefly, and she went in and closed the door, utterly relieved to be home and alone. What a disaster of an evening, and what bad luck about McDowall and his friends. What on earth must they think of such an uncaring daughter? *Damnation.*

Paul drove back to the house in North Camp that he rented with two male medical colleagues and a laboratory technician. What a disaster of an evening. It had been a mistake, and any hopes he had cherished of extending it in the privacy of her little place for an hour or two were well and truly scuttled. *Bugger.*

CHAPTER THREE

Winter 1962–1963

'Caput apri defero
Reddens laudes Domino!'

The high, clear notes rose up in the still air of St
Matthew's church, to lose themselves in the dark
vaulted ceiling. On any other cold November evening
the place would have been silent and empty, but
tonight a single electric light beamed down on the
Sunday-school piano at which sat Jeremy North, his
long fingers on the keys as he accompanied the singer.

'You have the most beautiful voice, Iris – you
should have been a concert soloist,' he said when
the last echo had died away. 'They're going to have
to learn the "Boar's Head Carol", so as to sing the
refrain while you take the verses.'

Iris did not reply, but trembled inside her quilted

jacket and fur-trimmed hood. He had asked her to come ten minutes early, to try out the 'Boar's Head', and the time had passed all too quickly before the west door opened and in came the rest of them, gathering round the piano and taking their places on the circle of chairs placed around it.

'Good evening, all! Very pleased to see such a good turnout on a winter evening.'

There was a varied response of 'Good evening's; they were all clearly eager to begin rehearsing for the Christmas choir.

'I think most of us know each other, don't we? I can see a new lady over there – an old friend, if I'm not mistaken.'

'Yes, I've brought Mrs Phyllis Maynard with me,' said Mary Whittaker.

'Yes, Mr North, Mary persuaded me to come,' Phyllis said shyly.

'Welcome, Phyllis! We're all indebted to Mary for that,' he smiled. 'Mrs Rebecca Coulter we all know for her splendid contralto' – he nodded towards a large lady weighing about sixteen stone at least, who bowed in acknowledgement.

'Mr Wetherby we know, a faithful member of St Matthew's who will add volume to our efforts – that's him over there with the Father Christmas beard – and all the way from North Camp, Mr Pritchard – I don't know if you will be able to help us out, Cyril – we need more male voices, a strong tenor or baritone.'

A thin-faced man of about fifty-five replied in a thin, whistly voice that Mr North could certainly count on him as a tenor.

'I've carefully preserved my voice, Mr North, and would come over for any occasion if needed.'

'Thank you, Cyril, I knew you'd step in. And if any of you have ever been to Everham Park lately as an outpatient, the chances are that you'll have met Sister Oates who works in that department – only we know her as Iris, a soprano to die for.'

He gave her a grateful look, and she responded with a self-deprecating smile.

'Now, then. We must decide on what we're going to sing. We all know the good old roof-raisers, "While Shepherds Watched" and "Hark the Herald Angels", but I'd like you to learn something different, like the French carol "Patapan" and the "Boar's Head Carol", dating from sixteenth-century Oxford, when the students would bring in the boar's head, roasted and no doubt with an apple in its mouth, to set before their masters at the high table. It's a splendid tune, do any of you know it?' There was a general shaking of heads.

'Right! Iris, you sing the first verse, and I want everybody to listen carefully.

"The boar's head in hand bear I,
Bedecked with bays and rosemary,
And I pray you, my masters, be merry
Quot estis in convivio!"'

51

An appreciative murmur rippled over the group, and Jeremy responded with 'Encore! Let's make her sing it again, shall we?'

This time she sang the verse and the refrain, while Jeremy sat at the piano, joining with her in a fine strong baritone.

'Right! So now come on, my masters, all join in!'

Their varied voices rose up to the roof, with Iris and Jeremy, the nurse and the teacher, leading them into a vision of Christmas, of sparkling stars in the frosty night, of remembered mystery and magic, seen through childhood's eyes.

How could Iris *not* fall in love with such a master?

It was after nine when Jeremy North unlocked the front door. He had called at The Volunteer, Everham's oldest pub, on his way home from the church, so as to sit and listen again, in his head, to Iris Oates leading the little amateur choir in their rendering of the 'Boar's Head Carol', and how quickly they had learnt to sing it in two parts, and how good it had sounded. But it was time to go home.

He heard Fiona's voice coming from the kitchen, and from familiar experience he judged that her mood was not good. She and their younger daughter Catherine were seated at the kitchen table, Fiona's face flushed and angry, Catherine's flushed and tearful.

'Hi, there!' he said, picking up the kettle and filling it from the cold tap. 'Who's for a cuppa?'

'A lot of use *you've* been this evening, just when I need all the help and support I can get!' replied Fiona. 'I'm going to see that manageress at Gibson and Price, she's thoroughly upset Catherine. I'll tell her I'm going to report her to their head office!'

'Sounds bad,' said Jeremy, standing waiting for the kettle to boil. He thought of asking Cathy if she had a kiss for her old dad, but her red and swollen eyes warned him against it. Instead, he asked her what was the matter.

'Come on, chick, it can't be that bad. Was it because she found you having a quick snog with Kevin behind the sale-rail?'

'Don't be so damned insensitive!' Fiona broke in, while Catherine sobbed that Kevin had had nothing to do with what had happened.

'It was that so-called friend who let him down, and now the shits have taken him in for questioning!'

'The shits being the boys in blue, I take it?' asked Jeremy, pouring boiling water into the teapot.

Fiona turned on him. 'You think you're so clever, don't you, making fun of our daughter's trouble,' she said, and he realised that she too was on the verge of tears. He sighed.

'Here's your tea, girls. Sorry it's nothing stronger, but Roy must have been at the medicinal brandy. Any chance of some light refreshment at this late hour? Shall I do egg on toast for us?'

'Oh, do yourself a damned egg on toast,' snapped

Fiona. 'Here's me trying to comfort a distraught girl while you've been lording it over that all-important choir.'

He made a conscious effort to stay calm. 'What about Denise? Is she anywhere around to lend a hand? And our devoted son?'

'You can be so hurtful,' said his wife. 'No, Denise has gone out with that nice new boyfriend to see that film on at the Embassy, and Roy's out with that boy from the garage. Well, you can hardly blame them, there's not much to keep them at home, is there?'

'And Peter-poppet? Didn't Denise bath him before she went out? After all, he's her child.'

'I bathed the poor little chap and put him to bed,' said Fiona. 'Thank you for the help you gave me with that!'

'His mother should care for him, not you, Fiona. And what about you, Cathy?' he asked, not unkindly. 'Couldn't you help sometimes with your little nephew – or lend a hand in the kitchen?'

For answer Catherine put her hands over her ears and screamed at the top of her voice.

'*I want to get away! Away from Everham, away from everybody who bullies me!*'

Fiona drew the girl into her arms and stroked a soothing hand over her hair as she gradually calmed down. 'Sssh, sssh, come to Mummy, dear, don't take any notice of him, he's like that with all of us. Sssh, ssh.'

Jeremy opened his mouth, closed it again and left the room. Quietly he climbed the stairs and went into his grandson's room. The boy lay sleeping, and tears pricked Jeremy's eyes as he placed a light hand on the fair head. 'Peter-poppet, you poor little bastard, you're the only one in this place I really love. And the only one who loves me.'

An idea came into his head. He thought of his sister and brother-in-law who lived at Basingstoke. He had a happy relationship with them – the lucky buggers had no children – and he decided to ask them if Catherine could stay with them for a week or two, as she'd lost her job and needed a calmer atmosphere than she had at home. Just until things were more settled, he would beg, a chance to get away from Everham, and possibly to save Fiona from having a nervous breakdown.

And avoiding one for me, too, he thought to himself. Bloody hell, that would scuttle the Christmas choir before it had really got started.

'There are two new admissions to be clerked in on Antenatal, Dr Hammond,' said Staff Nurse Moffatt. 'One's having her third and getting weak contractions, so we've given her an enema and hot bath. The other one's a primigravida who's overdue, for OBE.'

'What's that, Order of the British Empire?' asked Dr McDowall who had followed Shelagh into the ward. 'I always want to laugh when I hear those initials – oil, bath and enema! And when you consider that it's *castor* oil, it sounds so barbarous.'

'No more barbarous than the ARM she'll have tomorrow if the OBE doesn't work,' replied Shelagh coolly.

'You mean artificial rupture of the membranes? You'll have to show me how.'

'Thank you, Laurie,' said Shelagh, ignoring him. 'Anybody in labour?'

'Yes, we've transferred a girl to Delivery Room One, she's about two centimetres dilated, and the other – the one I told you about – getting a few pains, but it's early yet, we'll wait and see.'

Shelagh nodded. 'OK, I'll have a word with them both.' I can carry on as long as I've got work to do, she thought, but part of her brain was constantly thinking about her mother in the operating theatre with Mr Kydd and Dr Rowan. What was happening? How far had they got?

'Dr Hammond, Dr Hammond, where are you?' called a student midwife from the ward office. 'Oh, there you are – phone call from Sister Kelly.' She handed the telephone to Shelagh.

'Hello, Sister Kelly. Dr Hammond here.'

'Are you free to come over and see your mother, doctor?'

'Yes, of course, Sister. Is she in the recovery room?'

'No, no, dear, she's back on the ward,' said the sister whose friendly informality was not a good sign.

Shelagh began to tremble, her knuckles white on the receiver.

'Back on the ward already? That was quick. How is she?'

'She's coming round from the anaesthetic, and asking for you, doctor. Are you free?'

'Yes, I'll come over straight away.'

Shelagh replaced the receiver and hurried over to the gynaecological ward, trying not to think, not to imagine . . .

Bridget Hammond was lying flat, with one pillow under her head. An intravenous infusion of glucose/ saline was in progress, and a urethral catheter drained slightly bloodstained urine into a glass bottle on the floor. Her hands travelled restlessly over the sheet, as if trying to find something. Shelagh took hold of her left hand and held it to her cheek.

'It's me, Mother, I'm here with you,' she whispered, and as Sister Kelly took the patient's blood pressure, Bridget's eyes flickered and turned to focus on Shelagh.

'Shelagh – daughter – forgive me.'

'It's all right, I'm with you, Mummy, don't try to talk.' She had not said *Mummy* since she was a child.

'I'm sorry, Shelagh – my little baby – forgive me, please forgive me.'

'Ssh, Mummy, everything's fine. I'm right here beside you,' murmured Shelagh in bewilderment.

'Forgive me, my – f-forgive . . .'

Her words tailed off and her eyes closed as a pain-relieving injection took effect.

'I'm sorry, doctor, it's just that she kept saying your name, and I thought the sight of you might calm her,' apologised Sister Kelly.

'Of course, Sister,' faltered Shelagh, her blue eyes brimming. 'But what does she mean? Why does she ask me to forgive her? It's I who should ask to be forgiven, for my carelessness, my lack of observation—'

The sister put a warning finger to her lips and glanced at the patient. Shelagh bowed her head and covered her face with her hands. Then she felt a tap on her shoulder, and turned to see Dr McDowall, who had followed her.

'All right, Dr Hammond,' he said, and taking her arm led her out of the room and along to the ward office.

'Why does she ask me to forgive her? What for? *Why?*'

'Patients get all sorts of funny ideas when they're recovering from an anaesthetic,' he replied. 'But never mind, leave her to sleep now, and Mr Kydd will have a word with you later.'

'But why is she back from theatre so soon?' she asked, though dreading the answer.

'Because the operation's over, Shelagh. Harry Kydd will speak to you when he's finished the list. Oh, hello, Sister Kelly, good timing. Can somebody organise tea for Dr Hammond?'

'But what's he – what's Mr Kydd going to tell me?' Shelagh asked, her eyes staring into his – where she read the truth without being told.

'It's inoperable!' she cried. 'Oh, my God!'

'Stop that, Dr Hammond, stop it at once, do you hear? You're going to have to be strong for her, she needs you to be brave. Look, Sister's bringing you some tea. Look after her, there's a dear,' he muttered to Sister Kelly, and left the office.

Shelagh washed her face in cold water, combed her hair back into a coil secured with a clip, and returned to Maternity.

When Mr Kydd spoke to her at midday in his office, her found her surprisingly calm as she received the news that she had already guessed.

'Your mum's a tough lady, Shelagh. There's considerable secondary spread, and the wonder is that she's kept going for so long – sheer obstinacy, I expect!' He attempted a half smile. 'You mustn't waste what time you have left in vain regrets, my dear, on the contrary, she'll need cheering and supporting. Happily, you're near at hand, and whether she stays in hospital or goes home, you've only to let me know your wishes. Is there a relative anywhere who could come to stay with you to help care for her?'

'I really don't know, sir. She's rather lost touch with her relatives in Ireland – there's an unmarried sister, and I'll write to her to ask how things stand, whether she or any other woman member of the family could come over.' Shelagh paused, and asked the question that doctors have been asked for time immemorial. 'How long, Mr Kydd?'

He shrugged. 'Who can say, Shelagh? Your guess is as good as mine – a month, perhaps, or maybe two or three. You know how impossible it is to predict in terminal—in cases like this. The main aim is to keep her as comfortable as we can. There'll be a bed for her here whenever she needs it.'

'Thank you, Mr Kydd.'

'I can't help feeling pleased that you'll be staying with us for a while,' he said with a smile. 'Our patients will always be giving us new problems to solve. By the way, I intend to take our Mrs Blake to theatre on Friday, and we'll be under orders from Dr McDowall regarding her medication for the epilepsy – but he'll be under *our* supervision as obstetric surgeons, so we'd better not fall out!' He chuckled. 'I think we're going to have a few disagreements before he's finished his course, but I'm confident that he'll find the "old man" and the senior houseman – I mean woman – rather more than he bargained for!'

It was impossible not to smile, and Shelagh was grateful. 'I'd better get back to Maternity, sir – I need to carry on as normal, and I can see my mother at any time of the day or night. Thank you again, Mr Kydd.'

'Good girl, Shelagh.' His smile and handshake hid the pity he felt for her.

* * *

Ever since Jennifer Gifford had excitedly reported that she had started getting morning sickness, Phyllis had begun to experience unexplained doubts about the pregnancy, and was not surprised when she received Jenny's frantic phone call before seven two days later.

'Oh, Mum, I'm losing blood – a *lot* of blood, it's pouring out – oh, Mum, what shall I *do*?'

'Get Tim to send for whoever's on call at the surgery, straight away, Jenny dear – and try to keep calm. I'll be with you as soon as I can.'

'Oh, this is the end!' wailed Jenny. 'I'm no use, no good, I'm barren – *barren*! Tim'll have to divorce me and marry a woman who can give him a child! It's not *his* fault, he's had all those blasted sperm counts and froze his testicles in that icy water – but it's *me*, I'm the culprit, I'll leave him for his own good, I'm a failure!'

And so she continued for the rest of the day. Tim took the morning off from work, but was unable to comfort her. He turned to his mother-in-law when he too shed tears, not so much for the disappointment as for his wife's desperation.

'I've told her again and again, Phyllis, I don't mind if we don't have kids, as long as I've got her – only she won't listen, and I'm at my wit's end. What can I do to make her see that I love her, and don't *want* another woman, not if she had twenty bloody kids – oh, Phyllis, don't ask me to put my trust in God. He's been a cruel bastard to my poor Jenny!'

'Ssh, ssh, Tim, that sort of talk will get you nowhere, though I can sympathise with how you must feel,' Phyllis told him, cradling his head on her shoulder, just as she'd tried to comfort her daughter. Their GP, Dr James had called and said he felt fairly sure that the bleeding was menstrual, and not an early miscarriage, but either way it made no difference, and all he could do was inject a strong sedative to calm Jenny for the time being, write out a sick note and advise rest and reassurance.

Except that there was no reassurance to be had. Marion and her husband had sent their sympathy, and cards arrived from Jenny's colleagues at Everham Primary. Jeremy North phoned to tell her to take as much time off as she needed, though he knew she would be badly missed as Christmas was looming up with all its concerts, plays and parties; it couldn't have come at a worse time, he thought gloomily. At least he had managed to despatch Catherine to her aunt and uncle at Basingstoke, and his sister had assured him that the poor girl could stay with them for as long as she liked – even over Christmas if that was what she wished. 'As you know, Jerry, we've been disappointed in our hopes of a family, and we're only too glad to help out with yours. The poor girl's only seventeen, isn't she?'

'Thanks, sis, it really is appreciated,' he told her, fervently hoping that Catherine would not drive them crazy within a week.

And there was the choir – and Iris Oates and her adoration. He was, after all, only a man, and how could he look at the light in her eyes and remain unmoved, untouched, untempted? Tempted to do what? He was a married man, a *very* married man and a father and grandfather; and Iris was a Miss, which could mean single or divorced, aged somewhere between thirty and thirty-five, about a decade younger than himself. A nice girl with a pleasant face, not beautiful, a decent figure, nothing out of the ordinary except for that sweet, clear soprano voice and the effect it had on him – and the effect he clearly had on her. She was a newcomer to Everham, but where she lived and who, if anybody, she lived with, he had no idea. Now, if after the next choir rehearsal he asked her out for a quiet drink and she accepted, he would soon learn the answers . . .

'There's a packet for you on the table, Derek,' said Daphne as the Revd Bolt came in at the end of an afternoon of pastoral counselling, visiting parishioners who needed to talk. 'All the other post is on your desk. I had to sign for it, recorded delivery.'

'Hi there, my favourite wife,' he said, hanging up his coat and taking off his clerical collar. 'How've you been today?'

'Oh, well enough,' she answered with a shrug.

'Just the usual dead-tiredness and can't concentrate on all the Christmas preparations, all the things a good clergy wife is supposed to do – preside over the Mothers' Union, and listen to the deadly dull minutes of the last meeting, decide who's to give the vote of thanks to a God-awful speaker, while missing the documentary on BBC2. Oh, my God, Derek, is there anything more depressing than a menopausal woman? I'm sorry.'

'Poor old girl,' he sympathised. 'The boys'll soon be home for Christmas, and they'll do you good. You'll buck up when they come hurtling through the door, with all their left-wing ideals and stories of university goings-on, all the ribaldry – ah, youth, youth!'

'Bless them,' she said with affection.

'Why don't you join Jerry North's Christmas choir? They're making amazing progress, and attracting a lot more members. I looked in on them the other evening, and thought what a magician he is. He could get music from a chorus of cats.'

'No thanks, Derek, not for me. I couldn't stand all the chatter. The woman in the bread shop told me that peculiar woman Beryl Johnson has just joined, you know, the one who lost her mother a while back, and was so hysterical at the funeral. It'd do her more good than it would me.'

Derek froze. He stared at the packet on the sideboard, a small, square box that had come by recorded delivery. He mustn't open it in front of Daphne. He scooped it up with the other mail and winked at her.

'Better get the office work done before supper, then we'll have a nice, quiet evening.'

'Aren't you going to open that?' she asked.

'Oh, it'll only be a sample of something we don't need from the diocesan office,' he said, and left the room before she could answer. In his stone-cold study – the central heating of the vicarage was kept to a minimum – he picked up the silver paperknife on the desk, and cut the brown paper to find his fears confirmed. It was a red box with a well-known jewellers' name engraved on it, and it contained a gold tiepin, with a single diamond in the centre, nestling on a black velvet lining.

There was also a letter, and his initial reaction was to tear it up unread, but caution dictated that he should check the contents in case there were any threats or indications as to what she might do if he ignored her. Taking it out of its envelope and holding it between thumb and forefinger as if it were a stinging insect, he shook it open.

'*Dear Reverend Bolt, dearest Derek,*' he read.

Forgive me, I have to write because I cannot speak to you as I would prefer. Derek, you are starving me. All I ask is a crumb from your table, a word, a note, a letter, a telephone call, anything, just to acknowledge me and sustain me from one day to the next. Wear the tiepin and let me see it!

Out of the question, he thought. How could the woman expect him to take such a risk, a clergyman, and a married man with a family? The letter continued as if answering him.

I understand your obligations to family life, but I swear to you that Mrs Bolt cannot possibly love you as I do, nor with a quarter of my devotion to you. Every hour of every day your beloved face is before me. At night upon my bed I meditate on you, I hold you in my arms, I feel your body's warmth as I go to sleep, and in the morning when I wake – oh, Derek, you are still there with me!

For heaven's sake, she's obsessed, she's mad, he thought, and what might she do? He groaned inwardly. I can't possibly wear the tiepin, which must have cost at least a hundred pounds, possibly two, and I'll have to keep it in the safe. Suppose Daphne – ought I to confide in Daphne in case she finds out? What a disaster. And there was more.

If you only knew how much I long – oh, how I long for a sight of you, those glimpses of you in church, praying that you will send one brief glance in my direction, a crumb, a scrap from your bounty, one Good Morning among the many you have to say to those who do not appreciate it. You even deny me a handshake, a touch freely given to all except the one who pleads with you, begs you—

A few more lines in the same vein ended with '*your constantly devoted Beryl who beseeches you for an answer.*'

Derek glanced at his watch: Daphne was preparing supper and would soon be calling him to the kitchen table where they ate informally when alone. What on earth was he to *do*? He screwed up the letter in his hand and shoved it and the jewellers' box into the wall safe where he kept St Matthew's petty cash. Damn the woman, he would no longer be able to look in on Jeremy North's Christmas choir rehearsals, not without awkwardness and embarrassment, with her hungry eyes following his every move.

He glanced through the rest of the post – two circulars from the council, three charity requests and a few more Christmas cards. No doubt there would be one from *her* among the many that poured through the letter box, hand-delivered. His stomach gave a lurch as he imagined Daphne picking up the mail.

In the darkness of the hospital car park, on the back

seat of Paul Sykes' car, Shelagh laid her dark head on his shoulder; he encircled her with his arms, whispering in her ear.

'Darling, you need a good rest, right away from this place. Ever since this worrying time with your mother I've been longing to be near you – but you've seemed so far away.'

'Oh, Paul, if you only knew how much I've longed for *you* – I need you more than ever,' she answered. 'But I can't see how or when we can be together, now that the caravan's closed for the winter.'

'I know, Shelagh, I know only too well how you feel,' he said softly, letting his right hand cup her left breast and kissing her. She clung tightly to him, as if to draw strength from his body into hers. He chuckled quietly.

'Listen, when we next both get a Saturday to Sunday night off, I'll drive us down to a nice little B & B just outside of Eastbourne, hidden away, "far from the madding crowd" – how does that sound?'

'Wonderful, Paul, as soon as we can. I've written to my mother's sister in Donegal, hoping she'll be able to come over and stay with her when she's discharged – and as soon as that's sorted, we can head for Eastbourne.'

She gave a long, deep sigh, and Paul's body reacted sharply to her nearness.

'God, I want to make love to you, Shelagh! I hate these behind-the-scenes capers – but we'll make up for it, darling, won't we? Kiss me – and again.'

'I'll have to go now, Paul. McDowall's covering for me, and I don't want to give him something else to joke about.'

'One last kiss, then. Mmmm . . .'

When Jane Blake was wheeled into the maternity theatre, Shelagh knew she would need all her concentration. She was to assist Mr Kydd, and they stood together at the washbasins, 'scrubbing up', after which they put on surgical gloves and thrust their arms into sterile green gowns tied at the back by Elise the auxiliary 'runner'. Dr Okoje the anaesthetist had already sent her to sleep with an injection of pentothal, and Dr McDowall was adjusting the flow of the intravenous drip containing a measured amount of her anti-epileptic medication; the paediatrician Dr Fisher waited beside a heated cot with oxygen and aspirator ready if needed. Sister Tanya Dickenson was setting out her trolley with bowls of sterile water, gauze swabs and the swivelling Mayo tray on which lay the instruments to be used first: knife blade, dissection forceps and artery clamp. Mr Blake sat just outside the theatre, wearing a green theatre gown, ready to see his baby as soon as it was born. So, reflected Shelagh, there were nine adults, including the parents, anxiously awaiting the arrival of a small premature baby into the world.

It took only a few minutes for the surgeon to sever

the layers of skin, muscle and the shiny uterine wall containing the baby in its warm, watery nest; and as Shelagh held back the abdominal retractors, Mr Kydd deftly removed and held up a tiny baby girl, pink and slippery, and although she was undersized, she gave a mewing cry as if protesting against being thus disturbed. Her little legs jerked and her fists clenched as Shelagh clamped and cut the umbilical cord and handed her to Dr Fisher. Everybody in the theatre exhaled after a tense quarter of an hour.

'She seems to be in pretty good shape,' remarked Dr Fisher.

'At nine-seventeen precisely,' noted Shelagh.

'Weight one point seven kilograms,' added Fisher, and carried her out of the theatre, where her father stepped forward eagerly.

'Hallo, Dad, I'm a girl!' said Fisher as Blake gazed in awe.

'What a little peach!' he said shakily, but Fisher did not linger; he carried the baby away to the Special Care Baby Unit, where she would be placed in an incubator and assessed.

Mr Kydd, having done his vital work, left the suturing to Shelagh, while McDowall stayed at the mother's side, doing his own observations of her condition. They worked in silence until at a quarter to ten Shelagh placed an adhesive dressing over the line of stitches, wiped her forehead, and pulled off her gloves, mask and theatre cap. This, then, was her life as a doctor, she thought, her personal satisfaction at a time of personal sadness. She and her mother had grown much closer over the past week, and Bridget had said for the first time that she was proud of her daughter, for which Shelagh gave thanks that it had been said before it was too late, and would always be remembered.

Leigh McDowall touched her shoulder. 'Your mum's doing well, Shelagh.'

'What? Oh, er, yes, much as would be expected,' she said. 'I'm hoping that a sister of hers will be able to come over from Ireland to look after her when she's discharged.'

'Ah, that'd be ideal. She's quite a character, is your mum.'

A sudden thought struck her. 'Was it *you* who went to see her on Monday afternoon? I thought it must have been the anaesthetist, but obviously not Dr Okoje. Whoever he was, he talked a lot of nonsense, she said.'

'Is that what she said? And there was I, thinking she'd taken a fancy to me. Cruel world!'

It was impossible not to smile through her irritation. 'I see what my mother meant about the nonsense – but you certainly made her laugh.'

'It's the way they sing the refrain to "Patapan",' Jeremy North told Derek Bolt. 'The choir sings the verses, representing the children playing, and at the end of each verse old Mr Wetherby quavers up on a rising scale, "*Too-ra-loo-ra-LOO!*" followed by Cyril with a face like a hanging judge singing, or rather whistling on another rising scale, "*Pat-a-pat-a-PAN!*" It's hilarious, and sooner or later we're all going to collapse with laughter at the poor old chaps.'

It was time for rehearsal again, and Jeremy greeted his enlarged choir, noticing that poor soul Beryl Johnson, looking anxious as usual; perhaps she'll be as entertained as the rest of us are by the duo, he thought. He looked at Iris and gave her a broad wink, at which she held a finger to her lips; *don't laugh*. It was a silent exchange between them.

At the end of the rehearsal he glanced at Iris and tentatively offered a lift to any ladies going home. It was answered by a grateful 'yes, please!' from Rebecca Coulter who pushed herself forward with Phyllis Maynard and Mary Whittaker.

'Between us we'll fill his car,' she said, and it was only too true. The quiet drink with Iris would have to wait until next week.

'I'm not too happy about that poor Pendle kid,' said Leigh McDowall in the antenatal ward office.

'Trish Pendle with the toxaemia? Yes, she hasn't got much going for her, has she?' Shelagh replied. 'Only seventeen, illegitimate herself, deserted by her boyfriend, the usual story. It's hardly surprising that she gave in to the first boy who showed her any attention.'

Sister Dickenson interrupted sharply. 'That girl would do better to stay in bed instead of always hopping off to the day room for an illicit smoke. She's such a *silly* girl, says she can't eat the food here, and gets a girlfriend to bring her in a bag of soggy chips every evening. It's no wonder she's so overweight!'

'I'll try having a talk with her,' said Shelagh. 'And we'll get the dietician up to see her and discuss her likes and dislikes. Meanwhile I'll write her up for multivitamins and iron.'

Tanya sniffed, and continued speaking to McDowall. 'Her blood pressure's creeping up, Leigh, one hundred and forty-five over ninety-five, and one plus of protein in her urine. What she needs is a twice daily dose of methyldopa to slow her down, keep her in bed and control her blood pressure.'

'I'll speak to Mr Kydd tomorrow,' said Shelagh briefly, irritated by the sister's self-assumed role of diagnostician and prescriber of medicine.

'And let's get an intravenous pyelogram done before the old man's ward round on Thursday,' added McDowall. 'Can you book one for tomorrow morning, Tanya?'

'An IVP? – when we try to avoid X-raying pregnant women?' Shelagh queried.

'Do you want me to try to get one done tomorrow, Leigh?' asked Tanya, ignoring her. 'If we say it's urgent, they'll probably fit her in.'

'Yeah, speak to them in your most seductive tones, Tanya,' he grinned.

'Whatever for? There aren't any signs of renal failure,' objected Shelagh.

'I think there may be more to Trish's problems than meets the eye,' he said thoughtfully. 'Just a hunch. Put her on four-hourly temperature as well as blood pressure, and a fluid balance chart. We'll see if anything comes up. All right by you, Dr Hammond?'

She nodded assent, hardly able to contradict a medical registrar, and she knew that Mr Kydd respected his opinions. But the smile exchanged between him and Tanya infuriated her.

'Good. Then I'll go over to Gynae,' she said, and as she walked away she could hear them conversing in low, intimate tones. Such damned lovebirds were no asset on the team!

On Gynaecology her mother had wonderful news. 'Shelagh – oh, Shelagh me girl, wait till I tell ye! I've had a letter sent here from me sister Maura, and what d'ye think she says? She's comin' over to stay for a bit – isn't that grand? Just till I get back on me feet, like. It'll save ye a lot o' worry, Shelagh, bein' as busy as ye are!'

Shelagh was moved to see how her mother's pale cheeks flushed with pleasure at the prospect of seeing her sister again and being reunited after so long. At least *some* good had come out of this sad situation.

* * *

'I've just got to show you this cutting from the *Daily Mail*, Phyllis,' said Mary Whittaker over coffee. She took from her handbag a full-page story headed *Our Little Princess*, which showed a fortyish couple looking fondly upon a little girl of about four, holding a pet rabbit.

'This couple suffered disappointment year after year, Phyllis, and then they saw a documentary on TV about the number of children in care due to neglect – alcoholic parents, fathers in prison, all kinds of social deprivation – and there was a social worker looking for couples wanting to adopt or foster with a view to adoption. This middle-aged couple agreed to enquire further, and look, they've got this little girl, they've called her Sally, and they're *so* happy – look at the picture, isn't she a little sweetie? Phyllis, call me an interfering old busybody, but my dear, this is what your Jenny and Tim should do, give a good home to a child who needs one.'

'I'd never call you an interfering busybody, Mary, but – Tim's parents are dead against adoption. They say you don't know what you're getting, and they don't think they could ever love a child that wasn't Tim's actual son or daughter,' said Phyllis sadly.

'Listen, I'm sorry about Tim's parents, but they have no right whatsoever to inflict their opinions on a young couple like your Jenny and Tim,' said Mary Whittaker firmly. 'As for not knowing what you're getting, do *any* of us know how our children are going to turn out? Look at poor Jeremy North and *their* three – the elder girl has presented them with a fatherless child, the boy – or rather man – has been thrown out by his wife for drinking, so he doesn't see his child at all, and I hear the younger girl has become so out of control that Jeremy's sent her to stay with his sister and brother-in-law, just to get her out of Everham for a bit. No, Phyllis, you show this to Jenny, make her read it, and talk it over with Tim.'

Phyllis read the article through twice, and gazed at the photo of the little girl with her pet rabbit. Tears came to her eyes at the thought of unloved, neglected children when Jenny had so much love to give. The continuing disappointments of the Giffords was becoming a threat to their marriage, as Jenny no longer wanted to have sex because she said 'it didn't work'.

Phyllis Maynard's mouth set in a determined line. The 'little princess' was like a message of hope at a time of despair, and she resolved to do everything in her power to persuade Jenny and Tim that this was the answer to hitherto unanswered prayers.

CHAPTER FOUR

Trish Pendle's IVP report came back with a red star, indicating that urgent action was needed. Shelagh stood in the antenatal ward office and read it with consternation.

Left kidney small, poorly outlined, appears to be non-functioning, suggestive of congenital abnormality or chronic pyelonephritis. Right kidney shows moderate hydro-nephrosis due to reflux.

So McDowall's hunch had been right. The girl had a chronic kidney condition, possibly from before birth, and the 'good' kidney had to do the work of two. So far it had managed, but the additional strain of pregnancy, aggravated by a poor diet, was proving to be too great a burden, and it was beginning to show signs of pressure, and a backward flow of urine. The warning signs of rising blood-pressure, swollen legs and protein in the urine had been diagnosed as toxaemia of pregnancy, a fairly common condition, and not to be ruled out as additional to the kidney dysfunction. The newly begun fluid chart corresponded with the finding of the IVP, and Shelagh went straight to find Trish and ask her to get into bed for an examination.

'Just sit up for me, Trish,' she said, pressing the palm of her hand over the girl's left loin, in the region of the faulty kidney. 'Now, does it hurt here, my dear?'

'Yeah, a bit. I been tellin' 'em it aches round there, but they don't take no notice, they just say it's 'cos o' the baby.'

'And here, Trish?' Shelagh placed her hand over the right kidney, and Trish shouted, 'Yeah, that's sore – *ouch!* – Bloody hell!'

Shelagh was concerned. Tenderness over the right loin indicated that the back-pressure was causing some inflammation of the 'good' kidney, already overloaded with work.

''Ere, 'ave yer 'eard anything about that whatsit I 'ad yesterday?' Trish demanded.

'Yes, dear, and it does look as if you might have some kidney trouble,' Shelagh answered with the calm, matter-of-fact manner she used when imparting unwelcome news.

'What are they goin' to do about it, then? Any chance o' Dr Kydd startin' me off early?'

'I really couldn't say right now, Trish. We'll have to wait and see what Mr Kydd says on his ward round tomorrow,' Shelagh temporised. 'Meanwhile we'll get some blood tests done. Don't worry about it, dear, you're in the best place – though I believe you're having some problems with the food in here, so Sister says.'

'Yeah, it's muck – makes me feel sick.'

By the time Shelagh had finished trying to advise Trish about the importance of a healthy diet, it was visiting time, and Trish's scruffy girlfriend's arrival cut her short, though it was interesting to overhear the girls' comments to each other.

'Who's she, then Trish? Is she any better than the others?'

'She's not bad, at least she listens to yer, 'stead o' dronin' on about toxaemia an' stuff, so's yer can't make out what they're on about.'

Over in the doctors' mess, Shelagh found Paul Sykes drinking a solitary cup of coffee, so took a small cheese salad and went to join him.

'You look whacked out, darling,' he told her. 'What we both need is a night in that cosy little place at Eastbourne. How soon d'you think you'll be free?'

'Mother's being discharged on Thursday, and my Aunt Maura will be arriving tomorrow to stay with us – so perhaps next time we're both off at a weekend . . . we'll enjoy it all the more because of the wait, Paul!'

'Seems like years,' he said dolefully. 'How long is Auntie staying?'

'As long as she's needed, and that means – until my – you know,' she said bleakly, and he was immediately apologetic.

'Oh, darling, what a stupid question, I'm so sorry.' He put his hand over hers on the table. 'That'll mean over Christmas, I suppose.'

'How do I know? How do any of us know, Paul?'

As usual there was a pile of post on the hall table, and Derek Bolt's quick glance went straight to the backward sloping handwriting on the blue envelope. He picked it up at once and put it in his pocket. Daphne was in the living room watching television, and heard him come in.

'Derek, who *is* the person who keeps sending you these letters on posh paper? It looks like a female hand. Is it something to do with that Christmas choir of Jeremy North's?'

'No, just a poor soul I've been visiting, grieving for her mother and going through a phase of doubt. Let's get this stuff out of the way,' he said, sweeping up the rest of the post and taking it to his study, so that she would not notice the absence of the blue envelope. He went through to the kitchen and plugged in the kettle. 'I'm ready for a cuppa, aren't you?'

'Doubt? What sort of doubt? Has she lost her faith, d'you mean?'

'Oh, it's quite understandable when somebody loses the person closest to them – they feel that either God has deserted them, or doesn't exist at all. I try to give such reassurance as I can, but the words can sound a little hollow, even to me, when dealing with bereavement.'

Hollow indeed, you lying cleric, he told himself, and changed the subject to the date of the boys' homecoming. 'Will they be here by the Sunday before Christmas? Or are they staying on for the usual dinners and parties and pantomimes at Uni, and dashing home on Christmas Eve?'

'How should I know? I've written to say we're expecting them by the twentieth at least.'

Derek fervently hoped she would not be disappointed; her enjoyment of Christmas depended very much on the presence of Philip and Mark. Later, reading the unwelcome letter in the privacy of his study, heated by a one-bar electric fire, he experienced again the familiar mix of pity and exasperation.

Dear Reverend Bolt, dearest Derek,
My happiness, perhaps my sanity, waits upon
your pity, your kindness to me. All I ask for
is a note, however brief, a word of Christian
friendship to show that you understand the
plight I am in, longing for a drop of water

in the desert, a crust of bread to one who is starving. Whatever your responsibilities to your family, you cannot deny your duty as a priest to one of your parishioners, a sheep of your flock. If this plea from my heart cannot touch yours, you condemn me to despair, and you will be answerable to God for your cruelty.

Please, please, Derek, light of my life, send me a note to say that you care what becomes of me. Surely you cannot deny that much to a fellow human being . . .

He could read no more. What in God's name should he *do*? He had tried praying for guidance, but there had been no definite answer. Of course he could not possibly arrange to meet her anywhere – should he send a firm letter, suggesting that *she* should pray about it? Of course he pitied her as one of the flock entrusted to him by God, but he could not help her.

'*Blessed Lord Jesus, show me what thou wouldst have me do for this unhappy woman.*' He frequently found himself using the English of the Book of Common Prayer when dealing with a problem, and the words in themselves were consoling.

'You were right about Trish Pendle,' Shelagh admitted to Leigh McDowall when she met him in the corridor that connected the antenatal and post-natal wards.

He shook his head gravely. 'The poor kid will need to be thoroughly investigated after delivery, but we can do a full blood profile now for electrolytes, creatinine clearance and so on – and watch out for bugs in the urine.'

She nodded. 'I've sent the requests to the lab.'

'Good. D'you think the old man will go for an early delivery?'

'An early Caesarean section, I'd guess, to save her pushing,' she said. 'Her condition's only going to worsen as long as she's pregnant, isn't it?'

He sighed. 'Oh, it just isn't fair, Shelagh, that poor kid. Whatever kind of future has she got, if any? And the poor little beggar inside her, who's going to take *him* on, or her? She hasn't got a home for him, only a council flat with an alcoholic mother.'

'It'll be a case for the social workers to sort out,' said Shelagh. 'Foster care, most likely, while they wait to see how things go.'

'Wish I could meet the father of that poor little bastard – he wouldn't father any more!'

'Then you'd be had up for grievous bodily harm! Nobody ever *does* find out who's taken up one of these unlucky girls, get her drunk and then taken advantage of her. By the way, Dr McDowall, you're on call tonight, aren't you?'

'Yes, but I can take a couple of hours off this afternoon – to keep an appointment with a very special lady!' He gave a knowing wink, for they both knew that Tanya Dickenson had a half day.

'Enjoy yourselves,' she said coolly, putting away Trish Pendle's case notes in the file.

Miss Maura Carlin was scarcely able to hide her dismay when she saw her elder sister's fragile appearance; the two of them clung together on their first meeting after nearly thirty years.

'Sure, Bridie, none of us ever understood why ye upped and left us to marry that sailor feller, him that none of us ever saw,' she said, smoothing back her sister's white hair and looking reproachfully into the faded blue eyes. 'Well, they'll just have to manage widout me at home for a bit, so they will. I'm here to look after ye and little Shelagh until ye're better!'

The bustling Irish spinster was as good as her word, and Shelagh was filled with relief and gratitude towards an aunt she had never met. On her part Maura was open-mouthed when she saw that her little niece had become an efficient, attractive doctor.

'But why didn't ye write to me before, Shelagh?' she asked. 'How could ye let your mother face such an operation widout lettin' her family know?'

Bridget begged her not to blame Shelagh but herself, likewise for all the years without making contact.

'But never mind, I'm here now, and here I'm goin' to stay!' declared Maura, before they were interrupted by the arrival of a visitor.

'Bless yer, Dr Leigh!' cried Bridget. 'Meet me sister Maura!'

'Hello, Maura, pleased to meet you. I just bobbed in to ask how you're doing, Bridget, but I needn't have worried, you're looking fine! Let me explain, Maura. Bridget's my sweetheart, or at least I thought she was, but she won't give me any encouragement, says I'm too old for her – what a cruel world!'

Amid the laughter, Maura brewed a pot of tea and found some biscuits in a tin.

Shelagh felt a little awkward at such familiarity. 'Good heavens, Dr McDowall, what are you doing here?'

'Why, don't you remember, Dr Hammond, I told you I had a rendezvous with a very special lady? Thanks, Auntie Maura, I'll have another. Cheers!'

Shelagh was both baffled and annoyed. What on earth was he up to, going behind her back to ingratiate himself with her mother?

'I can't stay long, Mother, I only wanted to see how you are, and Aunt Maura. It looks as if I needn't have worried. Bye!'

Mr Kydd's decision to perform an elective Caesarean section of Trish Pendle resulted in the arrival of a small but healthy boy whom his young mother called Donovan. He was taken to the Special Care Baby Unit for assessment of his prematurity, and from there transferred to the care of a foster mother by the social worker under whose care Trish had been for several months. Trish herself was transferred two days later to Women's Surgical for a battery of kidney tests, prior to possible removal of the non-functioning kidney.

'My God, Shelagh, what a lump that Pendle girl is!' groaned Paul Sykes over lunch in the doctors' mess. 'Overweight, unintelligent and adding to the housing problems by producing a kid that she can't look after. I ask you, what can be done with creatures like that? There's something to be said for compulsory sterilisation, and I know you won't agree with that, but quite frankly it's my gut reaction.'

Shelagh was a little chilled by his words, though she knew that there were many who would agree with his argument. She paused before replying.

'In her case there might be no need for sterilisation anyway, Paul. With her serious kidney condition, she's not likely to become pregnant again, in fact she might not even survive. Let's just hope that little Donovan finds somebody to love him.'

'God, Shelagh, you make me feel such an ogre,' he protested. 'I'm just as concerned as you are for the little chap's future.'

The dark December days passed by, and Doctor Hammond was presiding at the last antenatal clinic before Christmas.

'Morning, Iris. There's quite a few here, so we'd better get started. Who's first?'

'A self referral. Her mother's with her.' Iris spoke a little breathlessly. 'Denise North, the doctor will see you now.'

'Good morning, Denise. I'm Dr Hammond. And – your mother?'

'Yes, I've come to support her.' Fiona waved a finger at the smiling little boy.

'And this fine little fellow is your son?'

'Yes, he's my grandson. Come here, darling, don't climb on the couch.'

'And is there a daddy around, Denise?' Shelagh asked quietly.

'No, and we don't need one. We're all devoted to him,' said Fiona North.

'And have you been referred to a social worker?'

'There's no need, I'll take care of my daughter, and see about maternity benefits.'

Shelagh turned to Iris. 'Sister, will you take this little chap out for a few minutes, I need to examine his mother.'

'There's nothing to feel yet, it's only been a month!' objected Mrs North. 'And *I'm* not going to be sent out of the room – my place is with my daughter.'

'Just hop up on to the couch, Denise, and let me feel your tummy.' Shelagh gently pressed her hand against the pubic bone.

'I think you're about ten or twelve weeks' pregnant, my dear.'

'But that's impossible!' cried Mrs North. 'Her last

period was in November.' Shelagh continued to speak to the daughter. 'I think your last true period would have been around mid-October. Anyway, we'll take a couple of blood samples today, and see you again after Christmas.'

'What's the blood test for?' demanded Mrs North.

'Oh, a whole raft of tests we do on our expectant mums, to check for anaemia and other conditions. A nurse will show you where to go, and make a further appointment. Good morning!'

She grinned at Iris as they left. 'I wonder what she'd have said if I'd told her we check them all for VD! What a woman – I can't help feeling sorry for that poor girl. But Iris, are you all right? You're as white as a sheet. You'd better sit down. I'll get you a glass of water.'

But Iris waved her aside. 'I'm all right, Shelagh, honestly. I'll call the next one in.'

Christmas Eve brought a clear, cold night, full of twinkling stars, *like silver lamps in a distant shrine*, Jeremy North half remembered from some old carol. His heart beat a little faster as he looked upon his special choir assembled at the west door of the church with their music sheets. Rebecca Coulter was a stately presence in a fur coat, Phyllis Maynard and Mary Whittaker were well wrapped up in woollen fleeces, scarves, gloves and knee-high leather boots. Beryl Johnson was muffled in a long scarf wound twice round her neck and over her mouth, above which her eyes peered anxiously, and Daphne Bolt, who had not attended any rehearsals, now appeared smiling broadly, with her sons Philip and Mark, home from University and looking for some entertainment. Cyril Pritchard immediately went over to welcome them to the choir and hand them each a carol sheet.

'I thought we might need a few extra copies, so I got these typed out by one of the ladies in the solicitors' office,' he said. 'I'll be leading you all in 'Patapan', that's a French carol written primarily for children, but has a very nice refrain, so take a look at it.'

The boys nodded and turned to grin at each other as soon as he turned away. 'What a weirdo!' muttered Philip behind his hand. 'Wouldn't care to meet *him* in the churchyard after dark, would you?'

'Poor old bugger, I bet he's as lonely as hell,' his kinder brother replied.

As always, Jeremy North experienced a tremor of mixed emotions at the mystery of Christmas: the medieval treasures of art and architecture to be found in this church that had stood here for over six hundred years, and where they were now celebrating the Nativity, the Incarnation of a holy child born in a stable. Memories of past Christmases when the children had been young came back to him, the feasting, the tree with its soft lights and wrapped presents at its base, the carols, the gifts given and received, the holly and the mistletoe – and the soft light in Fiona's eyes as they'd looked at each other over the tops of the happy children's heads, before it had all gone so wrong. As headmaster of a primary school he had the opportunity to see again the festival through the innocent eyes of a child; he enjoyed watching the parents' pride – and sometimes surprise – at seeing their children taking part in the annual nativity play, listening to their praise and shrugging off their enquiries about his own family. Now he prayed that the success of his Christmas choir would renew his own faith which was burning low. There was too much suffering in the world and not enough answers to prayer.

But now, surrounded by his singers, one face stood out from the rest: Iris Oates in her quilted red jacket with a fur-trimmed hood that framed her face smiled shyly at him, her eyes meeting his just for a moment, before she looked away.

O, God, is there a man who can resist a woman's adoration, especially when – but no, to encourage the girl in any way would be wrong. Wicked, in fact. And could lead nowhere. And yet, and yet . . . he longed to talk to her, tell her everything, for surely she would listen and understand.

He dragged his eyes from her, and addressed the group. 'Well, we're all here, plus a couple of – no, three new members from the vicarage. I hope we're all in good voice tonight, and festive mood. This is the night when Christ was born, and we need to keep a balance between reverent awe and rejoicing, so we'll start with "Good Christian Men, Rejoice" – and sing all three verses as we walk down to the square. Rebecca, you'll give us the first note, best ladies at the front, followed by the rest of us – and one of you Bolt boys can carry the lantern – thanks, Mark. Mr Wetherby and Cyril will bring up the rear, and see that nobody gets left behind. Off we go!'

The market square was ablaze with Christmas lights. The Volunteer was packed, and some came out to cheer them and throw a few coins into the bucket carried by Philip Bolt. They sang 'The Boar's Head Carol', and walked to the hospital singing 'The First Nowell', which they finished at the front entrance, near to Accident and Emergency.

'We'll need to keep out of the way of the ambulances bringing the sick and injured in from the pubs,' Mark Bolt remarked with a grin.

A woman representative of the Everham Park Hospital Management Committee met them and said she would guide them to the designated areas where they had permission to sing, starting with the children's ward, with a caution not to make too much noise, as some of the children would be asleep. The ward was quiet at first, and Cyril drew a few deep breaths, ready to sing 'Patapan'; but Jeremy quickly decided against the too-ra-loo-ra-loos and pat-a-pat-pans as being too loud and too unfamiliar. He chose instead 'The Rocking

Carol', two verses only, sung very softly. An older boy was fascinated and started to join in, as did a girl with a leg suspended in plaster. These two had no inhibitions, and belted out with gusto,

> 'We will rock you, rock you, rock you,
> We will ROCK you, ROCK you, ROCK you,
> Coat of fur to keep you warm,
> SNUGLY ROUND YOUR TINY FORM!'

The nurse in charge of the ward glared at the visitors who had sung so quietly that they had been drowned out by the rowdy boy and girl, and now hastily left the ward, followed by yells demanding their return. They were next led through men's and women's surgical wards, then men's and women's medical, where the older patients were mainly appreciative, some tearfully so, while others ignored them. Finally they climbed the stairs to Maternity, there being too many of them to crowd into the lift.

'Now for "Patapan",' said Cyril confidently as they approached the unit with some trepidation; they were led first into the antenatal ward where the women greeted them with smiles. They sang 'Once in Royal David's City' and were applauded, so Jeremy ordered 'While Shepherds Watched', also applauded. There were only seven patients in postnatal, one recovering from a Caesarean section, but they smiled and listened to 'Away in a Manger', with a few accompaniments from the five cradles beside the beds, the other two babies being in the nursery. Their guide then led them to the annexe which served the Delivery Unit and Theatre.

'I don't expect they'll want you in the Delivery Unit,' she said, 'but I'll go and see what's happening there. Wait here, please.'

She returned to say that a baby girl had been born ten minutes ago in Delivery Room Four. Dr Hammond had been sent for to put in stitches, and meanwhile the new mother had no objection at all to the carol singers, and asked for something nice and soothing for the baby. They moved up the annexe to the open door of Delivery Room Four, and Jeremy was about to begin 'Silent Night' when Dr Hammond breezed in.

'Good heavens, what's going on here?' she asked. 'What are you thinking of, Nurse Burns, letting these people into a sterile area? They must leave at once!'

By now the lady singers were at the door and smiling at the new mother, sitting up on the delivery bed, her baby in her arms. Mrs Coulter exclaimed, 'Mrs Peacock! Mrs Peacock, the new Methodist minister's wife! I knew you were expecting soon, but I didn't realise it was today!'

Another, heavier footstep was heard entering the annexe, and Dr McDowall appeared.

'I've heard a lot of disturbance going on here,'

he said with mock severity, 'and I've come to make some arrests. Who are these intruders, Marie Burns?'

'They're the carol singers, doctor, and Dr Hammond says they've got to go,' said Staff Midwife Burns clearly for all to hear. 'Mrs Peacock wants them to sing a carol for the baby. They're Methodists,' she added.

'Well, then they must stay, we've heard nothing detrimental about Methodists, have we?' he said, moving through the singers to the Delivery Room, where Dr Hammond stood waiting impatiently.

'Dr Shelagh, what a lovely surprise! A baby on Christmas Eve!'

'I'm simply waiting to suture an episiotomy,' she answered, trying not to show her irritation. 'And I've asked them to leave the department at once. Mr Kydd would be furious.'

'Oh, come off it, Shelagh, it's Christmas and these good people have come a-wassailing. We can't let them go without a carol.'

'Oh, *please,* let them sing 'Silent Night'!' begged Mrs Peacock.

McDowall nodded to Jeremy North, and they began to sing the carol. Iris Oates's voice rose up sweet and clear on the high note of *sleep in heavenly peace*, and Rebecca's bell-like contralto descended to the bottom note in the repeat of the line. No other sound was heard until all three verses were sung, and Shelagh saw that she had to capitulate. She formally thanked them for coming, but added that they must leave now because Mrs Peacock needed treatment. Ignoring McDowall who had overridden her authority, she beckoned to Nurse Marie Burns to prepare the patient for suturing.

'Thank you all, it was heavenly,' McDowall told the singers. 'Good night and a happy Christmas to you all – and a welcome to our new arrival!'

'Amen,' they repeated as they left and descended the stairs. Not much was said as they walked back to the church, apart from Cyril voicing his regret that they had not sung 'Patapan'. Jeremy whispered 'Thank you, my dear,' into Iris's ear, to which she could make no reply. She seemed to be floating somewhere between earth and heaven. All right, so Jeremy North was a married man with a family and was not for her – could never be hers – but that did not stop her from adoring him over the distance between them, and surely she would remember this glorious Christmas Eve until her dying day!

It was Christmas Day in the morning. The Reverend Derek Bolt did not expect the turnout for the 10.30 service to be large, because the church had been packed on the previous evening, swelled by a number of non-churchgoers who had thought it a nice idea to slip back to a time when they had believed without doubting, when there was still a chance that legends could come true, before the clamour of the world drowned out the angels' song. Daphne and his sons were sitting beneath the pulpit, and he hoped the boys would listen to him. He got nothing but good-natured teasing when he tried to talk to them as a father – as a *Dad*. He wanted to express his pride in them, the happiness they brought to their mother – oh, *hell*, there was that woman again, sitting two pews back from his own family. Now her presence would intrude on all the thoughts he tried to convey in his sermon on this special day of the year. For the next hour there she would be, gazing at him soulfully: she would completely spoil it for him.

Asking for forgiveness and God's help, the vicar proceeded with Morning Prayer. Seated at the organ, Jeremy North too had his unspoken thoughts. His eyes searched the sea of faces, but he knew there would be no sign of Fiona, Denise or little Peter. Somebody whispered, 'Its's a pity none of his family are here,' followed by a whispered reply, 'They say there's trouble with all three. Poor Mr North!'

Jeremy had in fact almost pleaded with Denise to come, but she had tearfully apologised, saying that she felt very ill, and Fiona had refused to leave her.

'Poor girl, just as she's found a decent boyfriend, and now this,' Fiona had sighed. 'And I'll get no help at all with the turkey and trimmings.'

'The turkey's in the oven on a low gas, and when I get back I'll take over in the kitchen, and you can take a couple of hours off,' he had reassured her.

'Somebody's got to stay around here in case the phone rings and it's Roy,' she said with a worried frown.

'As long as it's only Roy and not the police. Sorry, Peter-poppet, you won't hear Granddad making a joyful noise on the organ this morning.'

The Christmas service began; the hymns were lustily sung, the collection taken and Derek made the due preparation for Communion. The wafers and the wine, symbolising the body and blood, were taken from the altar; a queue of communicants formed, and Derek placed a wafer on the hand of each, then Mrs Whittaker offered them the chalice. Jeremy North went first, so as to get back to the organ and play softly while Communion proceeded.

'The body of Christ.'

'Amen.'

'The blood of Christ.'

'Amen.'

Derek braced himself as Beryl Johnson moved forward, and held out the wafer to her.

'The body of Christ.'

He waited for her 'Amen,' but instead she made a grab at his hand, pressing it to her lips, and moaning, 'Oh, my God, take pity!' The wafer fell to the floor, and he snatched his hand free, drawing back from her as if from a poisonous snake.

'Stop—be quiet—' Words deserted him as she stood before him weeping, but Mrs Whittaker, practical as ever, nodded to Phyllis Maynard who was next in the line of communicants, and a silent message passed between them. Phyllis stepped forward, took Miss Johnson by the arm, and led her down the aisle to a seat at the back.

'I'm sorry, I'm sorry, I'm sorry—' Beryl repeated on a rising note.

'Stop that, stop it at once,' ordered Phyllis. 'Listen, I'll take you home after the service, my car's just around the corner in the car park. Only you must be sensible.'

Phyllis got Beryl out of the church before the singing of the last hymn, 'O Come All Ye Faithful', led by the Christmas choir. They got into the car, and little was said on the journey to Angel Close and Beryl's little semi. Phyllis got out and walked arm-in-arm with her passenger to the front door. Beryl had quietened, but Phyllis went indoors with her and brewed a pot of tea which they shared.

'I know how you must miss your mother, Beryl, and I'm truly sorry, we all are, but it's really time to move on now. People will only give you so long to grieve, and then you must make the effort. I lost my husband less than three months ago, and I know how—'

Beryl Johnson turned and looked at her with streaming eyes. 'He was so kind and good to me when she died, but now he turns away, and I can't bear it.'

Phyllis stared at her. 'What do you mean? Who are you talking about?'

'Him. The love of my life, Derek Bolt. I can't live without a word from him.'

'Good heavens! You'll have to get over *that*, Beryl, or you could cause the vicar awful embarrassment, and besides, you'd make such a fool of yourself, people wouldn't sympathise. It's ridiculous.'

There was a pause, and Phyllis said, 'Look, I've got family coming for lunch, and I'd ask you to join us, but not if you're going to talk like this.'

'I don't want any company except his.'

'You're being extremely foolish, you know – what on earth would his wife think? Listen, I shall be at home for the rest of today, so here's my phone number if you need to—er, need help of any kind.'

Even so, Phyllis felt that if this poor woman 'did something silly', she would feel at least partly responsible, and it troubled her throughout the rest of the day. She said nothing to Jenny or Tim: they had other matters to discuss, arising from the newspaper cutting.

Thoroughly disconcerted, Derek completed the Communion; he saw Phyllis Maynard lead Miss Johnson out during the singing of 'O Come All Ye Faithful', and also saw his sons having a giggle over Mr Pritchard's disappointment at not singing 'Patapan'.

'That was a bit of bad luck,' said Jeremy as they disrobed in the vestry.

'God knows what I'm going do,' the vicar replied grimly.

'That makes two of us, then. Anyway, enjoy your dinner.'

'They won't be short of something to say over all the dinners in Everham today. Oh, bloody hell.'

Poor old Bolt, thought Jeremy on his way home. He's right, this'll spread for miles around.

Fiona was reproachful. 'Where on earth have you been? I've been half out of my mind. Roy's come home – that is to say he was brought home by two of his so-called friends who'd plied him with drink. I've put him to bed, but Denise is in an awful state, poor girl, I think she's picked up a tummy bug – and what on earth's the matter with Peter?'

For Peter had burst into tears, and was clinging to his grandfather's left leg. 'Wha's a matter, G'andad? Me naughty?'

Jeremy bent down and picked him up. 'No, no, my little man, you're a *good* boy. Granddad will see to the turkey, and then we'll all have a good Christmas dinner – won't that be nice?'

He turned back to Fiona. 'So you think Denise needs a doctor? It will be one from the emergency service, whoever's on call.'

'No need for a doctor,' said Fiona quickly. 'She

just needs a little love and care, that's all, and I'm here to give it, fortunately.'

Jeremy felt himself tensing in every muscle, a sensation of warding off something he could not name. He could not quieten an awful suspicion forming at the back of his mind.

'This decent boyfriend you mentioned, is she upset because he hasn't been around lately?'

'What's that to do with anything?'

'Put it another way, has she had her monthly on time? We'd better find out before we call out a doctor on Christmas Day, just to diagnose something she could diagnose herself, don't you agree?'

Fiona's face showed shock and disbelief. 'How – how on earth could you say a thing like that? How could you be so heartless and cynical? Oh, Jeremy, what's happened, you used to be so good to the children!' She burst into tears, and in spite of her words, he guessed that he had only confirmed her own suspicion. He began to tremble, and knew that he had to get away as quickly as he could, before he completely lost control of his tongue. He was still clasping his grandson to his chest.

'Come on, Peter-poppet, let's get your coat and scarf – mustn't forget your gloves – we'll go and see if the Indian restaurant's open on Christmas Day.'

His wife was now weeping piteously. 'Is this all the sympathy your own daughter gets? And your son? When the vicar drops in at Everham Primary and says what a wonderful school it is, how happy the children are, don't you ever feel *shame*? If only people could see what you're like in your own home – cruel, cruel!'

He did not answer but dressed Peter against the cold wind, and then marched straight out of the house, passing a curious neighbour at the gate. She stared at them.

'Happy Christmas, Mr North! And little Peter too, isn't it your dinner time?'

'Happy Christmas back to you, Mrs – er – sorry, can't remember your name. You'd better go in and comfort my wife, because I can't. I'm escaping.'

CHAPTER FIVE

'Was she the poor old soul who's lost her mother and her faith, the one you've been counselling, the one who writes the letters?' asked Daphne Bolt. They were seated at the table for Christmas dinner, and Derek was carving the turkey.

'Yes, what have you been up to, Dad?' asked Philip with a grin.

The Reverend Derek Bolt was glad that the boys were home, treating the unfortunate scene in the church with light-hearted irreverence.

'Think of all the talk going on as we speak, over the Christmas dinners in Everham,' said Mark. 'They'll be wagging their tongues right up to the Queen's speech!'

Daphne said nothing, but Derek knew that she

would return to the subject. Her expression boded no good to him; she clearly suspected that there must have been some encouragement on his part, for the woman to behave in such a way, and in public. When each of them had been served with a generous helping of turkey breast and stuffing, she started handing round the vegetable and gravy.

'Wow! This *good*, Mum! Nobody can roast a spud like you do,' said Philip.

'And so say all of us,' added Mark, in unspoken agreement with his brother to let the subject drop, remembering the despair in the woman's eyes.

After the huge meal, the family sat down to watch a programme on the newly acquired black and white television set, looking back over the past year, especially to the fear and anxiety of the Cuban crisis, thankfully ended by the courage of young President Kennedy, advised, so many British believed, by the more mature wisdom of Prime Minister Harold Macmillan. Prayers had been offered up in thanksgiving for the mutual friendship between the two men.

When the doorbell rang, Derek stiffened. What now, he thought, bracing himself for another scene.

'I'll get it, Dad,' said Mark hastily, intent on getting rid of any embarrassing visitors for his father.

A man and a small boy stood on the step. Mark recognised the choirmaster, and at first thought he was drunk, but then saw that he was in a desperate state of mind.

'Mark? Or is it Philip?' asked Jeremy North. 'May I speak with your father – please?'

Mark had been about to say that his father was resting, but quickly realised that this was something serious.

'Yes, come in,' he said, holding the door open and guiding them into the study, where he pointed to an armchair, and switched on the one-bar electric fire.

'It's the organist, Dad, and he's got a little nipper with him. He doesn't look too good, I've put him in the study, and – er – I'll hang around if you want to send the kid in here.'

Derek rose at once. 'Thanks. Could we perhaps lay on a cup of tea?' he asked, and Daphne rose to do her duty. Philip told her to sit down, and said he'd make the tea. 'That takes care of the TV,' he muttered to his brother. 'We mustn't let Mum miss the Queen.'

Derek greeted his visitors with a smile. 'Hello, Jeremy, hello, Peter. I expect you'd like a cup of tea or something stronger?'

Jeremy half rose from the chair. 'I don't want anything – only to talk to somebody who'll listen, preferably somebody with a bit of sense. I'm at my wit's end.'

'All right, old chap,' said Derek lightly. 'Shall we ask Mark to take Peter into the other room? The Christmas tree's all lit up, and you might find something nice on it, eh, sonny?'

Mark beckoned to the child who looked somewhat

bewildered, but he followed Mark, and the door was shut. Derek turned to his guest.

'Sit down, Jeremy, and I'll take the other armchair. I keep them for the truly troubled – the hard wooden ones are for the time-wasters.'

There was a pause while Jeremy briefly covered his eyes, and Derek saw that his hands were trembling. 'Take your time, Jeremy – whatever you say won't go beyond this room.'

Again there was a pause, and then Jeremy burst out with, 'I can't endure life at home any longer, Derek. My family is – is undoing me. My elder daughter had a son when she was twenty, that's Peter, apparently born without a father, but he's a dear little chap, as you can see, he lives with us at home, my one and only comfort at home. Now I suspect she's pregnant again with no father in sight, and she's lost her job at the coal merchant's because she was always off sick. My younger daughter looks like going the same way, can't hold down a job, boyfriend's in prison where at least he can't impregnate her and my son has been chucked out by his wife for drinking – so he's come home to be cosseted by his mother, leaving a poor little daughter fatherless – God knows what ghastly scenes she's witnessed. That's the family, Derek. My wife has so spoilt and indulged the three of them – she's *ruined* them in every sense of the word, can't see that they're responsible for the mess they're making of their own adult lives, and blames *me* for everything, says I'm cruel and heartless, a headmaster who's a saint at school and a devil at home. I've tried to make her see the harm she's doing, but I've lost all authority in my own home, she thinks the sun shines out of their arseholes, and I'm actually beginning to dislike them. She and I had a wonderful marriage while they were young, we had great sex, we *loved* each other, but now she'd throw me out if she could afford to. Oh, how I envy you your sons, Derek – I don't know what to do. Tell me what to do for Christ's sake.'

A light knock on the door announced Philip with a teatray. He set it down on the table and went out, closing the door softly and deciding that he hadn't seen poor old North blubbing.

Derek leant over and touched Jeremy's shoulder. 'That's better out than in, old chap. As it happens, you're not the only man in Everham with family problems. I'm not exempt myself, as you may have noticed this morning. What you need is a break from it all. Is there a relative or friend you could go and stay with until term starts again? You've got a sister, haven't you?'

'Yes, near Basingstoke, but she and her husband have already got Catherine, the younger daughter, since early December. They've managed to talk some sense into her, and got her a job in an old peoples' home.'

'So she'll be staying there, then, while you try to sort out the other problems?'

'Yes, but that won't change things with Fiona. She despises me for what she sees as my harshness, and I despise myself for having lost all authority. We loved each other once, but she's come to hate me.'

'Hm. It sounds pretty bad, but not hopeless. It takes two to fight, and your best course is probably to keep quiet. Don't rise to the bait, keep your head down and ignore whatever Fiona throws at you. It'll be easier when school starts again, and your position there will bolster your self-esteem. You're very highly thought of at Everham Primary.'

'That counts for nothing with a dysfunctional family, which is what mine would be called in a poor area with social workers and police on the doorstep,' said Jeremy dully. 'We Norths are a middle-class professional family, an image of respectability, and the more shame on me for failing to live up to that image.'

'Don't worry too much about images,' said Derek. 'It's what God sees and knows that's important.'

Jeremy gave a non-committal shrug, and hesitated; Derek waited for a sceptical response, but Jeremy had decided to make a further confession.

'There is something else I could mention, Derek, something weighing on my mind,' he said.

'Fire away.'

'There's a girl – a young woman in the choir who shares my love of music. I've been tempted to ask her out for a quiet drink after rehearsals.'

'But you haven't done so?' Derek had no difficulty in guessing the young woman's identity; he had seen the looks that passed between them in church, especially hers.

'Not so far, but – I feel I could confide in her, as if she would listen and understand without condemning me. It would mean so much.'

'Ah! Here I *can* advise you, Jeremy. Don't give in to temptation. It would only cause more trouble and would do no good to – to your soprano, and it would give Fiona a real grievance against you. Don't do it, old chap – it would be a great mistake.'

Your soprano. Was it that obvious? Did Derek suspect that he and Iris Oates were on the verge of an affair? Suddenly Derek spoke again.

'Look, Jeremy, I should ask you to pray about this, in fact we should both pray together while we have this opportunity. I too have a problem, something that could cause serious harm to my marriage, and I'm equally in need of guidance. So come on, down on our knees, *now!*'

Jeremy's sheer desperation overcame any sense of the ridiculous in the picture of two middle-aged men kneeling together on the worn carpet with an ancient ink-stain between them. He felt that he had been right to come here, and was almost relieved to know that the vicar had his own problems, no doubt to do with that interruption to the service that morning.

He waited for Derek to voice a prayer, while at

the same time Derek wondered what words to use. The Book of Common Prayer, the original version, supplied him.

Almighty God, unto whom all hearts be open, all desires known, and from whom no secrets are hid, cleanse the thoughts of our hearts . . . the ancient words sounded exactly right and appropriate, and Jeremy said a heartfelt 'Amen' at the end. They rose from their knees, and Derek recalled little Peter from his frolicking with the two young men. He and Jeremy shook hands. 'One day at a time, old chap,' he whispered.

It had been a good move.

Christmas was over, and the New Year yet to come. Mary Whittaker rang the doorbell of 25 Angel Close, half-hoping that Miss Johnson would not be in, but intent on doing her duty as a churchwarden. Beryl came to the door and stared blankly at her visitor.

Mary smiled. 'Ah, Beryl, I'm glad to find you at home. Would it be convenient for me to come in and have a little chat? I won't keep you long.'

'All right, yes, er – Mrs Whittaker.' Beryl opened the door and showed her visitor into a rather chilly living room, where Mary at once saw a photograph of the Vicar on top of the piano. Beryl noticed her glance, but said only, 'Do you want a cup of tea?'

'No, don't bother. If we could just sit down for a few minutes, I want to know how you are, my dear.

Tell me, how are you feeling now, Beryl? I mean after that little spot of bother on Christmas morning? Have you recovered? Forgive me, I don't want to pry, but I've been very concerned about you, and so has Mrs Maynard.'

'Yes, she brought me home in her car,' said Beryl dully.

'Yes. You do realise, don't you, Beryl, that such a scene was very embarrassing, not only to the vicar but to Mrs Bolt and their two nearly grown-up sons. It really mustn't happen again, you know.'

There was a pause before Beryl answered in the same flat tone, 'The only way to stop it happening again is to stay away from the church, and that I'm not going to do.'

'I'm sure nobody wants to make you feel an outcast, Beryl, though it might be a good idea to attend another church for a while. There's the Methodist church in Everham, that's very well attended, especially since Mr Peacock arrived – remember Christmas eve, when his baby girl was born?'

Mary gave a little chuckle, but Beryl stared at the floor and did not reply.

'Beryl dear, would you like to confide in me about how you feel? I promise you that it will go no further than this room, and you'd probably feel better if you can talk about it.'

She waited, and Beryl appeared to be debating within herself how to reply, but in fact she was exercising a rigid self-control. Mary tried again.

'We all know what a sad time you've had over the last year, Beryl, nursing your dear mother for so long, and then losing her and having to cope with all the formalities, the funeral and – everything. We all felt for you. Your brother came over from Canada, didn't he?'

Beryl's self-control suddenly gave way. 'Yes, George came over, not that it affected *him* that much. He's got his wife and kids, and kept telling me how much he missed them, couldn't wait to get back to Ontario. Not like Mr Bolt!' Her pale face flushed, and her voice rose. '*He* held me in his arms and kissed me. He comforted me as nobody else did, and I'll never forget the feel of his arms around me, and the touch of his lips on my cheek! How can you wonder that I love him? How could I not? I adore him, he's the love of my life, as God sees and knows. I don't want to go to the Methodists, I want to go where I can see *him,* listen to him – I know you mean well, but you'll never understand a love like this!'

Mary was taken aback, for this was a confession indeed, and she needed to proceed with caution. She got up from her chair, and went to place a hand on Beryl's shoulder.

'But my dear Beryl, he's a consecrated man of the church, a married man with a wife and two sons. *You* must try to see this from his point of view – he comforted you at your mother's funeral, but it meant no more than that. I'm sorry if I sound unkind, but you'll have to get over this – this, er, obsession. You must pray for help to get over it.'

'Oh, shut up! Don't pretend that you understand, because you *don't!*' Beryl shouted, so that Mary recoiled. 'Go and leave me in peace!'

Mary put on her gloves. 'I'm sorry to find you in this state of mind, Beryl, and I can see that I've been wasting my time and yours. Just think over what I've said, and if you are so strongly affected by Mr Bolt, keep away from him for his sake as well as your own. I'll leave now – don't get up, I can see myself out. And I'll pray for you.'

She chided herself as she got into her car. I've only made things worse, she thought, and done more harm than good. Her annoyance at her clumsy handling of a delicate situation was equalled by her apprehension of what the silly woman might do next.

Alone, Beryl fell to her knees, facing the armchair where Mary had sat.

'O Lord, almighty Father, *you* see, *you* know, take pity on me and lead *him* to pity me, too. I only ask for a kind look, a word, a touch, a handshake, even a little note, that's all I ask, anything to relieve this emptiness, this terrible longing!'

She remained on her knees for several minutes, then got up and went to the china cabinet, unlocked it and took out a paperweight of Venetian glass, a smooth, circular object with a swirl of rainbow colours expertly caught within it. She kissed it, and took a carved wooden box from the top of the cabinet, reverently placing the costly object upon its crimson velvet lining.

'My New Year present for you, my beloved, to stay on your desk and remind you of me every time you use it.'

Bridget Hammond called it 'No man's land', that week between Christmas and New Year too late and yet too early. Shelagh remembered her mother's words as Paul turned and seized her.

'God, Shelagh, I've been needing this!'

'And I too, Paul – oh, how much!'

From kisses they progressed to breathless culmination, and Paul groaned aloud as he climaxed. She wondered if anybody could hear beyond their locked door, not that it mattered, for they were unknown here. She felt his weight lie heavily upon her as his muscles relaxed and he slowly withdrew from her body. Outside the snow which had begun to fall on Boxing night continued to cover the whole countryside.

'Wonderful, darling,' he said thickly, lowering his head to lie beside hers on the pillow. 'And you, darling Shelagh, did you come with me?'

'Yes, yes, of course, Paul – you took my breath away!'

It was not true. She had not reached a climax.

The unfamiliarity of the room, her weariness after the drive, the knowing look of the woman who had booked them in as Mr and Mrs Thompson, and always the thought of her mother's decline and the dreadful possibility of her death during this one night away – it never left her mind. Suppose Aunt Maura were to phone the hospital – oh, God forbid! If only it were possible to wipe away all memory just for a day and a night, to let her enjoy their lovemaking without being racked by guilt: guilt because she was here with the man she loved, in a discreet B & B near the sea at Eastbourne, and guilt because she was deceiving her mother. She could not abandon herself to his urgent lovemaking, and had to pretend that she had.

Slowly, gently, she rolled herself from beneath him – he was already asleep – then lay on her back, looking towards the darkened window, hearing the distant sound of waves upon the shore and his deep, contented breathing. A couple taking time off in No Man's Land to commit adultery – but *no*, neither of them were married, which made it the lesser sin of fornication, though just as bad in her mother's eyes; but her mother did not know, and would never know. Shelagh's thoughts whirled round in her head, and sleep evaded her for what seemed like hours. Paul did not stir until the knock at their door at eight o'clock warned them that it was time to get up.

'Shelagh darling,' he murmured, reaching out to

touch her, but her head ached and she needed the lavatory and the shower where he joined her, holding her tightly against his body beneath the cascade. They towel-dried each other and went down to breakfast where they were served by the same woman who had booked them in, and who obviously saw them as an unmarried couple celebrating the approaching New Year with a snatched night in each other's arms.

But Shelagh had come to a decision. While he ate eggs and bacon and she had toast and coffee, she suggested that they went for a walk along the shore – 'to clear our heads and get some fresh air into our lungs' – and he agreed, though added that they would have to leave by ten at the latest to get to Everham by midday; they were both on call for the afternoon and the rest of the day and night.

Beneath a grey sky, beside a grey sea, they strode against the whirling snowflakes.

'Paul.'

'Yes, my love – you'll have to shout!'

'Paul!' She raised her voice. 'When will you take me to meet your parents?'

'Not yet, darling. It's a long way to Carlisle, but we'll go there all in good time. It's a case of finding the right moment.'

'What about when we get officially engaged?'

'Not yet, Shelagh, not just yet. There are all sorts of factors – money, a home, our careers – as we've always agreed,' he shouted, holding his scarf in the teeth of the wind.

'My mother's dying,' she said, loudly enough for him to hear. 'And it would be wrong to tell her that we have definite plans for the future when we haven't. She'd be heartbroken if she knew that we – if she knew about this. But I'd like you to meet her before she – she goes, just as a close friend of mine.'

She had said rather more than she had intended, but he had heard what was *not* said, and knew that an answer was required.

'Listen, Shelagh my love, I'd like to meet your mother, and I'll tell her that we're getting engaged at midsummer – and married by the next midsummer. Is that how you want it to be?'

'Oh, Paul, dearest Paul, you know I do! I'm sorry – I'll take you to meet her just as soon as you like.' She stopped to kiss him. 'Only – she mustn't know that we – that we are more than friends – you do understand that, don't you?'

''Course I do, darling, just as you wish, as soon as you can fix it up. Come on now, it's time we were on the road, especially with this snow piling up!'

Talk of the scene in St Matthew's church on Christmas morning rumbled on.

'What an exhibition! She must be completely infatuated with him.'

'Poor soul.'

'Silly woman, behaving like that in public!'

'What on earth must Mrs Bolt think? And those two nice-looking boys!'

'What d'you think he'll do about it?'

'Don't know. What I say is, there's no smoke without fire.'

'What d'you mean by that?'

'He may have led her on in the first place, we don't know.'

'He was kissing her at her mother's funeral.'

Daphne Bolt could not keep silent. 'You've been seen outside her house, talking to her in the street, walking together in the churchyard like a couple of lovesick teenagers. It's hard enough being a vicar's wife without this sort of humiliation. Let me tell you, if anything like this ever happens again, I'll deal with the woman myself.'

Derek Bolt saw that she meant it. He understood her fury, but what could he do? He could hardly forbid Beryl Johnson her right as a parishioner to attend her church.

'Bridie darlin', here's your tea.'

'Ah, Maura, you're a saint! What time is it?'

'Nearly eight o'clock, and gettin' light. How did ye sleep, dear? I didn't hear ye movin' around at all.'

'Sure I had a grand night – just out to the commode once, and then I slept again.'

'No pain?' Maura helped her sister to sit up and

drink her tea. Her thin fingers clasped around the mug looked almost transparent.

'None at all, Maura. In fact I had a wonderful dream, it was so real! I was layin' here, and the room was full o' light, like bright sunshine. Then I seemed to be floatin' up in the air, so calm, so peaceful it was. Yeself and Rose were with me, and ye were cryin'. I told ye not to cry, and ye stopped and put your arms around each other—'

'Holy Mary, Mother o' God!' breathed Maura, crossing herself. 'Ye should have called me, Bridie, I'd have phoned the hospital, and asked Shelagh to come!'

'No, no, Maura, there was no need to call Shelagh, when she was probably helpin' a poor woman givin' birth. This was so beautiful, I thought I was near to heaven, but then there was a voice or somethin' inside me, that said I must come down to earth, the time wasn't ready yet.'

'Oh, sweet heaven, it must've been an angel drawin' ye back.' Maura wiped her eyes. 'Shelagh should've been here.'

'Not in the middle o' the night, Maura, but some time today ye can send for Father Orlando from Our Lady of Pity, to bring me the Blessed Sacrament. We can receive it together with Shelagh.'

Maura nodded. 'I'll call Father Orlando straight away.' And I'll make sure Shelagh's here too, she added to herself. Bridie was getting near to the end, and Maura knew that her sister's daughter would want to be summoned if this strange experience happened again.

For Maura was certain that Bridget's guardian angel had drawn her back to earth in time to bid her daughter farewell.

Shelagh hurried to the doctors' quarters, threw on her white coat and activated the pager which immediately began to bleep. She practically ran along the corridor leading to the Maternity Department, almost twenty minutes late, Paul's car having been held upon the journey back from Eastbourne by the still heavily falling snow. She went straight to the office of the Delivery Unit, where Laurie Moffatt sat at the desk.

'The switchboard's been looking for you, Dr Hammond,' she said. 'We told them that you were expected back by two' – she glanced at the wall clock which showed twenty minutes past – and Dr McDowall said he'd take over until you arrived.'

'Heavens, I'm terribly sorry,' panted Shelagh. 'So where is he now? I must relieve him as soon as possible.'

'There's no emergency here, doctor – but when he phoned the switch, they told him there was an outside call for you,' said Laurie with a curious look.

'Oh, my God,' Shelagh whispered, thinking of her mother. 'I'll ring switch now.'

With trembling fingers she dialled the number, to

be told that Dr McDowall had taken the call on her behalf.

'We couldn't locate you anywhere, Dr Hammond,' said the girl on the switchboard. 'Dr McDowall said he knew the person who was calling, a Miss Carlin, and he told her he'd pass the message on to you.'

Shelagh froze with fear. 'I must find him, then, as soon as I can – oh, my God!' She felt suddenly faint, and sat down heavily on one of the plastic office chairs.

'Are you all right, Dr Hammond?' asked Laurie, and Shelagh shook her head, conscious of the thudding of her heart.

Which was when Dr Leigh McDowall strode into the office. '*There* you are, Dr Hammond, we were about to send out a search party. Where the dickens have you been?'

He nodded to Laurie who got up and left the office, closing the door behind her.

Her face chalk-white, Shelagh asked, 'W-what was the message you took from my aunt Maura, Leigh?'

'Nothing desperate, though it sounds as if your mother had a very strange dream in the night, and Miss Carlin has sent for a priest to give them Holy Communion. She wants you to go home this afternoon and share it with them, so you'd better go now.'

Shelagh almost wept with relief. 'What? Well, no, I can't, I'm back on duty. I'll ring my aunt now.'

'I wouldn't do that if I were you, Shelagh.' He spoke seriously, and she looked up.

'Why not?'

'Your good aunt informed me that you had been on call for the past day and night, so she believes you to be free this afternoon, and able to spend this hour with your mother.'

'Oh. Oh, I see.' This time she did not look up. 'You've caught me out in a lie, then.'

'So it would appear, although your affairs are no concern of mine. I didn't give you away, I just told Miss Carlin that you'd be there this afternoon. So give me your bleep, and I'll take over for the next hour.'

She knew that he had been on call for the past day and night, and should now be free for the rest of the day. She got to her feet, her knees weak.

'I have to thank you, Leigh.'

'Don't bother. I'd lie in my teeth to spare your mother distress. And keep quiet about everything. I won't ask you where you've been, or who was with you, it's no business of mine – but be careful, Shelagh. You might not get off so easily another time.'

She could hardly meet his unsmiling eyes.

'Happy New Year, Mum!'

Phyllis Maynard welcomed her daughter and son-in-law on New Year's Day with hugs and kisses.

It was good to see Jenny's eyes looking bright, and Tim gave her a conspiratorial grin. Something was afoot. She waited.

'This is for you, Mum,' said Jenny, taking a bottle of her mother's favourite sherry out of her bag.

'And so is this, Phyllis,' added Tim, producing a box of high quality chocolates.

'Oh, my dears, you really shouldn't!' She deeply appreciated their kindness at such a time, no longer having Ben to share the New Year with her. 'You've been much too extravagant, but I'll share them and enjoy them. Thank you!'

'And we – er – wonder if you could give these to aunt Mary,' Jenny went on, producing another bottle of sherry and another box of chocolates, 'just to thank her for that *Daily Mail* cutting.'

'Mary? Oh, you mean Mary Whittaker? Does this mean—are you going to—'

'Yes, Mum, we've got ourselves on the books of an adoption agency, and we both feel that it's the right thing to do, don't we, Tim?'

'That's right, Phyllis, we do,' he smiled and nodded.

'But Tim, your parents aren't in favour of—'

'My mother will come round to the idea, and my father will follow,' he replied with conviction. 'And in any case, my wife's wishes come before theirs – so we have to thank you and Mrs Whittaker for getting us started!'

'It's the answer to all our prayers, Mum, like a

ray of light in the darkness,' added Jenny, and Phyllis saw tears in her daughter's eyes.

'Oh, my dears, let it be! May it all go well!' More hugs and kisses followed, for she realised they were setting out on a journey that might have setbacks and disappointments along the way, and possibly unforeseen expense if they adopted from another country.

With hope in her heart, Phyllis prayed that they would attain their hearts' desire.

CHAPTER SIX

When Maura Carlin took the coffee tray up to Bridget's room, she found her seated at the window in a pool of winter sunshine. She wore the flowery quilted housecoat that Shelagh had given her in place of her old candlewick-cotton dressing gown, and looked up with a bright smile.

'Was there ever a winter with this much snow, Maura? How will the snowdrops get through, buried under these drifts? D'ye remember Grandmother callin' them the Fair Maids o' February, bringin' in another spring?'

'I do, and it's a promise of another spring for *you*, Bridie, never mind the snow. It's a miracle, thanks be to God.' Maura set down the tray on a small circular table, and marvelled yet again that her sister, who had seemed near to the end of her life at New Year, was now gazing over the snowy back gardens of the terraced houses in Alexandra Road. The strange dream she'd had about coming back to earth after being close to death seemed to have done her good, for she had regained some of her appetite and had even put on a little weight. To Maura it was a miracle, even though Shelagh had gently told her that terminally ill patients sometimes appear to rally for a while, but that it is a reprieve rather than a recovery. How long it would last could not be guessed, but Shelagh had decided to take advantage of it and introduce Paul Sykes to her mother.

'I've made a fruit cake and some o' them cheese scones you like split and spread wid butter,' said Maura. 'D'ye think I ought to make sandwiches as well?'

'Like those chicken sandwiches you made when Father Orlando called? Yes, let's have some o' those as well. It's really good o' ye, Maura.'

'But not too good for Shelagh's young man, we want to make him feel welcome,' replied her sister. 'I've put me best skirt and jumper on, and the mother-o'-pearl brooch.'

'If he's who we hope he is, he won't want anything too fancy,' said Bridget, and they chuckled together, anticipating news of an engagement between two doctors.

But when the doorbell rang that afternoon, Shelagh

stood on the doorstep with a good-looking man they had not seen before.

'Hello, Auntie, I've brought Dr Paul Sykes to see Mother,' she said. 'This is my aunt Maura, Paul – she's come over from Ireland just to look after Mother, and it's a great blessing to us all.'

They followed Maura up the stairs and entered the bedroom, made bright by flowers, books and photographs of Shelagh as a baby and a schoolgirl.

'I've brought my friend Dr Paul Sykes to see you, Mother. He's a registrar on Mr Fielding's surgical team, and he's been asking to meet you.'

'Hello, Mrs Hammond. I've been looking forward to this,' Paul said pleasantly, holding out his hand. 'Shelagh's told me so much about you that I feel we've already met. Ah, I can see where she gets her looks!' He turned to Maura, bustling around setting out the refreshments. 'How is it that all Irishwomen are beauties?'

He sat down beside Bridget, and Shelagh stood behind her, pleased that Paul and her mother were meeting at last, though they had agreed that Bridget was not to be told how long they had been friends, nor the nature of their relationship.

'Shelagh is very highly regarded at the hospital,' Paul said, but soon discovered that Mrs Hammond wasted no time on pleasantries.

'I'm proud o' her meself, doctor, and if the pair o' ye are lookin' towards the future, ye'd better put a ring on her finger, before another steps in and takes her off ye.'

He looked slightly taken aback, and glanced at Shelagh who blushed but was not sorry about her mother's straight talking. Maura handed him a cup of tea and a cheese scone.

'Mother has a way of getting to the point, you'll notice, Paul—' she began.

'The fact is, I haven't got that much time left, Dr Paul,' Bridget broke in. 'The Almighty is lettin' me stay to see another spring, but there's no time for shilly-shallyin', and I'd like to see her settled before I go. If the pair o' ye are plannin' on gettin' engaged, I'm happy if she is.' She smiled on them, and Paul knew he had to give an answer.

'I echo that, Mrs Hammond,' he said with all the charm he possessed. 'I'm happy too, if Shelagh is. The reason we haven't announced it yet is to do with practicalities – our careers, our savings and so on, and also I'd like to get my Fellowship of the Royal College of Surgeons, which should be by midsummer. I've already told Shelagh that we can get officially engaged then.' He looked at Shelagh who nodded shyly.

'What about an unofficial one, then?' asked Bridget. 'What about *now*?'

'Of course, but we'll keep it under wraps for the time being,' he answered. 'Until I get my FRCS, and have something to offer her.'

'Oh, Paul.' Shelagh's eyes filled with tears of happiness at hearing these words which carried a promise, a commitment; there were kisses all round, between her mother and Paul, herself and Paul and herself with her mother and aunt.

'God bless ye, Paul, and thanks for comin' to see me,' said Bridget. 'We'll be meetin' again soon, I dare say!'

When the couple had left, Bridget begged to go to bed. 'Sure and I'm worn out wid actin' the dear old lady, Maura. Give me a hand – that's right, thanks. And if that's the feller she wants, I'll call him son-in-law. But I could wish he was Dr Leigh.'

Thursday again. Blessed Thursday, the night of choir rehearsal, and Jeremy's escape from home life. Since its Christmas success, the choir of St Matthew's church had grown, and they had been asked to sing at local venues like the church hall and the old people's home. There were the stars, Iris Oates and Rebecca Coulter, who encouraged the rest; there were the stalwarts, Phyllis Maynard and Mary Whittaker, and Beryl Johnson whose thin chirp was often drowned out by the others. There was the usual shortage of men, Wetherby and Pritchard being better than nothing, and a new acquisition, Tim Gifford, a passable baritone pressed into service by his wife Jenny, and Jeremy's own versatile voice. The Bolt brothers had gone back to university, and Daphne Bolt no longer came; Derek absolutely refused to join, which was a pity, Jeremy thought, because the man shouldn't let Beryl Johnson keep him away, if indeed it was she who was his problem.

'Good evening, friends!' His confident smile belied his inner turmoil. 'Are we all in good voice tonight? I've got plans for Easter, when we might do something from Stainer's *Crucifixion* for Good Friday, and there are some beautiful pieces for Easter Sunday. But tonight we'll do some hymn practice, to get ourselves into shape.'

He glanced towards Iris Oates in her fur-trimmed hood, looking straight at him with such love in her eyes, such sheer adoration, that he stopped speaking just for a moment, then recollected himself and got through the evening without looking in her direction again. But his mind was made up, and at the end of the rehearsal, he approached her.

'Er – Iris – I'd like to sound you out on one or two matters to do with our repertoire, how we can best plan for the next quarter – perhaps over a quiet drink – would you mind? Have you got time this evening?'

Waiting for her answer, he held his breath, sure that she was going to refuse, until she smiled and said, 'Certainly, Jeremy, that would be nice. Thank you.' He was able to exhale, unaware of her own hope and fear.

Tim Gifford offered his car to ferry another couple

of ladies to their homes, while Jeremy drove Iris to The Volunteer, where they sat on a bench seat in a corner of the lounge bar. She asked for a sweet white wine, and he ordered a pint of Guinness.

'It's been a good evening, hasn't it?' he said.

'Yes, everybody really seemed to enjoy it,' she agreed, pushing back her hood. 'Our choir – your choir is easily the best in the area.'

'Yes, thanks to you and Rebecca Coulter – you're the stars, and I'm grateful. You make it all worthwhile.'

She hesitated, not knowing how to reply. What sort of an answer did he expect? To say that she was grateful in return? So she just smiled and inclined her head.

'What brought you to Everham?' he asked. 'It's been about a year, hasn't it?'

This was easier. 'Not quite a year. I was looking for a job away from – from where I was living, and saw the advertisement in the *Nursing Times* for a second sister in Outpatients at Everham Park. The hours are from eight in the morning till five or six – it varies, but I get free evenings and weekends. There are a few evening clinics, but not many.'

'And that's what you wanted?'

'Yes, as soon as I saw the advertisement I realised that I'd be able to join a club or an evening class – or even a choir! – and be able to attend regularly.'

'A lucky break for St Matthew's, then. And are

you enjoying life in Everham? Is it better than where you were living?'

'Much better, and I've made new friends.'

She hesitated, and he asked, 'Did you have a special reason for leaving your last job?'

'Yes, I simply couldn't stay in Chelmsford – that's where I was born and brought up, and my parents still live there.' She looked straight at him, and went on, 'It was a broken engagement, the usual story, I suppose you'd say.' She gave a little self-deprecating shrug.

'I see. Had you been engaged long? I'm sorry, Iris, I seem to be interrogating you—'

'It's all right. Three years. We were saving up to put down a mortgage on a house, and well, he just got tired of waiting – said it was like a staled-off marriage. And he'd found someone else.'

'Had he? Presumably a lady who wasn't willing to wait that long before . . .' He tailed off with a significant look.

'Presumably, but it doesn't matter now. I believe that I was led to Everham Park Hospital and to St Matthew's – and to the choir. A new start at thirty-three!'

'Lucky for us, then.' She shyly returned his smile. 'Where are you living?'

'A bedsitter near the station, though not for much longer. I'm moving into a ground-floor flat, a very nice one. It's on the Everham Road, on the way to North Camp. After all, I've been saving up for the past two years, and can afford somewhere decent as well as convenient. But this must be boring you.'

'Not in the slightest, I'm all ears.'

'But you said you wanted to discuss the choir.'

'Ah, yes, the choir. My Thursday evening refuge, my escape from the joys of family life, especially since—' He broke off, and she waited with tumult in her heart.

'You're a married man with a family,' she heard herself say.

He nodded grimly. 'Yes, so I am. And I'm also a headmaster who runs an excellent school, well spoken of by the children, the parents and the Education Committee. And yet in my own home I've been a failure, and now I'm having to face the effects of that failure. I'm sorry, Iris, I shouldn't be burdening you with all this, I can't expect you to understand.'

She heard a bitter edge to his voice, and saw that his fists were clenched under the table. Something told her that she was on the brink of taking a step that would change her life.

She remembered Denise North and Dr Hammond's opinion of the girl's mother.

'Don't worry, Jeremy,' she said softly. 'You don't have to tell me, but I'm listening if you want to talk. Whatever you say will be in strictest confidence.'

Suddenly he put his head between his hands, his elbows on the table. His voice shook as he went on,

'Oh, God, Iris, I don't know what to do – I'm at the end of my tether.'

Iris regarded him, longing to draw his head on to her shoulder, but they were in a public place. She decided to tell him about Denise's visit to the antenatal clinic.

'Don't worry, Jeremy,' she said again. 'As a matter of fact, I've met your daughter Denise – and her mother.'

He raised his head and stared in astonishment. 'How? When?'

'Don't forget I work in Outpatients. I don't normally take antenatal clinics, but sometimes when the midwives are all occupied – in fact I was there when Denise came on her first visit with her mother, and the doctor and I were in complete agreement that the girl was under her mother's thumb, and had never been allowed to grow up. Her little boy was with them – he's a perfect poppet, isn't he? So I can quite believe what you say.' Leaning across the table, she held out a hand which he quickly took and held in both of his.

'My dear Iris, what a relief, you *do* understand – I thought you would, but I couldn't be sure. You can see what a mess my life is in, it could hardly be worse, but knowing that *you* know and understand, that makes it easier to bear. Oh, bless you, my dear, thank you!'

Iris's heart leapt, but she hardly knew how to reply. She could not tell him of Dr Hammond's words on Denise's latest visit to the antenatal clinic, that the girl was big for her dates, and the doctor had wondered if she was carrying twins. Nothing had been said to her or her mother, for to be sure they would need to wait until at least thirty weeks into the pregnancy, when two foetal hearts could be heard, and two foetal heads palpated abdominally.

She glanced at her watch. 'We'd better be going now.'

'Yes, though I'd rather stay here with you.' They stood up. 'First I must take you home.'

'You know that I'll be thinking about you and praying for you and all the family – Jeremy.'

'Thank you, Iris dear, you've helped me enormously.' He pressed her hand, and held it briefly against his cheek.

When they arrived at the Edwardian house where she had her bedsitter, he led her to the communal front door and kissed her. It was only a brief touch of his lips on her cheek, but it sent her spirits soaring. Married man though she knew him to be, Iris Oates also knew herself to be in love again.

'Who goes home? Climb aboard!' Tim Gifford invited the ladies of the choir to accept a lift, and Mrs Coulter and Miss Johnson got in, leaving one available seat. Cyril Pritchard would have taken it, but was on his bicycle.

'Come on, Mary, let's walk and leave the seat for

a more deserving case,' said Phyllis Maynard with a smile. 'Rebecca's such a size, she takes up two seats, and frankly I feel embarrassed in Beryl Johnson's company – she just sits there looking anxious, and doesn't say a word.'

'But we know what she's thinking, don't we?' said Mary. 'Or rather, who she's thinking about. Frankly I think she should be referred to a psychiatrist.'

'Poor soul.'

'Poor Derek Bolt, I'd say – you never know what a woman like that is going to do next. Everybody's talking about her. I'm surprised that she still attends St Matthew's.'

'For all we know, Derek may have had words with her, you know, warning her off.'

'Changing the subject, Phyllis, what a nice son-in-law you have, a real asset to the choir.'

'Yes, Tim's a sweetie. Jenny talked him into it, it's the evening she goes to Keep Fit.'

'And is there any news of the adoption plans yet?'

'Not so far, apart from correspondence, sheaves of forms to fill in, and they've got to find two non-related referees before their names can even be considered. It's going to be a long haul, Mary, and needing a solicitor makes it quite expensive. Never mind! It's such a relief to see both of them looking so much better. I was really worried about Jenny, and I just hope and pray that it won't be too long before they hear some good news.'

* * *

'Your mum's had one of those strange remissions, Shelagh,' remarked Leigh McDowall, 'and she's giving thanks for living to see another spring. Nice to see her and Maura having a good old sisterly argument!'

'Of course we're all pleased,' said Shelagh coolly, 'though it means she'll have to face the inevitable decline again.'

'All the more reason for enjoying the present, I'd say. Her sister thinks it's a miracle.'

'Yes, unfortunately. Poor Miss Carlin is going to be disappointed.' She turned back to studying Mr Kydd's theatre list for the following day, irritated by his familiar way of speaking about her mother and aunt. Perhaps they'd told him of Paul Sykes' visit, which might lessen his disapproval of their night away. Even so, she still felt embarrassed, knowing herself to be under obligation to him, and wanting him to realise that she cared nothing at all about what he thought.

Staff Nurse Moffatt came into the office to check on a patient's medication, and seeing Shelagh, she said, 'By the way, Dr Hammond, there's a storm brewing on Postnatal. The night sister's in trouble with the paediatrician over the breast-or-bottle controversy, and she's terribly upset.'

'Tell me more,' said Shelagh, turning to give Laurie her full attention. 'I know that Dr Fisher is adamant that all mothers should breastfeed their babies, but perhaps he makes the bottle-feeders feel unnecessarily guilty. What's happened, then?'

'We all know that there are mothers who genuinely haven't got enough milk to feed their babies, but he insists that if they persevere the milk will increase. Apparently he's furious because Night Sister Hicks has been giving the babies top-ups in the night.'

Leigh McDowall, still in the office, said, 'Dr Fisher knows his stuff, and his wife breastfed without any fuss when she was delivered here. The mothers are lucky to have a paediatrician who takes such an interest in infant feeding.'

Shelagh spoke to the staff midwife. 'I'll look into it, Laurie. Sister Hicks on postnatal night duty has had years of experience, and I can understand how she feels if Dr Fisher comes round telling her how to do her job. I'll have a word with her.'

McDowall shrugged and left the office.

It was at the Wednesday market in Everham's market square that Phyllis Maynard met Fiona North at the greengrocery stall. Snow still hung around in drifts, and a few flakes were falling.

'Hello, Mrs North,' she said. 'Are you surviving this delightful winter weather?'

'It's just one more trial to put up with,' was the dour reply, and Phyllis thought she ought to sympathise.

'Sorry to hear that – er – Mrs North – I'm sorry but

I'm hopeless at remembering names,' she apologised. 'You'll have to remind me.'

'Fiona, though I'm not bothered what I'm called.'

'Phyllis, and I'm not bothered either! I'm a member of your husband's famous choir – Jeremy could get a joyful sound out of a chorus of cats!'

'Don't talk to me about his precious choir,' snapped Fiona. 'All very well for you old ladies to swoon over him, but if you had any idea of the way he treats his own family, you might not be so enamoured.'

Phyllis was taken aback by such uncalled-for rudeness, but wanted to remain civil.

Fiona continued on a rising note, 'He's got no sympathy, no understanding of the problems of young people, even his own children. For all that he's a headmaster, I could tell you things about your wonderful Mr North that would make your hair stand up on end!'

People were turning round to see who was speaking so loudly, and Phyllis took her by the arm. 'We can't stand here in this snow. Come on, what we need is a nice hot cup of coffee, so let's go to Edward's, it's always nice and cosy in there.'

Fiona allowed herself to be led to the popular bakery that also had a café at the back. Phyllis chose a corner table, and told Fiona to sit down while she went to order coffee. The proprietress Mrs Pearce stepped forward to serve her, having taken in the situation with interest.

'Having a bit of trouble, Mrs Maynard?' she asked in a low voice. 'She's the headmaster's wife, isn't she?'

'Yes,' answered Phyllis briefly. 'We need two coffees with milk – and I think a couple of toasted teacakes would be nice.'

Mrs Pearce sniffed; no chance of a piece of juicy gossip from this churchy woman, but she'd heard the talk about the North's grown-up children, none of whom had been to university, and the eldest girl had a child with no father.

'There we are, Fiona, let's both enjoy a little break from all this snow. Let me see, now, didn't your eldest girl go to school with one of my daughters?'

'No, she couldn't have, yours are much older. My poor Denise was let down by a rotter when she was only twenty, so her chances went by the board. I've stood by her, and helped her to bring up the boy – and now the poor, sweet, trusting girl has been let down for a second time,' said Fiona, bursting into angry tears. 'And all *he* can do is complain about how much it's going to cost. Poor Denise worked very hard at Trencher's before she became ill.'

Trencher's. The coal merchant's. Phyllis remembered hearing that Denise had been sacked for being frequently off sick. She decided not to get too involved with this woman, and to avoid asking questions about Denise or any of the family. From what she knew of Jeremy North, she doubted that he could be such a monster as his wife had described, for he was as well respected at Everham Primary as he was at St Matthew's. Other people's lives, thought Phyllis, so often not what they appear to be, but she had no wish to hear anything more from this woman about her husband. They drank their coffee and ate their teacakes, for which Phyllis refused to accept any payment, and as Fiona now looked more composed, they went their separate ways.

Shelagh put on a smile and a deliberately relaxed air as she sauntered into Postnatal before going for her lunch. All twelve beds were occupied in the main ward, and apart from one howling baby there was a peaceful atmosphere. A couple of mothers were contentedly breastfeeding their babies, others were sleeping, their babies having been returned to the nursery. A middle-aged nursing auxiliary, Connie, was helping a new mother to fix her sleepy baby on to the nipple, and in the last bed sat Mrs Shirley Gainsford, struggling with a yelling ten-pound boy born the previous day by caesarean section.

'Hello, mums, how're we doing?' asked Shelagh easily. 'My word, young master Gainsford's making his presence felt! – aren't you, young man?'

Mrs Gainsford, flushed and frowning, did not look up from her task. The baby's arms and legs were flailing as he resisted her efforts.

'I'm determined to get Justin to fix onto the nipple and stimulate the milk ducts,' she said. 'He's got to learn who's boss!'

'It's early days as yet, Shirley,' said Shelagh, sitting down on the side of the bed. 'Caesarean babies often take longer to learn the art of suckling, and you've got a sore tummy which doesn't help, and he's a big baby, isn't he? Added to which, you won't have much milk for him yet. I suggest a little bottle of boiled water to help him to settle.'

Out of the corner of her eye Shelagh saw Connie the auxiliary grimace and roll up her eyes, but she was unprepared for Mrs Gainsford's reaction.

'What? A *bottle*? No way, doctor, you're as bad as that tiresome sister on night duty. Justin is *not* going to have a rubber teat shoved into his mouth, and in any case, there *will* be colostrum for him, the forerunner of milk, with valuable protein. Dr Fisher explained it all to me. Come on, Justin darling, show the doctor what you can do!'

But Justin steadfastly refused to show the doctor anything but his rage, and Shelagh sighed inwardly. Shirley Gainsford was a teacher of mathematics at Everham College, in her middle thirties, and this was her first baby. She was an articulate woman who had come to the Delivery Unit wanting a natural delivery without pain relief, but after six hours of excruciating contractions with no progress, Dr Rowan had performed a caesarean section and extracted a big baby who had opened his mouth and roared right from the beginning, and had scarcely stopped since, or so it seemed to the other mothers in the ward. The walls of the postnatal ward carried posters of smiling mothers and babies, all proclaiming that *Breast is Best*, and Dr Fisher the consultant paediatrician visited the postnatal ward from time to time, to promote this excellent dictum.

'Very well, Shirley,' said Shelagh gently, 'I'll leave you to deal with Justin yourself.'

She followed Connie into the ward office, and the auxiliary shook her head.

'Oh, doctor, you shouldn't have mentioned the word *bottle* to her, it's like red rag to a bull. She goes berserk at the very mention of it!'

'So I see,' said Shelagh. 'The trouble with the Mrs Gainsfords of the world is that they've read all the textbooks, been to the relaxation classes, and then reality sometimes comes as a shock, not as straightforward as they'd been led to expect.'

Connie nodded in agreement.

'So, what do we do about Justin and his mother? Come on, Connie, you've had three children and you must have *some* suggestion!'

'Try letting her give him a little boiled water with a plastic spoon? He'll spit it all over the place, of course, but it might get a little fluid into him. We have to avoid upsetting her at all costs. If she hadn't been so influenced by Dr Fisher, we could give him a few ounces of half-strength formula milk, just to settle him, and give us all a break – Sister Hicks said he kept the whole ward awake last night, because Mrs Gainsford wants to have his cot beside her day and night, so it's no wonder the other poor mums want to go home!'

Shelagh was thoughtful. Should she try to have a word with Dr Fisher? No, because he wouldn't listen to a mere house officer. His wife had recently given birth to her first baby in this hospital, a normal delivery, and had breastfed like a dream from day one. Even so, Shelagh was worried about Mrs Gainsford; she owed it to all the mothers to maintain a happy atmosphere, and remembered being told by an old midwife that there should be no such words as *must* or *can't* on a postnatal ward, especially to the first-timers who were having to adjust to a complete change of lifestyle, and often felt anxious and inadequate. In the end she telephoned Mr Kydd's office, and left a message. He phoned her back that same afternoon.

'It's the matter of breastfeeding, Mr Kydd. The mothers just aren't getting enough sleep, thanks to baby Gainsford the ten-pounder delivered by section yesterday. His mother insists on having his cot by her bed night and day, so the other mothers can't sleep, and the night sister's at her wit's end, thanks to Dr Fisher lecturing them on *Breast is Best*.'

'Ah, yes, Mrs Gainsford, I'm not surprised. She's not likely to have much milk yet, anyway. You know I usually hand over feeding problems to the midwives, they know better than I do as a rule. So what exactly is the problem?'

'The baby's big and hungry, with a voice like a foghorn, and won't suck, but Mrs Gainsford won't allow him to be given a top-up, to tide him over until the milk comes in. I don't know whether to approach Dr Fisher—'

'And get a flea in your ear? No, go ahead and do what you and the midwives think best, Shelagh, and if Fisher complains, let me know. How's Bridget, by the way? McDowall says she's having a remission.'

'Yes, Mr Kydd, she is, though of course it won't last.'

'Then make the most of it while it does last, Shelagh. And good luck with Mrs G!'

Two deliveries took place that evening, managed by student midwives under supervision, and Shelagh retired to her narrow bed in the doctors' quarters, on call for admissions and emergencies. It was two-forty when the bedside telephone roused her, and she switched on the light and lifted the receiver. It was Night Sister Hicks, sounding agitated. She had fallen out with Mrs Gainsford, she said, and 'words' had been exchanged.

'And the worst of it is, doctor, she's telephoned her husband and asked him to come and take her home – I ask you, a two-day caesarean! And all the women are awake!' She was on the verge of tears.

Oh, heck, thought Shelagh, and said, 'All right, Sister Hicks, I'll be over right away. Get your auxiliary to make tea and toast for the patients.'

She threw her white coat over her pyjamas, and stepped into her shoes. On the ward, she noticed that baby Justin was quietly sleeping, and went to the office where Sister Hicks sat, flushed and untidy, hairpins flying out of the twisted grey coil at the back of her head. She rose when she saw Shelagh.

'She was sleeping, Dr Hammond, in fact they were all asleep when that baby started crying again, so I brought him into the office and gave him two ounces of half-strength formula milk. 'He wolfed it down as if he was starving, doctor, it was pitiful.'

A shadow at the door signalled Mrs Gainsford coming into the office in her nightgown and bare feet. 'I won't stand for it, Dr Hammond! This ignorant woman picked my baby up and gave him a bottle of formula rubbish, knowing that I had expressly forbidden it, and in defiance of Dr Fisher's orders!'

'Which is why he's gone to sleep at last!' retorted Sister Hicks, emboldened by the doctor's presence. Shelagh saw that she must be firm, or the two women might come to fisticuffs.

'Stop it! Stop it, both of you,' she ordered. 'Think of the other mothers.'

'Dr Fisher will hear all about this!' said Mrs Gainsford angrily. 'And my husband's on his way to take my baby and myself home, out of this place, whether you like it or not!'

'You have a perfect right to take your own discharge, Shirley,' said Shelagh calmly. 'This hospital is not a prison. All we ask is that you will sign a form stating that you are discharging yourself against medical advice.' She winked at Sister Hicks. 'How's the auxiliary getting on with the tea and toast, Sister?'

'I shall write to the *Everham News* about this,' went on Mrs Gainsford angrily. 'I don't intend to let this outrage drop!'

In fact Mr Gainsford turned out to be bewildered and anxious, and not at all willing to take his wife and newborn baby home on a snowy February night, but Mrs Gainsford was adamant. She had already retrieved her toilet bag and birth-congratulation cards – the flowers would have to be left behind – and Shelagh said she had better take two hospital blankets, one to wrap around herself, the other to keep Justin warm on the car journey. The other mothers, wakened and disturbed by all the comings and goings, were not sorry to see them go. Justin, replete with his top-up, slept soundly as he was carried away.

Inevitably there were repercussions when the news got round, and Sister Hicks was called to the Midwifery Superintendent's office to explain what had happened. Shelagh found herself facing Mr Kydd and Dr Fisher; Leigh McDowall had also been asked to attend in Mr Kydd's office.

'I'm absolutely furious,' declared Dr Fisher, and was immediately reminded by Mr Kydd that he hadn't been there when it happened, and also that Sister Hicks was a reliable and observant midwife with years of experience of caring for newborn babies. He turned to Shelagh.

'Why did you allow this woman to leave the ward in the middle of the night with her baby, scarcely two days after a caesarean section, Dr Hammond?'

'I had no choice, sir. Mrs Gainsford was determined to leave, although her husband made an attempt to persuade her to stay. In my opinion she was showing warning signs of possible puerperal depression, and it would have been unwise to antagonise her further. I had to choose the lesser of two evils.'

Dr Fisher broke in. 'You should have telephoned me at home, Dr Hammond, to let me know what was going on.'

'With the greatest respect, sir, that would not have made the slightest difference.'

'Hm,' grunted Mr Kydd. 'You may leave us, Dr Hammond, because I don't think we're getting any further forward. Mrs Gainsford's general practitioner has been informed, and the district midwives will be calling twice daily. Matron will need to hold an inquiry about this, and I shall give my opinion then.' He gave her a smile as she left.

As she walked down the corridor towards the lift, McDowall hurried after her.

'I say, Shelagh, I wish you'd called me. I could have dealt with the couple, and persuaded her to stay. I've imbibed a lot about Dr Fisher's ideas. As it is, he's absolutely furious and not without reason, I'd say.'

Shelagh stopped and turned round to face him. 'And *I'll* say that I'm not afraid of some know-all paediatrician who comes interfering on the postnatal ward. Sister Hicks knows her job inside and out, and she's been devastated by all this.' She turned and continued walking. He continued to follow her.

'Look, Shelagh, be reasonable. Fisher's wife was delivered here a couple of months ago, and we didn't have all this caper, she was an example to the mothers that breast is best.'

'Don't talk to me about that man and his wife,' she retorted over her shoulder. 'He needs to learn that all mothers are not clones of Mrs Fisher.'

'For heaven's sake, *we* know that *breast is best*, and it's up to us to help the mothers achieve it.'

'Up to us, eh? An average, sensible woman who has tried her best to breastfeed her baby knows more about it than half a dozen male doctors.' She stopped, having arrived at the lift. Having completely lost his patience with her, he made no attempt to hide his exasperation.

'But Fisher's a consultant paediatrician, for God's sake!'

'Big deal. And I'm a woman.'

'Listen, Dr Hammond, have you ever breastfed a baby?'

'Not yet, Dr McDowall. Have you?'

The lift arrived with a clank, the doors opened and she stepped in. She pressed the 'down' button, and disappeared from his sight.

CHAPTER SEVEN

Well into February the snow continued to lay, where it froze overnight, making the paths treacherous in the morning. The elderly frequently slipped on trodden freezing snow, especially where the paving stones were uneven. It was outside Edward's that Miss Johnson fell, sending her walking stick flying. A group of shoppers congregated around her.

'Are you all right, dear?' 'Has she broken anything?' 'Does anybody know about first aid?' 'Can she stand up?'

Beryl was lying on her side, and gave a moan of pain. 'I can't pull myself up,' she gasped. 'Somebody will have to help me.' She quickly checked that her skirt was well pulled down, not showing her knickers. The contents of her shopping bag were spread around on the pavement.

A couple of shoppers raised her head and shoulders, which made her groan out loud.

Mrs Pearce from Edward's bakery shook her head. 'What we need is a good, strong man to heave you up, dear – oh, look, there's the vicar on the other side of the road – he'll help you!' She raised her voice. 'I say, Mr Bolt, this lady's had a fall, and needs somebody to help her to stand up. Could you come and oblige?'

Which was exactly what Beryl had planned when she apparently slipped and fell; in fact she sustained a bruise over her left hip which was unplanned but none the less painful.

With extreme reluctance Derek Bolt crossed the road. 'What's the trouble?' he asked. 'Can she not get up on her own?'

A moan from Beryl was the only reply, but she held up her right arm for him to take hold of, and with Mrs Pearce supporting her at the back, she managed to sit upright. Another heave brought her to a standing position, still clinging to Derek's arm.

'She can't walk in this state,' said Mrs Pearce. 'Just let's get you into the shop, my dear, and we'll brew you a nice hot cup of tea. Can you keep hold of her, Mr Bolt? Just so's we can get her into the bakery.'

Derek could find no way of escape. Beryl laid her head on his shoulder. 'Stay with me,' she whispered, 'don't let me go!'

The women exchanged glances, remembering

what had happened in church on Christmas morning. Everybody had heard about it.

'If we can support her just as far as the shop, she can sit down and rest,' said Mrs Pearce, happy to take charge of a tricky situation. 'Can you just put your arm around her, Mr Bolt, so that she can lean on you? That's right, we'll soon be there.'

But not quite soon enough. Daphne Bolt was just emerging from the chemist's when she saw her husband, half-leading, half-carrying Miss Johnson towards Edward's bakery, while a few other women watched and commented. It was the last straw: enough was enough. She stepped forward and faced the couple squarely.

'Let go of her at once, Derek. Stop making a fool of yourself,' she said loudly. 'And as for *you*, Miss Whatsername, you can stop this ridiculous carry-on, and take your hands off my husband *at once*, or you'll regret it. I won't stand for it!'

Derek had removed his supporting arm from Beryl's waist, and drew away from her, and her head drooped with no shoulder to rest on. The onlookers stared in fascination: this was a scene to tell and retell! Mrs Pearce stepped forward to support Beryl in place of the vicar.

'You needn't think you're going to get away with this!' Daphne called out to Beryl. 'You're going to hear from my solicitor tomorrow, let me tell you – you'll be ordered to stop this nonsense once and for all!'

Beryl was trembling all over as Mrs Pearce steered her into the bakery.

'Come on, my dear, let's get indoors,' said her rescuer, casting a contemptuous look back over her shoulder at the vicar before she shut the door.

Ignoring her husband, Mrs Bolt headed for the vicarage. Derek took the opposite direction, and found that he too was trembling. Daphne was more than capable of carrying out her threat, and he needed time to consider how he should act. Hitherto he had not thought it necessary to consult the Bishop of the Diocese, but if Jamieson the family solicitor was to become involved, he would be well advised to get his own story ready. That evening he wrote a letter to Bishop George Grieve, outlining the problem, rather than telephoning him out of the blue and having to launch into the ridiculous details.

The Matron of Everham Park Hospital, and the Medical Superintendent Dr Brooks, met together with Miss Coyle the Midwifery Superintendent at an informal meeting in Matron's office, to discuss the self-discharge of a maternity patient with her baby in the middle of a cold February night, two days after a caesarean section.

'If the Gainsfords send in a formal complaint, or if the incident appears in the *Everham News*, there will have to be an official tribunal,' said Matron, 'and we would be in a much stronger position if we hold an internal inquiry as soon as possible, and have a written record of it at hand.'

Dr Brooks agreed, and asked who should be present in addition to Dr Hammond.

'Harry Kydd, of course, as she's on his team, and Night Sister Hicks?' he suggested. 'And what about Fisher?'

'He'll make an enormous fuss if we don't,' she replied, 'and will no doubt give us his lecture on secrets of successful breastfeeding. I shall ask Miss Coyle to speak on behalf of Sister Hicks who has been thoroughly upset by this whole business, and has had to go to her doctor because of it. Miss Coyle considers that she has been punished enough, if indeed she has been at fault.'

'And we don't invite the Gainsfords to attend?'

'Oh, no, Dr Brooks, they would only be required to attend a tribunal, which we hope will not be necessary, as we've agreed.'

So Dr Shelagh Hammond was summoned to attend the meeting which took place two days later, at ten o'clock in the morning. She held her head high and was outwardly composed when asked to describe what had happened, beginning with being called to the postnatal ward at 2.40 a.m. She recalled it to the best of her ability, reporting that baby Gainsford was asleep when she arrived in the ward, having been given a small diluted formula feed by Sister Hicks. Mrs Gainsford, however, was very displeased.

'A bottle given to a baby whose mother was determined to breastfeed?' Dr Fisher cut in. 'Utterly irresponsible!'

'You will have your turn to speak, Dr Fisher,' said Dr Brooks. 'And so was this small bottle-feed the cause of Mrs Gainsford's self-discharge, Dr Hammond?'

'That and her state of mind, sir. She came near to physically attacking Sister Hicks for giving the baby a drink that finally settled him. He was a very large, hungry baby, and wouldn't suck at the breast because his mother's lactation was insufficient – in fact she had scarcely any milk, two days after a section.'

'And did you make any attempt to persuade Mrs Gainsford to stay?'

'No, sir. By this time she was hysterical, and had already telephoned her husband to come and take her home. And in my opinion, sir, she was showing signs of puerperal depression, and was incapable of listening to any reasonable explanation.'

'And when the husband arrived, was he equally insistent on taking her home?'

'No, sir, he'd have tried to persuade her to stay if she had been capable of listening to reason. I felt that she was mentally disturbed, and in letting her go, I chose the lesser of two evils. I lent her two hospital blankets to keep herself and the baby warm in the car.'

'And could you not have telephoned Dr Fisher at home to ask for his advice?'

'With respect, sir, it wouldn't have made the slightest difference.'

'Rubbish!' said Dr Fisher contemptuously.

Dr Brooks ignored him, and went on to question Miss Coyle about Sister Hicks, exonerating her for giving the bottle-feed. When Dr Fisher had his turn to speak, he condemned all concerned, and said that Mrs Gainsford was a sensible woman who wanted to do right by her baby son, and gave his opinion that she had been badly let down by insensitive midwives. Mr Kydd gave a good account of Dr Hammond's practice on his team, and mentioned that her mother was terminally ill. Dr Brooks immediately offered his sympathy, but Shelagh assured him that her mother's illness had nothing to do with her actions on that night. 'I would have acted in the same way, whatever my private problems.'

The meeting ended after twenty-five minutes. Dr Brooks gave Shelagh a mild reprimand, and a warning that in future she should not take too much responsibility into her own hands. 'Consultants are there to be consulted, doctor,' he said, though Dr Fisher clearly thought the outcome of the meeting was unsatisfactory.

'It will be a different story at the tribunal,' he said, 'when the Gainsfords are able to speak for themselves, and it's all in the local press. *Then* you'll hear the verdict of the local community,' he said with a certain relish.

When the outcome of the meeting became known, Shelagh met with both blame and sympathy.

'Congratulations, Dr Hammond, on getting off with just a slap on the wrists,' said Dr McDowall when she met him and Tanya Dickenson in the antenatal ward office. 'Only mind your step with Dr Fisher in future – he thinks the whole thing was mismanaged.'

'Thank you, doctor. I haven't anything further to say,' she replied coldly.

The next day she was summoned to Mr Kydd's office.

'Very sad news, Shelagh. Mrs Gainsford's GP has phoned to say she's been admitted to Bridge House as an emergency. It's a small private hospital, as you know, actually a psychiatric unit. The poor woman went completely berserk when she got home, and her husband thought the baby might be in danger, so their GP sent for an ambulance straight away, with a provisional diagnosis of puerperal psychosis. We can only hope that rest and sedation will restore her to normality. Her mother has come to look after the baby who's apparently thriving on formula milk. It's as well that you let her go when you did, but it's a sad business.'

'I'm so very sorry to hear that, Mr Kydd,' said Shelagh, thinking of the mother, the husband and the baby. She made no comment about it to any other members of staff, but when they came to hear of it, there was a great deal of commenting and head-shaking.

'Well done, darling!' enthused Paul when the story reached the doctors' mess. 'What a slap in the eye for that know-all Fisher!'

'What a tragedy for the family, just after the birth of their first baby,' she replied. 'Let's say no more about it, Paul.'

'When that wretched woman receives a letter from Jamieson, she'll find out that her pestering of you is to cease forthwith,' said Daphne Bolt.

'Can you hold your horses until I've spoken to the Bishop?' asked Derek. 'I've asked for an appointment with him to discuss the problem and what best to do about it.'

'Good. And you can tell him the whole truth – that you've never encouraged her in any way,' his wife replied sceptically. 'There are those who hint that it isn't all on her side, you know, and if you are completely blameless, we need to hear it. And *I* need to hear it – in court, if that's the only way to stop this nonsense.'

'Only wait until I've spoken to Bishop Grieve,' said Derek wearily. 'If it *does* turn into a public scandal – which it will do if she's taken to court – I want to get my story in first, and the Bishop on my side. And of course I want *you* to know that I'm not guilty of any wrongdoing, Daphne. I've been a fool, it's true, and I've regretted trying to be kind to the woman, but that's the extent of my fault, and nothing worse than that.'

* * *

Jeremy North was finding life easier to bear. The snow still lingered, but as the days began to draw out, the enlarged church choir still met on Thursday evenings to practise, and it was common knowledge that the choirmaster met Miss Oates from time to time, usually after choir practice in a public place like The Volunteer, where they talked. And his car had been seen in the hospital car park, and Sister Oates emerging from Outpatients, having changed into her usual neat hooded jacket and getting into his car.

'I don't think there's anything in it,' said Phyllis Maynard. 'It's all open and above board – they're never seen doing anything other than talk, and it's probably all about music.'

'They don't *have* to say or do anything untoward, you've only got to look at them,' retorted Mary Whittaker. 'See the sparkle in her eyes and the spring in her step. And he's happier, nobody can deny that. He was looking dreadful at Christmas. None of his family come to church, which is a pity, when you consider there are three of them, plus the wife and that dear little boy. They say the eldest girl's expecting again.'

'We mustn't jump to conclusions,' said her friend, though she too had heard the rumours. 'But if it's true, poor Jeremy!'

'Jeremy, I need a word,' said the vicar to the choirmaster after evensong.

'Is it about something I've done, Derek? – because if it is—'

'Nothing whatever to do with you and your soprano,' replied Derek, 'though I reckon that's being well chewed over and giving rise to all sorts of rumours. No, this is my problem, and I think you may be able to help me out. I hope so, anyway.'

'Mysterious,' said Jeremy, raising his eyebrows. 'Is it by any chance about a certain lovelorn spinster?'

'How did you know?' asked Derek quickly.

'The gossips of Everham talk of nothing else, old chap. What do you want me to do? – take her off your hands?'

'I only wish you could. You should see the letters, desperate love letters, gifts which I have to keep in the safe, out of sight – and the stalking, the sudden confrontations in public or in the church grounds, the pleading – it's intolerable, Jeremy. It's reached a point when something's got to be done, and if I won't do it, Daphne will. I decided to see the Bishop and ask for guidance—'

'Ah, that was a good move. What did his lordship say?'

'Frankly, he wasn't much use, and was inclined to treat it as a joke – "oh, come on, Bolt, use a bit of common sense, be firm with her", that sort of thing – he said that clergymen and doctors must accept that lonely and lovelorn women fall for them. He actually said that I took the situation too seriously – "you must

161

face the fact that for her you're just a masturbatory fantasy"—'

'Is that what he said? I've heard some name-calling in my time, but *that* one has to be a first,' said Jeremy, unable to keep a straight face.

'Yes, he thought it was funny, too, and I told him it was no joke. When I said that Daphne was going to see a solicitor, he said it would be much wiser to ask the woman to attend me in the vestry by appointment, and let her know that if she doesn't stop it forthwith, she'll be hearing from my solicitor and threatened with a court injunction.'

'But it'll just be her word against yours, won't it?'

'No, because I shall have a strong third-party presence there as a witness, an authoritative figure, preferably a man who will stand there looking suitably grave while I speak sternly to her – and who will not leave us alone on any account.'

'That sounds like a good idea. What about one of the churchwardens?'

'I'd like a man who's had some experience of domestic tension, Jeremy – and who has successfully pulled himself up, somebody liked and respected in Everham, articulate and – oh, you know who I mean, Jeremy!'

'Are you telling me that you mean myself, by any chance? No way, I'm no heavyweight here, Derek, on the contrary I'm gossiped about because of Iris Oates – and don't ask me to give her up, because she's the one individual who keeps me sane. No, *I'm* not the strong third-party presence you're looking for.'

'But I think you are, Jerry. You're *human*. People *like* you. And I'm asking you nicely to do this for me as a friend!'

'Well, if you really can't think of anybody else—'

'I can't. Name a day and a time when you can nip out of school.'

'Wednesday, say about ten?'

'Yes, that'll do.'

'Let's make it Wednesday week – give you a chance to think what you're going to say to the woman. That's er—' He took out his pocket diary. 'That's February 20th.'

'OK. And thanks a million.'

The continuing snow and ice brought in a stream of casualties, mainly elderly, who had slipped and broken hips, wrists and ankles. Paul looked tired, not surprisingly, thought Shelagh, after days and nights of overworking. And he was impatient.

'When can we have another weekend, darling?' he asked her. 'Or just a night away? This bloody snow keeps laying around, but we can get down to Eastbourne before dark. Or find some place a bit nearer?'

'It seems as if this winter is never going to end,' sighed Shelagh. 'Actually I'm off the second weekend in March, if that fits in with you.'

'I can make it fit, no problem. Seems like a hell of a time to wait, but make it the Saturday and we're as good as there. Oh, Shelagh, you need to get away just as much as I do. Your mother's still holding on, so you've got no immediate worries where she's concerned. I just want to – need to – we both do, darling.' His eyes looked into hers, and she felt almost guilty. Her mother might have a relapse at any time, in which case their night of love would have to be postponed for an indefinite period, but meanwhile she owed it to him to show that her feelings were unchanged, though she wished they could be officially engaged before midsummer. Perhaps after another tender lovemaking, it might happen . . .

Fiona North was in tears, the cause of her distress being Roy's two-year-old daughter Sally, to whom they were not allowed access.

'And the situation's not helped by your attitude to Roy,' she accused him, shrugging away the arm he had put around her shoulders. 'You won't let him stay here, your own son!'

'I've got him to join Alcoholics Anonymous, and found him a flat in Everham – he has just got to stand on his own two feet, he's twenty-three, not a child but a grown man – a married man, can't you see that? And I've got him this job as a garage forecourt attendant.'

'Do you call that a job?'

'Yes, it's a job that he can do, and will bring in a small wage – give him a chance to build up his self-respect. You never know, Amy might be persuaded to have him back.'

'That wicked woman, he's better off without her.'

'My dear Fiona, there's Sally to consider, and his responsibility to her – and *we* want to see her, she's as much our grandchild as Peter-poppet.'

'Amy refused him his rights, and threw him out!'

'Yes, because he was lurching home belching and hiccuping – what woman would want him in her bed, for Christ's sake? You'd throw *me* out if I was a drunk.'

'She drove him to drinking!'

'Oh, come on, Fiona, he was always drawn to the booze. Remember how we copped it when he was caught trying to buy liquor at the wine shop, underage? Anyway, I've done what I can for him, and now I want to see little Sally. I'm going to ask Amy if she will let her come to see us for one day a week.'

'Well, I'm not having that woman in my house. If I saw her I think I'd give her a fist between her eyes – and don't expect me to drive over there and grovel to her!'

'And Roy's lost his licence, so he can't go, so it'll have to be me, then.'

'I don't think it's asking too much of you. Roy has a right to see his daughter.'

'And we all want to see Sally, poor mite. Right, then, I'll ring Amy and fix a day. I'll make it Saturday if that's all right with her; I'm a bit tied up on Sundays with the choir.'

'Thank you,' she said in unsmiling acknowledgement.

'Oh, Fiona, if you only knew how much I long to be as we were,' he suddenly confessed, reaching out to take hold of her hand. 'If you could only see beyond your own family and realise that other people also have rights – it would make such a difference to us.'

'If you're telling me to chum up with that bitch of an Amy, you can save your breath.'

Don't say anything more, Jeremy North told himself. And thought of Iris Oates.

The snow of the longest winter since 1947 still lay in the churchyard when the Reverend Derek Bolt had summoned Miss Beryl Johnson to a meeting in the vestry of St Matthew's. He was there at half past nine, expecting that she would be early, and Jeremy North appeared at twenty to ten. Miss Johnson arrived five minutes later. The stage is set for the play to begin, thought Jeremy, noting Derek's nervousness and giving him a broad wink.

When Beryl had seen the envelope lying on the doormat, with her name and address neatly typed, she had no idea what it was or where it came from. It was not a utility bill or a begging letter from a charity, there being no such printed indication on the front or back of it.

When she picked it up and slit it open, she thought she would faint for joy. Derek Bolt was requesting a meeting with her in the vestry of St Matthew's church on Wednesday the 20th at ten! The typed letter was brief, and mention was made of Mr North who would also be present, but Beryl thought only of the main contents, that the man she loved as much as life was summoning – inviting? – her to a meeting with him.

What should she wear? Her choice settled on her best coat of brown-and-white tweed, and a brown beret in place of a hat. None of her shoes seemed right, and she bought an expensive pair of soft brown leather boots that almost matched her handbag. A light silk scarf completed the ensemble, and she set off with mixed eagerness and apprehension in equal measures, hoping that Mr North might not yet have arrived; but he was already there in the vestry where the two men had been talking. She smiled uncertainly at them, but their faces were serious as she entered the vestry.

'Please sit down, Miss Johnson,' said the vicar, though both men remained standing.

'I've asked to see you about the unsolicited letters and gifts you persist in sending to the vicarage,' Derek Bolt began. 'I have to keep the gifts in the safe, so that they will not be seen. My wife is very annoyed at the number of letters I receive from you, and it is partly due to her understandable anger that I have called you to this meeting. It is very disrespectful towards her, as well as the sudden meetings we have in the town, clearly planned by you, for example, when you slipped and fell in the market square.'

'Oh, Derek, you don't – you can't really know how I—'

He held up his hand. 'Let me finish, please. Your behaviour has become a joke in Everham, it's made me into a laughing stock, which is embarrassing for me and Mrs Bolt. I want no excuses, no pleading, I only want this nonsense to stop. Do you understand what I'm saying, Miss Johnson?'

'Please, Derek, if you'll only listen—'

'No, I don't want to listen. You must listen to me. I want this nuisance to *stop*, and I want your assurance that it will. Do you hear me? Do you understand?'

She began to cry, and her voice broke on a sob. 'Please, Derek, please will you ask Mr North to step outside for a minute—'

'Certainly not. Mr North is here at my request, to be a witness to everything said by either of us. I want him to hear your promise that you will stop harassing me. I don't want to exclude you from St Matthew's, though I think it would be advisable for you to attend another church while all this gossip is going on. So will you give me your assurance that you will stop following me?'

There was no intelligible reply. She continued to weep into a handkerchief, and Derek looked helplessly at Jeremy. Although Jeremy had been told there was no need for him to speak, he decided that he had better step in.

'Now then, Miss Johnson, Mr Bolt has put it to you fairly and squarely. You are not to pursue him any longer, because if you do he will take legal advice to force you to obey. You wouldn't like to be summoned to appear in court, would you? But that's what will happen if you persist in annoying him and his wife. Think of all the local newspapers, the embarrassment to all concerned. Come on, Miss Johnson, pull yourself together and be sensible. I know it's hard to feel as you do, but if you have any regard at all for Mr and Mrs Bolt, you will cease annoying them.'

Beryl now gave way to loud, uncontrollable sobs, and the two men looked at each other helplessly.

'What on earth am I to do, Jeremy?'

'You go, and leave her with me. Go back to the vicarage or whatever, and I'll drive her home. Go on, there's nothing more you can do, she wants you to comfort her, but that would be fatal. *Go!*'

And Bolt obeyed, leaving North to take a firm hold on Beryl's right arm and lead her, sobbing, out of the vestry, down to the west door, and out into the cold air. Holding firmly on to her, he took her to his car and pushed her into the passenger seat. He clicked her safety belt into position, then climbed into the driver's seat and started up the engine.

What was said on that short journey was a

repetition of what had already been said in the vestry, and finally ended when he made her promise to stop pestering the vicar. She finally answered with a despairing 'yes', which he made her repeat.

'You promise to – to keep this promise?'

'Yes. All right, yes.' It was barely a whisper.

He let her go, with pity in his heart, reflecting that his was not the only unhappy house in Everham.

How the news got out, nobody knew, but the three-way meeting in the vestry became known and talked about. Most of the women sympathised with the vicar and thought Miss Johnson a silly woman; others felt sorry for her and thought him unnecessarily harsh. Everybody praised Mr North's involvement, and approved of his role as referee, adding to his popularity as headmaster and choirmaster.

But . . .

'He and Miss Oates were seen together at that concert in the school assembly hall,' said Mary Whittaker.

'Yes, and seen by everybody there, all open and above board,' answered Phyllis Maynard who had her own happy thoughts. Tim and Jenny Gifford had been visited by a social worker following their application, and were due to attend an adoption panel on the ninth of May Phyllis could think of nothing else.

CHAPTER EIGHT

Spring 1963

Sunshine at last, lifting Shelagh's heart as she walked into the living room where Bridget sat by the window; Maura was in the kitchen, washing up after their lunch, but she at once put the kettle on to make another pot of tea for her niece.

'No, honestly, Auntie, I can't stay. I've just nipped in to see Mother,' Shelagh said, smiling. 'Isn't it heaven now that the snow has gone at last? I see the daffodils are out, and there are catkins on the tree at the corner.'

'Lambs' tails,' said Bridget. 'That's what we always called them.' She sighed. 'And there've been too many real lambs lost wid their poor mothers this year, buried under the snow on the hillsides, so I was hearin' on the wireless. It's been a terrible time for farmers, wid everythin' behind time.'

'But it's over now, and we can look forward to more days like this one – blue skies and bare arms!' Shelagh laughed, but covertly regarded her mother: the cancer still seemed to be in remission, and Maura was trying to believe that her sister was miraculously recovering. Shelagh was heeding Mr Kydd's advice to accept the temporary reprieve that had been granted, and did not discourage her aunt, though she shrank from the thought of Maura's disappointment and distress when her hopes were unfulfilled. Bridget herself did not refer to her condition, but there was a peacefulness about her, a calmness of heart and mind that seemed to fill the air of the whole house. Shelagh felt sure that her mother knew the truth, but was letting her sister continue to hope, enjoying these early spring days.

'Will ye be comin' to us over the weekend?' asked Bridget. 'Ye said ye were goin' to be free.'

Shelagh tried to reply easily, 'I can come over tomorrow night, Friday, but I'm, er – I've arranged to go out with friends on Saturday, and we'll be late back. So I'll be here until Saturday lunch.' She forced a smile to hide her troubled conscience, but it was of no use. She would not be any more relaxed than on her previous escape to Eastbourne with Paul; she would constantly worry, not only about the possibility of her mother's condition suddenly deteriorating, and also the fact that she was deceiving her mother and aunt. But she had promised Paul, and it would be for just one night – and she was determined that by the time they returned to Everham on Sunday morning, he would have agreed to an official engagement. And then she would bring him to visit her mother again.

She looked at her watch: she would be assisting Dr Rowan with a short theatre list this afternoon, a couple of D and Cs, a cone biopsy and removal of a Bartholin's cyst. It shouldn't take too long, and there would be time to make a quick visit home; she was on call tonight, Thursday, before her free weekend.

As it happened, the gynae list had to be cut short because of an emergency caesarean section sent over from Maternity with an antepartum haemorrhage. Dr Rowan took over, with her assisting him, and a healthy baby girl was duly delivered. As she removed her theatre gown, cap and gloves, the telephone rang in the theatre office, and a staff nurse came running to report what the switchboard had said.

'There's been a major incident,' she told them, 'an accident on the A325, an articulated lorry ran into a London coach, and cars piled up behind them. They're bringing the casualties here, and all medical and nursing staff who are free are asked to go down to Casualty to help. They say Diane Devlin's been seriously hurt. She was in a car with her boyfriend – and to think I was watching her on the television last night!'

'I'm on my way.' Shelagh hurried to the changing room to put on her white coat, threw her stethoscope round her neck, and checked that she had a tourniquet in her pocket – a length of stout rubber tubing to tie round a limb to stop haemorrhage; then she and Rowan ran down the stairs and along the bottom corridor to Casualty.

Never before had she seen such chaos as met her in Casualty that afternoon. The whole outpatients department had been taken over for the injured, the examination rooms being used for the more seriously hurt, while others sat or were laid on stretcher trolleys. There were the sounds of weeping and groans, orders being given and supplies of morphine and tetanus vaccination arriving in batches from the pharmacy, with a crate of intravenous saline. The X-ray staff had returned to their department, and Father Naylor, the hospital chaplain, hurried from one to another, giving such reassurance as he was able. Over all was a pervading smell compounded of blood, dirt, vomit and an element that Shelagh thought was the very odour of pain and fear. She braced herself.

Sister Oates was attempting to deploy such medical and nursing staff as were available, including two local GPs. She thankfully welcomed Dr Rowan and Shelagh.

'Dr Rowan, will you help with the late arrivals unloading from the ambulance – sort out stretcher cases from walking wounded? Dr Sykes is in Room Three, Dr Hammond – will you see if he wants any help? I had to take his nurse away – can you take him this pint of glucose saline and an IV-giving set?'

Shelagh took the set and entered the room, to find Paul Sykes examining a woman who lay on the couch. She was deathly pale, her red hair was bloodstained, and her clothes were dirty, torn and dishevelled. In spite of this, Shelagh recognised Diane Devlin, the well-known TV actress who played the female lead in a popular soap opera. She appeared to be unconscious, and made no movement as Paul Sykes lifted each eyelid in turn, and shone an ophthalmoscope into the pupils. He straightened up.

'Oh, hello, Shelagh – ah, thanks. My nurse has been called to some other vital need, so can you help me put up the drip?'

Shelagh nodded and handed him the giving set. She opened the bottle and pushed in the top end of the plastic tubing, letting the fluid flow through, and then clamped it off, hanging the inverted bottle on a portable drip stand. Taking the tourniquet out of her pocket, she tied it loosely round Diane Devlin's forearm. A faint moan of protest came from the white lips, and Paul leant towards her.

'Diane? Diane, can you hear me?' he asked softly, his lips close to her right ear. She gave another sighing moan, and then very slowly nodded.

He looked up at Shelagh with relief. 'She's recovering consciousness, so I don't think there's any serious head injury, just a badly fractured tibia and fibula, and multiple lacerations. And of course she's badly shocked.'

'And – her companion?'

'DOA,' he mouthed silently, and Shelagh experienced a hollow sinking of her heart. *Dead on arrival.* She thought of the suddenness with which this calamity had struck the busy arterial road. In just a few short moments of havoc death had claimed lives, and irrevocably changed others.

She watched while he whispered into Diane's ear. 'Don't worry, Diane, you're safe with us at Everham Park Hospital, and we'll look after you. You'll be all right, Diane.' He turned to Shelagh. 'Right, put on the tourniquet, let's get that drip up and going.'

He inserted the cannula into a prominent vein on the back of the right hand, and then the end of the giving set was connected, and the flow adjusted to about thirty drops per minute.

'Plaster,' he said, and Shelagh cut off a length of micropore tape. As she handed it to him, Sister Oates put her head round the door.

'Dr Hammond, will you go to Room One at once,' she said without ceremony. 'Dr McDowall has got three patients to attend to, and needs help.'

Shelagh nodded, and left Paul to attach the micropore tape to the tubing. 'Sorry, I'll have to go.'

'Yes, don't keep the great white chief waiting – and send me a nurse if you can find a spare one.'

As soon as she entered Room One, she felt the tension, and a smell of blood and perspiration rose to her nose and throat. Dr McDowall and a student

176

nurse were cutting off the bloodstained trousers of a pale-faced man of about forty to forty-five, lying on one of two couches, and his wife sat beside him. Her face was streaked with tears and dirt, and a rough dressing above her right eye was held in place with a hastily applied bandage. On the other couch a girl of about eighteen writhed from side to side, gasping and moaning at intervals. Shelagh summoned up all her self-discipline and professionalism, and as if in answer to a wordless prayer, she experienced a certain sense of calm in the midst of havoc; she was a doctor, and this was where she was needed.

'Right, Dr McDowall, what's to be done?'

He looked up and smiled as if he were greeting her in the bar of The Volunteer.

'Hi, Shelagh, you're as welcome as a win on the pools. Meet Mr and Mrs Hartley, Alfred and Grace. They've been chucked around on the road quite a bit, and Alfred has lost a fair amount of the red stuff. Dear little Nurse Kitty here has been giving out tetanus jabs like free biros, and I want to get a drip going as soon as we've cleaned up Alf.'

'Yes, I see. And the young lady?'

'Ah, yes, that's Cathy Hartley, their daughter who was with them in the car.'

'Not Hartley, doctor, she's my niece, and her name's North,' cut in Grace Hartley.

'We haven't any children, more's the pity.'

'Correction – niece. And if you could get some

177

sense out of her, it would be a godsend, Shelagh. She's either got internal injuries or a bad attack of the vapours, and I'm inclined to go for the latter.'

'Cathy's obviously in pain,' said Shelagh, picking up the girl's hand and feeling for her pulse.

'If you mean that she's throwing herself around as if she's been stung by a hornet, you'll find that her pulse and blood pressure are normal, and she won't answer a single question. Could you calm her down for us, Shelagh? It would do us all a favour, because quite frankly I haven't got time for an in-depth counselling session right now.'

Shelagh sensed his irritation and lack of patience with the girl as he reapplied himself to Alfred Hartley's needs.

'Kitty, me darlin', hand me that Venflon cannula – keep still, Alf – there we are! We'll get a couple of pints of blood cross-matched for you, but meanwhile here's a nice drop of Everham Park Special Brew running in – OK?'

He adjusted the flow of intravenous glucose and saline solution, and Shelagh turned her back on the group to give all her attention to the girl.

'Easy now, Cathy – ssh! Stop making that noise, and tell me where the pain is.'

The only response was an agonised grimace and an even louder groan as the girl clutched at her abdomen.

Shelagh looked down at her, and in a flash realised what was happening. She began to remove the girl's

178

stockings and knickers, and sure enough, there was fresh blood on them.

'Did you know that you were pregnant, Cathy?' she whispered in the girl's ear.

'No – I don't know – oh! – I wasn't sure – oh, *help* me!'

'Keep calm, Cathy, and hold tightly on to my hand. You're having a miscarriage. Be brave, now, it'll all be over soon.' Raising her voice she said, 'Nurse, I shall need some ergometrine – will you go and ask Sister Oates for an ampoule from the OPD drug cupboard?'

'Good God, whatever for?' asked McDowall. 'This is a multiple road-traffic accident, Shelagh, not the delivery unit – and I need Nurse Kitty to help me with these two.'

Shelagh spoke quietly and levelly to the student nurse. 'Go and get me an ampoule of ergometrine, nurse – *at once*, do you hear me?'

There was an authority in her voice that demanded instant obedience. The nurse glanced doubtfully at McDowall, and then hurried from the room. With her left hand Shelagh continued to hold the girl's hand, and with her right she laid gentle pressure on the lower abdomen. With the next expulsive pain, a fetus about the size of a closed fist emerged, still in its membranous bag, and with a tiny placenta attached. Shelagh judged it to be of about ten to twelve weeks' gestation. She reached for a kidney dish from a shelf, and quickly scooped up the aborted fetus to place in it, covering it with a paper towel and depositing it under the couch. The nurse hurried in with the glass ampoule which Shelagh snapped open, and asked for a 2cc syringe and needle to draw the contents up and inject into the girl's right buttock.

'*Ow!*' protested Cathy.

'Sorry about that, dear, but it will stop the bleeding,' she said. 'It's over now, and you won't feel any more pain.'

The student nurse watched open-mouthed, and so did Leigh McDowall.

'Oh, *heck*!' he exclaimed. 'Thanks a million, Shelagh – thank God you got here in time. I shall have to resign and get a job as a plasterer's mate—'

Shelagh turned blazing blue eyes upon him, and mouthed the words, 'Shut up!' with a meaningful glance at Cathy's uncle and aunt.

'Have I – have I lost it?' whispered the girl, gazing up at her.

'Yes, dear, you have – don't worry – ssh!' Shelagh whispered back. 'Your relatives don't know.'

'Is Cathy all right, doctor?' asked Grace Hartley. 'I've been so taken up with my Alf that I haven't paid much attention to my niece. We were taking her back to her parents in Everham. Is she badly injured?'

'No, Mrs Hartley, she'll be fine. We'll admit her to a bed here overnight, and then she can go home tomorrow.'

'Alfred will need to be admitted to a surgical ward, too, Grace,' said McDowall. 'Is it possible that you could go to your relatives tonight, the ones you were on your way to? We're going to be awfully short of beds, I'm afraid.'

'Well, yes, I suppose so, doctor, though I don't like leaving my Alfred.'

'Can we telephone your sister and ask her to come for you?'

'It's my brother, doctor – Mr Jeremy North. I can remember his number.'

Shelagh suddenly gasped at hearing the name, but quickly composed her face.

'Good, I'll call him up when I can find a free phone,' said McDowall. 'And – er – did you say that her niece will be staying in overnight, Shelagh?'

'Yes, Cathy's feeling much better now, but she'd better be observed. After all, she's had a nasty shock, though there aren't any other injuries.'

She noted Leigh McDowall's raised eyebrows, and shook her head slightly. If Cathy decided to confide in her aunt later on, that would be up to her, but Shelagh did not consider it her duty or her business. She hoped that McDowall too would keep his mouth shut.

Once the intravenous drip was running, Alfred Hartley visibly improved, and he was admitted to Male Surgical with a provisional diagnosis of internal haemorrhage from an unknown source, possibly a ruptured spleen. When Grace's brother arrived, McDowall told him that his sister could go home in his car, and straight to bed; his brother-in-law would have to stay in hospital, and so would his daughter, just for one night's observation.

Shelagh felt thankful for the family's sake that Cathy's miscarriage need not be disclosed; her elder sister, now at twenty-two weeks' gestation, was carrying twins.

By six o'clock the casualties had all been seen and assessed. Sister Oates reported that there had been two deaths and one not likely to survive. The miscarriage won't count as a death, thought Shelagh, for only live births, however premature, have to be registered as births; even so, Shelagh had been strangely affected by the lifeless, undeveloped fetus, already recognisable as a human being, which she had placed under the couch, out of sight. Seven men and ten women, including three children, had been admitted to wards, while a further nineteen had been discharged home with minor injuries. The outpatients department had been cleared of extra trolleys and wheelchairs; the examination rooms had been cleaned and replenished, and the floor mopped over with a detergent that was also a disinfectant. The staff were now drinking cups of tea dispensed by the Women's Royal Voluntary Service who had come in specially to reopen the refreshment bar.

'Oh, Dr Hammond, that North girl has been sent home with her aunt,' said Sister Oates. 'Sister Kelly on Gynae says that they're full to overflowing with surgical cases, and so I said she had better go home.'

Shelagh could hardly insist that room be found for Cathy; but she feared that the parents would be more likely to discover the truth if Cathy went home now, without a chance to calm down and conceal a pregnancy that had ended due to trauma.

She knew that she should now go back to Maternity to see if there was anything happening that would need her to be there, but for the moment her knees felt weak, and she sat down heavily on one of the plastic chairs of the OPD.

'Shelagh! There you are! How can I ever thank you for turning up to attend to that abortion? You were an angel sent from heaven!'

There was not much of the angel in the look she gave him. 'I think the less said about that, the better, Dr McDowall,' she said with ice in her eyes.

His shoulders slumped apologetically. 'Yes, I know how you must feel, Shelagh, and I'm never going to forget missing out on that girl,' he confessed. 'I'm thankful that you came in when you did, and I just want to acknowledge the fact, that's all. And let's face it, it *was* a lucky break for her!'

Shelagh thought this remark uncalled for, but knew it to be true, so let it pass. She stood up and faced her junior house officer, tight-lipped and unsmiling.

'I can forgive you for missing a fairly obvious abortion, Dr McDowall, but I object to your general attitude – your total indifference and impatience towards that girl, who was clearly very distressed. And your infuriating compulsion to crack feeble jokes on every occasion, no matter how inappropriate, is *not* appreciated in such a sensitive field as obstetrics and gynaecology.'

'Oh. I see. Good of you to let me know how you feel, Shelagh. Thank you. But look, we've got to go on working together for another four months, so we might as well be friends, don't you agree?'

He held out his hand to her, but she ignored it and said, 'Just remember that we are doctors, and not stand-up comedians. I'm not much good at one-liners.'

All of a sudden her voice broke, and tears stung her eyes. Good grief, she mustn't cry in front of this man! She quickly rose and turned her back on him, walking briskly towards the lower corridor and the lifts up to Maternity. She might be needed in the Delivery Unit.

When Jeremy, his sister and his daughter arrived home in Jeremy's car, Fiona at once seized Catherine in her arms.

'Whatever happened to you, darling? Was it very dreadful? Oh, thank heaven to see you home again and safe!' It was left to Jeremy to welcome his sister into his home.

'Oh, hell, Grace, this has all been our fault, after you've kept Catherine for so long!' he said in self-reproach. 'If she'd come home earlier—'

'No, don't blame yourself, Jerry, it was time for her to come back to you.'

'Well, you'll want a hot bath, I expect, and then go to bed. We'll put you in Roy's room. And tomorrow we'll visit Alfred.'

'It looks as if we'll have Grace here for a time, Fiona,' he said a little later. 'While Alfred's in hospital. How's Cathy? She seems a bit subdued.'

'Well, can you wonder at it, after all the child's been through?' Fiona retorted. 'I've put the poor girl straight to bed, with a hot drink.'

'The same for Grace, I'd guess. I'm putting her in Roy's old room.'

'And what if our son turns up needing his room, may I ask?'

'He can't have it. He's got that flat with his boozing buddy, and he's not going to come back and live here, as I've told him and you. God knows my sister and Alfred have done us a good turn for taking Cathy off our hands for so long.'

'My Cathy has just told me that she's wanted to come home for weeks, so it couldn't have been *that* marvellous with the Hartleys, being put to work at that old people's home. She needed her mother!'

Jeremy did not reply, but went to see if his sister needed any assistance with her bath. Here at least he was appreciated. He'd had to cancel choir practice this evening, and felt the lack of it.

Shelagh answered the phone in the antenatal ward office. It was Paul.

'It's no good, darling – the hospital's chock-a-block with all these accident casualties. Fielding's going to be around all weekend, and I have to be here, too.'

'Of course, Paul, I understand, we simply have to call it off. It's a big disappointment, but – how's Diane Devlin?'

'Only so-so. That tib and fib are well and truly smashed at the ankle. Fielding will do what he can for her, working with the orthopaedics, but she could be left with a limp.'

'Poor girl. At least she's survived. Does she know about—er—?'

'Not yet. We'll wait until she asks about him. Better ring off now.'

'Of course. Bye, Paul.'

She replaced the receiver. Disappointment? But she would not have to deceive her mother again.

'Catherine's staying in bed today,' said Fiona the next morning. 'She's got her period, and it's unusually heavy and painful. The accident must have brought it on early.'

'Poor kid. I'll pop up to see her before I go to school.'

186

Cathy was sitting up in bed. 'Hi, chick, how're we doing? Got over the shock yet?'

'I don't feel at all well, Daddy. I've got the most awful period pains.'

'Oh, poor you,' he said with a smile, noting her pallor. 'When was it due to come on?'

'I don't know, in a couple of weeks. Daddy, can you get me a cup of tea and a couple of paracetamol?'

'OK. And when exactly did this one start?'

'When I was taken into hospital, after being thrown from one side of the road to the other – Daddy, can't you stop asking questions, and get me tea and paracetamol, please?'

'Sorry, chick. D'you think we ought to ask Dr James to call?'

'Oh, for heaven's sake, *no*! There's no need for *him* to come round asking me a load of questions! After all, it's only a period.'

'Hm. All right, I'll send your mother up with the tea and tablets. I'm off to school now. Bye, chick – hope you'll feel better when I come home.'

He sent Fiona up to her, and decided to walk to school and enjoy the warm spring weather after the long and snowy winter. He also decided to have a word with his sister.

Alfred Hartley's operation was performed on the night of his admission, a laparotomy to examine his internal organs. Mr Fielding told his wife and brother-in-law

187

the next day that there had been severe bruising of muscles, and some trauma to the liver and spleen, though not severe, and it should heal spontaneously. The only treatment had been to aspirate out the stale blood and clots from the abdominal cavity, and to start a course of antibiotics. They were told that he was to stay in hospital for rest and a light diet until the course was completed, and then if satisfactory to be transferred to a hospital in Basingstoke. Grace Hartley recovered well from the shock and minor abrasions; a long gash across her forehead at the hairline had to be redressed, cleaned and bandaged by a district nurse. Although she had pain from this and a persistent headache, she made no complaints, so great was her relief at the outcome of Alfred's injuries.

But on the subject of her niece she was not very forthcoming. 'All went well up until Christmas,' she told her brother. 'In the New Year she started to be moody, said she was fed up with working at the old people's home. Alfred and I urged her to stick at it, and he told her that if she gave it up she would have to return to you.'

'And did her moodiness improve?' asked Jeremy.

'Not really. She was irritable and off her food – and I thought she didn't look well.'

'Gracie, tell me the truth. Did you suspect that she might be pregnant?'

'It crossed my mind, Jerry, but I couldn't ask her outright – that's for her mother to do. This week I asked her if there was anything troubling her, and could I help – but she rounded on me and told me to mind my own business. That's when Alfred said she must go home.'

'Oh, Grace, I'm so sorry. And it's led to all this—' Jeremy was conscience-stricken at what his sister and brother-in-law had suffered because of his wilful daughter.

'Don't blame yourself, Jerry. If Cathy *was* pregnant, she isn't any more. There was a lady doctor who was attending to her, but I couldn't think of anything but my Alfred. There was certainly a lot of blood around, and the doctor sent a nurse for a special injection which she gave to Cathy. It *might* have been a miscarriage, Jerry, but that's all I can say.'

'Bloody hell,' said Jeremy.

'Look, Jerry, as soon as Alfred is ready to transfer to Basingstoke, I'll go with him, and get out of your way.'

'Good God, Gracie, you're not in anybody's way here.'

There was a pause while they looked at each other, and then Grace spoke again.

'Jerry dear, you've got a lot on your plate right now, what with Denise and Roy, and I only wish I could help in some way, but – well, you know how it is with other people's marriages. Outsiders just must not interfere.'

He sighed deeply. 'Bless you, sis, you'll be glad to

get away from here. And glad that your marriage is so different from ours.'

'Yes, but we didn't have children, Jerry, which was a big disappointment to us.'

He laughed shortly. 'And now you realise what a lucky break that was!'

It was coffee time in the doctors' mess two days later. Paul Sykes was in a towering rage. 'I'm absolutely incandescent!'

'Why, what's up?' asked Dr Fisher.

Sykes spread out the *Everham News* on one of the tables. 'Look at that!'

Right across the front page was the headline:

BRAVE DIANE MOURNS IN HER HOSPITAL BED

There was a photograph below it, showing Diane Devlin peeping over a mountain of flowers, cards and letters from well-wishers.

'Wow! I say, that's a bit over the top, isn't it?' one of the doctors remarked.

'And that isn't all. Look, here, inside!'

He turned a page, and there was Diane again, looking tragically into the camera. Two nurses stood one on each side of her, their hands upon her shoulders. The caption ran:

NURSES IN BEDSIDE VIGIL WITH HEARTBREAK DIANE

There was a murmuring among the onlookers, and glances exchanged.

'Who took the pictures?' he was asked.

'It must have been that damned photographer who clicks on the newborns in Maternity, what's his name, Roger somebody. God only knows how he got in. If I see him, I'll strangle him.'

Dr Leigh McDowall studied the photograph. 'What a villain, Paul, to force his way in to upset the lovely Diane – though I must say, she's beautifully made up.' He turned and left the mess before Sykes could come up with a rejoinder, and made his way to the antenatal ward, where both patients and staff were having mid-morning coffee.

'Has anybody got an *Everham News*?' he asked, and found that Tanya and Laurie were already poring over the pictures in a newspaper borrowed from a patient.

'It must have been an inside job, one of those two nurses let him in, probably at night,' said Tanya. 'Oh, good morning, Dr Sykes! Coffee?'

Sykes, who had followed McDowall over from the mess, ignored her invitation, and said he was looking for the baby photographer. 'And if those nurses were responsible for letting him in, I'll have them reported to Daddy Brooks.'

Shelagh Hammond, quietly sipping coffee in a corner, asked him how Miss Devlin had taken the news of her fiancé's death. He replied angrily,

'That's another reason why I object so much to this heartbreak stuff. The fact that he was still – er – married to somebody else, but was going through a divorce, should be entirely private. What a nerve, plastering details of her life all over the newspaper! The national tabloids will take it up next. I'll throttle the bastard.' He looked to Shelagh for support, but she put down her cup and beckoned to Laurie. 'We'd better get on with those two ARMs, Nurse Moffatt.'

'They're all ready for you, doctor,' replied the staff midwife. Artificial rupture of the membranes was an uncomfortable and quite painful procedure for the mother, but labour usually started within the next twenty-four hours, especially if the woman was overdue.

And it got Shelagh out of the office.

Elm Grove was a handsome, five-storey Edwardian house on the Everham Road, just south of the town. A hundred years ago it had been the residence of a wine merchant and his wife and five children which had increased to eight, with a hierarchy of servants.

Times had changed, and soon after the end of the Second World War, an enterprising estate agent had bought Elm Grove and turned it into three self-contained flats, plus the basement for storage and an attic for letting out to students. The spacious ground-floor flat, designated as Number One Elm Grove, now belonged to Iris Oates, and she had taken a week of her annual leave to be free for the all-important day of moving in, from her bedsitter in Everham.

'The removal van will be coming on Tuesday,' she told the choir members. 'That will take the furniture, including my little piano, and they've left me six tea chests to pack all my belongings in.'

'Six!' exclaimed Phyllis Maynard. 'Surely you won't need that many.'

'I didn't think so, but when you think of what I must pack carefully in crumpled newspaper – clothes, shoes, bed linen, tablecloths and towels – kitchen utensils, crockery, cutlery, glassware, ornaments, pictures and photographs – and all my books—'

'Stop! It sounds as if you'll need all six chests,' laughed Phyllis. 'Well, I'll be happy to come round and help with packing. Shall I come at ten o'clock on Tuesday?'

'Oh, Phyllis, that would be so kind,' said Iris. 'I've got a nurse friend who'll be able to come for a couple of hours in the afternoon, and another friend who's a physiotherapist is coming in the evening – so it looks as if there'll be willing hands enough, but I'd be most grateful if you could give me a little help. Thank you!'

'And on the Wednesday there'll be everything to unpack and put in its new place,' Phyllis reminded her. 'Count me in for that, too.'

'And we'll have a fish and chips supper, my treat,

to show my appreciation,' said Iris happily. 'We'll get it from Sammy's, that shop in the square.'

With the move and the unpacking completed, Iris and her three helpers sat down to eat the supper that Phyllis had fetched in her car from Sammy's.

'Doesn't it look cosy and homely with all the pictures and photos up?' said the physiotherapist, and Iris's heart beat a little faster. This would be a proper home, a place of her own to which she could invite friends. And of course she could ask Jeremy North to come here, with the benefit of being able to talk freely in privacy. And perhaps practise a hymn or a song or two, she thought, sitting at my little piano. What bliss! What absolute joy . . .

CHAPTER NINE

Summer 1963

May came in with the latest news of Diane Devlin's progress at Everham Park Hospital; she had had two operations on her injured leg, and was still having to stay in bed to avoid any weight-bearing on it. She was able, with assistance, to leave her bed and be helped into a wheelchair, so that members of staff could wheel her to see other parts of the ward and chat with staff and other patients. When she acquired a stick resembling a shepherd's crook, to which she tied a large pink bow, Mr Fielding started calling her Little Bo Peep.

At Everham Primary School and St Matthew's church, there was tension in the air; Jeremy North's face showed increasing strain, and when Rebecca Coulter asked him if he were ill, he shook his head and admitted that life was a bit difficult at present, but that it was nothing to do with the choir. Iris Oates looked on helplessly: should she invite him to visit her in her new home, and then perhaps he would confide in her, so that she might comfort him? The reason she did not was because she knew that such a meeting, such an opportunity, would lead to an inevitable consequence, and there would be no way back. This was something that he must decide, not she; she was there for him when he needed her, that was all. So she stayed silent, her heart yearning for him.

Then, at choir practice one Thursday evening, Jeremy's eyes were shadowed by dark rings beneath them, and his mouth was set in a grimly straight line, suppressing any tendency to tremble. For once he did not seem to be enjoying the music, and when the practice was over, he offered lifts to the ladies as usual; Phyllis and Rebecca squeezed into the back seat, and Iris was about to sit down in the passenger seat, but noticed Miss Johnson standing near them looking desperately unhappy, and felt she had no choice but to give up the seat to her, hoping that the three others in the car would encourage her to talk, and perhaps give her some comfort. She told Jeremy that she was perfectly happy to walk home on such a beautiful May evening, and they exchanged a wordless but meaningful glance.

Walking home while revelling in her own secret

thoughts, anticipations and seemingly impossible dreams, she turned on the radio when she arrived, but was unable to concentrate on the news which continued to focus on the rumours around Westminster and Mr Macmillan's government.

When the doorbell rang at half past nine, she rose and went to answer it with a trembling heart. She knew who would be standing on the doorstep, and held back the door to invite him in.

'I can't stand it any longer, Iris,' he told her with a sort of quiet desperation. 'So I've come to you. I don't know where else to go. Will you let me stay?'

She held the door open, and he stepped over the threshold. She closed the door and drew the bolt across, then turned to him and held out her arms. He embraced her and kissed her cheek; then his lips found her eager mouth, and they stood locked together in a kiss that changed Iris Oates' life, a kiss to drown in.

When at last they separated, she led him to the living room and invited him to sit down on one of the two armchairs. She went into the kitchen, and switched on the electric kettle, setting out two mugs on a tray.

'D-do you want anything to eat – egg on toast, or—' she began shakily.

'No, tea'll be fine, thanks.'

Such a mundane question and answer, no endearments, not even names, for there was no need for lovers' talk. He had come to her and she had welcomed him into her home and her heart. And when he lay naked in her bed, she lay beside him, ready and willing for him to enter her body.

Jeremy knew her to be a virgin, and held himself back, not without difficulty, while he gently explored her with his forefinger and then a second finger, to open the entrance to her body. She gasped with pleasure, and hardly felt a brief spasm of pain; when he considered her to be ready, he inserted his swollen member, and within seconds they achieved climax together. For her it was so simple, so easy, the most natural thing in the world.

Daphne was waiting for her husband, the opened letter in her hand.

'Right, this settles it, this is the last straw! Read it and deny it if you can, then show it to our solicitor and take this madwoman to court!'

Derek had half a mind to tell his wife that she had no right to open his mail; as a clergyman he had to keep the secrets of all who confided in him, but on this occasion she had recognised the handwriting and was about to take action. He looked at her hopelessly.

'Have you heard what I said? If you won't see reason, I'll go and see Jamieson myself, and the *Everham News* – I'll ask them to print it, so that everybody can read it. Will you answer me, please?'

'Daphne, I'm sorry about this – and sorry for that poor woman—'

'Poor woman my foot! Will you answer me *now*, this minute?'

'All right, I'll make an appointment with Jamieson as soon as he can see me.'

'Today, if possible – and at the very latest, tomorrow.'

'All right, Daphne, I'll phone him now.'

'Good. And you'd better keep this ridiculous letter with any others you've got, to use as evidence of harassment.'

He read the letter in his study. It was desperate indeed.

I cannot endure this emptiness, your stony face, your cruel words. I can neither eat nor sleep, I'm starving, I'm pining, I'm fading away. I cannot obey your order to stay away from all that makes my life bearable. Oh, Derek, love of my life, greater than my love for God, if he exists, which I'm not sure of, though I'd gladly worship him if he would soften your heart towards me. I respect your wife and her legitimate demands on you – but even she could hardly begrudge me a word, a touch, a smile, anything to show me mercy. I go to bed at night, and can no longer imagine your arms around me because you have withdrawn yourself from me. I'm the sorrowing woman in the Song of Songs:

'By night on my bed I sought him whom my soul loveth. I sought him, but I found him not. I opened to my Beloved, but my Beloved had withdrawn himself and was gone. I sought him, but I could not find him. I called, but he gave me no answer.'

Oh, let these words speak to you, touch you, make you relent, my only love.

And he was about to betray her – and might find himself in a storm of gossip like that now surrounding Jeremy North – or like the persisting rumours of an illicit affair between a government minister and a young blonde model who was also entertaining a Russian diplomat, which might constitute a security risk. The minister concerned had stood up in the House of Commons to deny the rumours, but the newspapers continued to be full of it.

Over coffee and toast, Jeremy told Iris how his life had worsened in the North household.

'My younger daughter has miscarried, due to the road accident, thank heaven, but the elder – my daughter Denise—' He could not go on.

'Don't be afraid to tell me, Jeremy,' she said softly. 'I already know that she's carrying twins.'

'You know? Oh, yes, of course, from the hospital. When Fiona told me just as I got home, I lost control of myself, and we had a bitter row. I blamed her to her face that she'd ruined the children and our marriage with it. She asked what the hell was I talking about, and why I was so unloving towards our children. That was when I said, "Our children? Do you mean that useless drunk we call our boy, and those couple of sluts we call our girls?"'

'And what happened then, Jeremy?' she asked quietly.

'She went for me like a wildcat – see this scratch under my eye? She clawed at me, she pulled at my hair, she tried to kick me in the crotch – I had to fend her off as well as I could, she was screaming her head off, and I thought of Peter-poppet upstairs, perhaps hearing it – so I shot out of the back door, and – and – oh, Iris, what shall I do?'

'Stay here, of course, Jeremy. Move in with me while you decide what best to do. Oh, Jeremy my love, stay with me for as long as you like – forever!'

'Dearest Iris, how can I ever repay such kindness—'

'Kindness has nothing to do with it, Jeremy,' she replied truthfully. 'It's my pleasure, my joy, my love for you, my happiness because you've come to me.'

As May progressed, the ongoing saga of Jeremy North and Miss Oates continued to rage. Opinions were divided as to who was most to blame, and those who, like Mary Whittaker, considered the headmaster's behaviour unforgivable expected that he would be discharged from his duties at Everham

Primary. She and others reckoned without his popularity with pupils, staff and parents, and while not condoning the fact of his leaving his family to live illicitly with another woman, they hoped that the situation would be resolved, as they did not want to lose him. The parishioners of St Matthew's were also in two minds about what should happen to the talented choirmaster; the choir continued to meet and practice on Thursday evenings, though their soprano Iris ceased to attend.

'If there are those who don't want to sing in the same choir as myself, Jeremy, I'll settle their dilemma for them, and stay away,' she told him, though he begged her to stay, for the sake of her sweet soprano voice, the best in the choir.

'There may come a time when I shall feel able to join again,' she said, 'but for now it's best if I stay away, to save embarrassment.'

'*I'm* not embarrassed, Iris,' he said. 'Let them say what they like about us.'

'But some of them *will* be embarrassed, and the vicar will be criticised for tolerating us,' she replied, refusing to change her mind. She continued to attend church regularly, but refrained from partaking of Holy Communion, as did Jeremy, to Derek Bolt's relief, because as vicar he could not countenance open and unashamed adultery. His own private thoughts were very different, knowing Jeremy's domestic situation as he did. He gave no public opinion, and when directly approached and asked to say what he thought and where he stood as regards Mr North, he replied that only God must be the judge. He knew that when his case against Beryl Johnson for harassment came up in court, he too would be at the centre of a scandal, albeit of a different kind, and to take a high moral stand against Jeremy North would lay himself open to a charge of rank hypocrisy. In the town, Fiona North had no compunction whatever in letting her husband's perfidy be known to all who would listen.

The Education Department of Everham Borough Council sent for Jeremy to question him, but not to condemn him out of hand. They had no wish to lose an excellent headmaster, and there was no suitable person, male or female, to take over the headship at the present time. At the end of the interview the Education Committee made him wait outside the boardroom while they discussed his case among themselves; and by a vote of three to one decided to leave him in his post until the end of the school year in July, in the hope that circumstances might have changed by then, and he restored to his family and responsibilities as a husband and father.

Shelagh Hammond and Paul Sykes had reopened their caravan at Netheredge, but had not yet used it themselves; they had let it out to friends and acquaintances for early holidays. Both of them were busy at their work, and had not yet had the same time off together, even for just one night. Shelagh was not sorry; Bridget had been showing signs which indicated that her time of remission was coming to an end, and Shelagh could not risk leaving her for a night. She wanted Paul to visit her mother again, and reassure her of their engagement, to become official at midsummer, but the days went by without an opportunity, and he confessed that he was reluctant.

'I *want* to visit your mum again, Shelagh, but things are a bit hectic on surgical at present,' he apologised. 'Diane's had two operations on her leg, and will need another – that tib and fib were smashed to bits, and she won't be able to walk without crutches for some time. And to be honest, darling, she's rather taken to me, in fact she told Mr Fielding about her preference, and he agrees that we mustn't do anything to lessen her confidence in herself and her career. I know you'll understand.'

'Of course I do. I saw you pushing her in her wheelchair in the grounds yesterday afternoon,' Shelagh replied drily; 'and I've heard the rumours, of course, but I discount them. We all know that female patients often fall in love with their doctors.'

'Oh, I wouldn't say *that*, Shelagh,' he said with a slight, self-deprecating shrug. 'Don't forget, the poor girl has only just lost her, er, boyfriend. She's desperately worried about her injury, and the effect it might have on her career if she's left with a limp. Mr Fielding mentioned the possibility to her, and she's got this idea that I'll be able to put it right for her – I only hope that I can, for her sake. But it's good of you to be so sweet and understanding.'

Jenny and Tim Gifford were jubilant after their interview with the adoption panel.

'We think we did well, Mum,' said Jenny eagerly. 'There were two men and two women on the panel, and they asked us lots of questions – and we must have given them the right answers! There are quite a lot of poor little mites in care and available for adoption, they said. They prefer the adoptive parents to live a long way away from the birth mother, to prevent the children being followed by relatives – so we might get one from the north or the South West, maybe Wales or Scotland. The social worker told us we have to go and visit the child and the foster home at some point, to see how we get on, and if we take to the child – and he or she to us! – oh, Mum, that won't be a problem – I feel that I love this little one already, even before we know who he or she is!'

'Me too, Mum,' added Tom.

Phyllis Maynard shared the happy anticipation of her daughter and son-in-law, as did Jenny's colleagues at Everham Primary, glad to see her happy after the bitter disappointments of the past.

'Jeremy North says he's thrilled for us, Mum – he's *such* a nice, decent man, in spite of all the talk about him leaving his family and going to live with a sister from the hospital. All *we* know is that he looks happy again, after being so tense and strained for so long. Good luck to him, we say!'

It was a warm summer afternoon. Shelagh's head throbbed, and she closed her eyes momentarily, then made an effort to concentrate her mind on the matter in hand: assisting registrar Dr Rowan at an afternoon list in the gynaecological theatre. She had hardly slept during the preceding night, the Delivery Unit having been busy: even when midwives had delivered a baby, a doctor was still called upon to suture episiotomies and tears of the perineum. And she had waited around for two hours for a first-time mother to give birth: a nervous student midwife conducted the delivery under the supervision of a particularly garrulous midwife who kept exhorting the woman to push down. Early on, Shelagh had suspected that help would be needed, and finally intervened to tell the midwife to prepare for a forceps delivery. The head was high and a local anaesthetic had to be given between contractions; a long, steady pull had been required, and a baby boy was born, rather limp and slow to breathe; the midwife had taken him to clear his air passages and gently blow upon his body to stimulate him to gulp in air, and meanwhile Shelagh had to deal with a brisk blood loss which continued until expulsion of the placenta, amounting to a post-partum haemorrhage; the student midwife had given the injection of ergometrine to cause the uterus to contract, but it had been a traumatic delivery, and Shelagh wondered in retrospect if she should have sent for Dr Rowan who might have decided on caesarean section. After suturing the episiotomy, she had returned to her bed but sleep was impossible. And here she was, almost falling asleep in the gynae theatre. Dr Rowan glanced at her across the operating table.

'You all right, Shelagh? You were up half the night with that "forks", but you did well. The mum and baby are fine.'

'Yes, it was a long, hard second stage for the mother – we were all exhausted.'

'And how's *your* mum these days?'

'Not so good, Dr Rowan. The remission seems to be coming to an end.'

'Yes, so Mr Kydd was saying. Look here, you go and have a rest. Sister can assist with these minor ops, can't you, Sister?'

'No problem,' the theatre sister answered.

'Off you go, then.'

Thankfully she stepped aside from the table, peeled off her gloves, and wriggled out of her green gown. She could have gone for a rest on her bed, but decided to use the unexpected break to call in on her mother.

Arriving home in the mid-afternoon, she was met by a dismayed Aunt Maura who put a finger to her lips and whispered, 'Hush, Shelagh, your mother's got a visitor!'

'A visitor? Who?' asked Shelagh in surprise. 'Has Dr McGuinness called? Or Father Orlando?'

'No, no, neither o' them, Shelagh. I've put 'em in the front room,' said Maura in some agitation. 'The fact is, ye see, Shelagh, she wants to be left alone, not to be disturbed.'

'What's going on? Are you keeping something from me, Aunt Maura?'

'No, but – ye see, we weren't expectin' ye.' Poor Maura looked like a naughty child accused of wrongdoing. 'It – it's the doctor.'

'What? Oh, yes, I think I see,' said Shelagh in relief. It must be Paul! He had decided to visit Bridget after all, and reassure her about his intentions. Bless him! And before Maura could say another word, she opened the door to the front room and stepped inside. And then stopped dead. Maura followed and stood behind her. Her mother and Dr McDowall were seated together at the table, on which a number of documents were spread out.

'What on earth is going on?' she demanded with an annoyance that sprung from anxiety and fatigue. 'What are you doing here, Dr McDowall? What right have you to come here in my absence to discuss private matters with my mother? What's *this*?' She stepped forward to seize an official-looking certificate from the table, but McDowall covered it with his hand.

'Not so fast, Shelagh. It's not how it looks. There's nothing "going on", as you say. Your mother and I have every right to hold a private discussion if she so wishes. We weren't expecting you—'

'Obviously not!' she retorted, her face flaming. 'I'm only her daughter, after all! Mother, I demand to know what you've been saying to this man—'

'Will ye *shut up*, Shelagh!' Bridget almost shouted. 'I sent for him, so I did! I asked him to come while ye weren't here – and can't I ask who I please to me own house?'

She covered her face with her hands. Shelagh stared in shocked amazement, and McDowall put his arm around Bridget, drawing her head against his shoulder, and whispering gently into her ear. He then looked up at Shelagh with quiet but unanswerable authority.

'Will you kindly leave us, Shelagh?'

Incredulously she stared at him, then turned and left the room. Maura closed the door, and followed her niece into the kitchen, where Shelagh collapsed on to a chair.

'What have I done, Auntie, for her to send me away and let *him* hear all her private matters? If she wants to make a will or something, why doesn't she send for Jamieson?'

'Sure, there's no harm in the man,' soothed her aunt. 'She sent for him, and I wasn't to be tellin' ye – but Bridget would *never* plot against ye, Shelagh, ye know that.'

'I know, or I thought I knew,' said Shelagh with a

sob. 'Oh, my poor mother, something's troubling her, and why can't she tell me?'

She was wiping her eyes when the door opened and McDowall came in. He smiled at Maura.

'Is the kettle on, Maura? I reckon we could do with a good strong Irish brew all round, and your sister is to rest.' He took hold of Shelagh's hand. 'Now, my dear, you must promise me never to mention this business to your mother. She's suffered quite enough. I can assure you that we were not plotting anything against you, quite the contrary. You'll just have to trust me. Can I have your word on that?'

She nodded dumbly. 'I've got no choice. I won't have her upset for anything.'

'Good. What have you been up to? You look like a ghost. Did you faint in theatre or something?'

'Nearly. Dr Rowan sent me off to rest.'

'Good man. And now you can. Go to bed, and stay there till morning. I'll cover for you tonight, OK?'

'All right.' Shelagh capitulated, afraid that she might start crying again if they argued.

When he had put all the documents away in a locked metal box, and Bridget had been settled down in her bed, Leigh McDowall left the house. Maura looked thoughtfully at her niece.

'Sure, it's plain to see that doctor cares about ye, Shelagh,' she said.

* * *

'Will she have to appear in court, Jamieson?' asked the Reverend Derek Bolt. 'Because if she does, I honestly don't think that I could go through with it.' He pictured the thin, pale, fifty-year-old woman standing there before a magistrate, and felt that he would not be able to meet her eyes.

'She doesn't have to appear, but it would be in her best interests to do so,' replied the solicitor. 'If she's as pathetic as you say, the magistrate is more likely to be lenient, even though he'll have to issue a restraining order. And if you're thinking of withdrawing the charges at this stage, Mr Bolt, the case would collapse and you'd be back at square one, as would Mrs Bolt – and you'd continue to be harassed, *and* have to pay the costs!'

'So what will happen?'

'She'll be sent a summons to appear at Winchester Magistrates' Court on the specified date, and told to present herself, usually about an hour before the time scheduled.'

'Will she have to wait in the same room as—?'

'No, you'll be separated from the start, before and after the hearing.'

'Should I wear my clerical collar?'

'You don't have to, but I think you should. We need to emphasise that you're a man of, er, Christian beliefs, and wouldn't have brought this action lightly.'

'But it could have the opposite effect, and make me a figure of ridicule.'

'It's just possible, but on the whole it would probably be to your advantage. Miss Johnson hasn't got her own defence, and there's no doubt that you'll win the day.'

'My wife wants to attend, and I can't stop her,' said Derek gloomily.

'There again, it could be a good thing. She'd be your chief witness – your only witness, in fact, if called upon. On the other hand, we don't want to give the impression that your wife forced you to bring the case by delivering an ultimatum.'

'Even though it would be the truth.'

Mr Jamieson cleared his throat. 'Sometimes there's an occasion to avoid awkward truths, but if you want to win this case and preserve marital harmony, I'd rather not involve Mrs Bolt.'

Derek's face reflected his real distress, and the solicitor clapped him on the shoulder.

'Come on, Rev, you can't back out now – or if you did, you'd regret it!'

So the vicar decided to go ahead. The date of the hearing was fixed for Monday, the twenty-seventh of May.

CHAPTER TEN

'Yes, she's going to give a huge farewell party when she's discharged from Women's Surgical,' Laurie Moffatt told the maternity staff. 'Matron was not too keen on her taking over the hospital grounds for an evening, but she fluttered her eyelashes at Dr Brooks, and showed him her chequebook, so he gave her permission. She's going to have a big marquee set up at the back, and a posh catering firm to do the refreshments. It'll be the biggest do in Everham since the Coronation, so Roger was telling me – he'll be taking the photographs.'

'And who's going to be invited?' asked a student midwife.

'Everybody. Medical and nursing staff from all the wards, on duty or off. Those on duty can take it in turns to go for ten or twenty minutes, depending on how busy they are, so everybody will have a chance to hear a fond farewell from the lovely Diane Devlin!'

'I'll go if there's smoked salmon on the menu, not otherwise,' said Dr McDowall.

'Oh, of course we must go, Leigh!' protested Tanya Dickenson, laughing. 'There'll be actors from the TV studios – you'll be there with Paul Sykes, won't you, Dr Hammond?'

'If I'm asked,' replied Shelagh briefly. She found it impossible to concentrate her mind on anything other than her mother's decline, and as soon as she could get away for her half-day, she drove home.

'She sleeps most o' the time, Shelagh, but she's peaceful, and even smiles in her sleep,' said Maura. 'It's ever since Dr Leigh came to see her that time – and I know I'm not supposed to mention it, but it's true – it's as if she was ready to – to – oh, Shelagh, she seemed to be gettin' better, I was so sure it was a miracle—'

Shelagh put an arm around Maura's shoulders. 'Bless you, Auntie, for all your loving care, but it was only a temporary remission. I didn't say anything, I didn't want to upset you, but the end is near now. We must be grateful that she's peaceful, no worries and no pain, thanks to the injections.' She was about to add, 'of morphine', but avoided naming the drug associated with terminal illness. Father Orlando had visited to hear Bridget's whispered Confession, and administer the Last Rites. The thought occurred to Shelagh that she could ask Paul Sykes to visit her mother and reassure her about his intentions, but she decided not to do so. No, it was too late now.

When Mr Kydd saw Denise North in the antenatal clinic, he said she was to be admitted for rest and observation. He reckoned that the babies were now at about thirty-five weeks' gestation, and a good size. However, Denise's blood pressure was rising, and her ankles were swollen, warning of possible toxaemia of pregnancy; he wanted to keep a close eye on her, he told Shelagh. 'We might have to consider getting them out sooner, and that would mean caesarean section,' he said. 'But if she rests, lightly sedated, we should be able to get her through another couple of weeks at least.'

Knowing that Denise's father had left home and was living with Sister Iris Oates, Shelagh felt that Iris should know about this, and went to look for her in Outpatients. She had not spoken to Iris on the subject of her relationship with Denise's father, simply because it was none of her business, nor was it her place to judge, though other members of staff had voiced their disapproval, and Iris had been summoned to Matron's office on account of it.

'Did you know that Denise North has been admitted to Antenatal for rest and observation?'

Shelagh asked in a matter-of-fact way, and saw how Iris stiffened.

'Yes, Mr North told me,' she replied. 'It means that he's got one more thing to worry about, on top of all the rest. He wants to visit her at a convenient time, but doesn't want an encounter with – with the wife, which could lead to a scene in the ward.'

'But that needn't affect you, Iris,' Shelagh gently pointed out.

'It wouldn't help,' the sister replied with a tightening of her lips. 'Matron has only agreed to let me stay in my job as long as there are no "repercussions", she says, and told me I wouldn't get a reference if I left, not while I'm "living in sin" with the man I love. Anyway, thank you for telling me, Dr Hammond.'

'Repercussions' were not long in occurring. Mrs North visited her daughter every afternoon, and listened to a series of complaints about the hospital and the ward staff.

'It's *awful* in here, Mum, I've hardly slept a wink. The other women talk till past midnight, and then they snore like pigs. It's no good saying anything to the night nurses about it, all they do is sit in the office, talking.'

'The food's terrible, Mum. They came round with so-called beef casserole today – all fat and gristle, with a few carrots. I couldn't eat it, and what do you think they offered me? A ham sandwich! Can you bring me in some of those little pork pies? And some pickle?'

'The staff here couldn't care less, Mum. That blonde sister who's supposed to be in charge of the ward is an absolute bitch. She told me to stay in bed, though I have to get up to go to the toilet, and she told me that I grumble too much!'

'This is too bad!' cried her mother. 'I'll go and find somebody to speak to, now!'

There were no nurses in the ward office, only Dr Hammond looking through a pile of laboratory reports and putting them into case notes. She looked up when Mrs North came in.

'I can't say I'm very pleased with the treatment my daughter's receiving in here, doctor,' Mrs North began. 'After all, she is supposed to be in here for a *rest*, but she isn't getting much, what with the other patients talking half the night, and snoring. And the food is simply dreadful! I've had to bring her in some cold chicken and a fresh salad.'

'I'm sorry to hear that Denise isn't satisfied with her treatment, Mrs North,' said Shelagh. 'Perhaps if you had a word with the nursing staff—'

'There's not much use in complaining to *them*,' sniffed Mrs North. 'That blonde sister is thoroughly insensitive to those she's supposed to be caring for, and she's been downright rude to Denise. I thought midwives were supposed to be caring! – I intend to complain to the Matron about her.'

'I've never heard any of the mothers complaining about Sister Dickenson,' said Shelagh evenly, aware

217

of the irony of her defence of a woman she resented. 'She's a thoroughly competent midwife and ward sister, and I suggest you speak to her personally before reporting her to Matron.'

'If *that's* all the response I get, I might as well take my daughter home now – she'll get more rest there!' retorted Fiona North.

'You can please yourself, of course, Mrs North – only I must advise you that to take Denise home would be most unwise. She could end up with eclampsia, and start having fits, which would be fatal to the babies. It's up to you.'

She turned her attention back to the desk, and refused to listen further.

'I'll write to the Matron and the Hospital Management Committee!' shouted Mrs North, but Shelagh did not raise her head.

The great day dawned, accompanied by brilliant sunshine. During the morning and afternoon a team of organisers arrived to put up the marquee and erect the tables on which the feast would be laid out by a firm of caterers.

'Just like a wedding reception,' commented Laurie Moffatt, standing at a window in the maternity department, overlooking the area. 'And look at that raised open-air platform in front of the trees – with fairy lights strung across it, for when the daylight starts to fade, it'll be just like a stage setting!' She turned to see Dr Hammond behind her, also looking out of the window.

'I say, Shelagh, would you like to go over to the bun fight with me this evening?' she asked. 'My Roger'll be photographing everybody and everything in sight, and your Paul will have to be up there on the stage with Little Bo Peep when she starts thanking everybody – so shall we go together and be first in the queue for the grub?'

Shelagh was about to say no, but recollected that her absence might look like ill will, as if she were jealous of the actress and Dr Sykes' involvement with her.

'OK, Laurie, let's go over at about seven, shall we? I shan't want to stay long.'

'Long enough for the buffet,' giggled Laurie. 'And we mustn't miss the speeches!'

As it turned out, there was only one speech of significance, Diane's own. Shelagh and Laurie followed the crowd from the lower hospital corridor into a warm summer evening. A record of Acker Bilk's clarinet filled the air with 'Stranger on the Shore', enhanced by the sound system, and Mr Fielding and his surgical team were about to take their seats on the platform.

'Look, there she is,' said Laurie as Diane Devlin came into view, leaning on her beribboned walking stick and Dr Sykes' arm. She wore a long white gown with a gold belt, and on her left foot a dainty, flat-heeled ballerina shoe, also in gold; her injured leg was encased in plaster below the knee, though her full-length skirt hid most of it. Her red hair tumbled over her gleaming shoulders, and an enormous cheer arose when she was carried up onto the stage by Dr Sykes, and set down on the armchair ready for her, well padded with cushions. When the applause died down, she rose with the aid of her Bo-Peep crook, and exchanged a kiss with Mr Fielding. Taking the microphone, she began to address her guests.

'Listen, everyone, I love you *all* for coming to my farewell party – and I want you all to know that Everham Park Hospital will always hold a special place in my heart, and I shall remember Mr Fielding's amazing surgical team as long as I live. But it has been Dr Paul Sykes who has changed my life. Words cannot express—' Her voice broke, and her listeners waited while she regained her composure, and continued, 'Words cannot express my gratitude to him, this fantastic surgeon who has earned my lifelong obligation for saving my right leg, and therefore my career – and therefore my *life*! Ladies and gentlemen, please stand for Dr Paul Sykes, my doctor! My wonderful doctor!' She threw her arms around Paul's neck and they kissed while cameras clicked and the spectators cheered and whistled. It was then that Shelagh heard Dr McDowall's voice, standing with Tanya Dickenson only a few feet ahead of her and Laurie.

'Stirring stuff, eh? Our TV actress has sunk her claws into Sykes, and is letting us know that she doesn't intend to let him get away!'

'I wonder what Dr Hammond will say when she hears about this,' said Tanya. 'If I were in her place, I wouldn't stand for it.'

'What I can't understand is why a woman as beautiful and intelligent as Dr Hammond should throw herself away on a creep like him – what a waste!' McDowall answered. Tanya raised her eyebrows and Shelagh stiffened at hearing these words; she wanted nothing more than to get away from this crowd before McDowall saw her. Laurie too had heard, and was clearly embarrassed.

'Honestly, what an exhibition, Shelagh! Pass the sick bag, will you? Let's get out of here, I've had enough of this, haven't you?'

They slipped unnoticed through the applauding crowd, now surging towards the marquee, and once back in the hospital corridor, Laurie muttered, 'Sorry, Shelagh, I'd no idea that she was going to lay on such a spectacle.'

'Not your fault, Laurie, and don't miss the grub,' replied Shelagh lightly. 'You go back to the marquee, and I'll pop up to the Delivery Unit to see what's cooking.'

'Are you sure?' asked Laurie. 'Would you like me to bring you over some smoked salmon or whatever's on offer?'

'No, thanks, I'm OK. You just go back and get your supper,' replied Shelagh who only wanted to reflect on what she had seen and heard. She began to climb the stairs to the department, rather than use a lift that might be occupied, and tried to organise her thoughts. She could not doubt the evidence of her eyes and ears, the way that Paul and Diane had kissed so passionately and publicly while the guests roared. Had Diane planned it to lure Paul into a trap? Surely he had not expected the announcement of the actress's feelings for him, her overwhelming gratitude? No, he must have been taken by surprise, and would come to her to explain and apologise, for after all, he was *hers*, he had declared his love for her and persuaded her to give herself to him, to agree to be lovers . . .

And then she heard again in her head, like a record replayed, the contemptuous tones of Leigh McDowall: *a woman as beautiful and intelligent as Shelagh Hammond . . . throw herself away . . . what a waste!*

She stood still on the staircase, feeling suddenly uncertain of what she should think, what she should do; let me get back to my work, she told herself, hoping that there would be patients in labour, mothers in need of her skill. She took a couple of deep breaths, and reached the top of the stairs. A telephone was ringing somewhere, and Dr Rowan appeared.

'Ah, there you are, Shelagh,' he said, and there

was a sympathetic tone in his voice that made her suddenly afraid: what was he going to say? Surely he couldn't have heard about her humiliation already?

'Your aunt has phoned,' he said gently. 'You're to go home at once, my dear.'

Her mother. In a moment every other emotion was swept away: she must go home.

'Will you be all right to drive, Shelagh?' asked the registrar. 'Would you like me to ring for a taxi?'

'No thanks, David, I'll be OK.'

'Give me your bleeper. I'll be on call for you tonight.'

She handed it to him, and then retraced her steps to the lower corridor and out to the car park.

Bridget had died peacefully, without a struggle. 'I went in to close the curtains and take her a milk drink,' said Maura, wiping her eyes. 'And I went over to the bed, and saw that she had gone. Your dear mother was at peace when she drew her last breath.'

She had sent for both Father Orlando and old Dr McGuinness, who greeted Shelagh when she arrived and knelt beside the bed. She looked upon the calm face, the wax-pale fingers holding the silver crucifix that she had worn around her neck for so many years. Father Orlando said a prayer for the repose of her soul, and they all joined in the 'Our Father'. Dr McGuinness signed the necessary certificate, giving the cause of death as uterine cancer.

'Shall I ring for the undertakers, Maura?' asked the old GP.

Maura glanced at her niece, and replied, 'No, thank you, doctor, we'll keep her here till mornin'. Shelagh and meself will do the last duties for her.'

So Bridget's daughter and sister carried out the last offices, reverently washing her body, combing her hair and putting on a clean white nightdress. Neither of them spoke, apart from Maura sighing, 'Sure, she's finished wid the troubles o' this world, Shelagh.'

She then made tea, and they kept silent vigil beside the still form until midnight, when Shelagh said they should go to bed. Sleep soon came to her, no longer hurt or humiliated by the events of the evening, but only thankful for her mother's life and peaceful death.

'There's Dr Sykes on the phone for ye,' said Maura as her niece sat talking with the undertaker, deciding on the wording of the notice in the *Everham News*.

'Will you tell him that I'm busy, Auntie, and say I'll ring back when I'm ready?'

'I'll tell him that for sure,' said Maura, hurrying back to the phone with a certain satisfaction. It rang again ten minutes later.

'It's Dr Leigh, Shelagh. He says he'll be here in ten minutes.'

'Oh, did he? Will you tell him I'm busy right now?' answered Shelagh, who had finished talking with the undertaker.

'He hung up the phone, so he'll be here soon. He says he needs to talk wid ye.'

Shelagh frowned. 'I suppose it's to do with that afternoon when I came home and found him here with her, when he ordered me out of the room. He's got a nerve, inviting himself round at a time like this. I shall tell him that my solicitor will deal with my mother's affairs.'

Maura pursed her lips. 'It was your dear mother who sent for him that afternoon, Shelagh. She asked me to phone the hospital and ask him to come and see her, and then she wanted me to get out the strongbox from under her bed. He'll be wantin' it again, and I'll have it ready for him. Ye'll have to see him, because she trusted him, Shelagh, and asked him to take care of her affairs.'

'Well, for her sake, then – but it annoys me, Auntie. Mother didn't have that much to leave, only the house and whatever she had in the Post Office. All right, I'll see him when he comes, but not willingly.'

Maura hurried off to put the kettle on and get out the biscuit tin. Shelagh stripped the bed on which her mother's body had lain. When the doorbell rang, she heard his voice speaking quietly to her aunt, accompanied by a kiss. Maura showed him into the front parlour, where she stood waiting for him.

'Hello, Shelagh. This is a very sad time for you,' he said, holding out his hand which she briefly shook. 'You'll be busy making the usual arrangements, but first I need to discuss some matters with you, pertaining to your mother's wishes.'

'I shall consult Mr Jamieson my solicitor about any legal matters,' she replied coldly. 'I suggest you contact him if you have anything to say about her wishes.'

He looked at her pityingly. 'I can understand how you feel, Shelagh, but your mother entrusted me with a matter about which I must inform you before you see your solicitor – before you register her death. Might I suggest that we sit down with a cup of Maura's tea, and that you let me tell you what your mother told me?'

'She should have told *me*,' she said. 'I am her daughter, after all.'

'But she told *me*, my dear, and you must listen,' he replied, in a voice that was kindly but firm. 'Shall I go on?'

'If you must.'

'Good, so let's sit down. You'll know that your mother's private papers were kept in a strongbox under her bed. I've asked your Aunt Maura to bring it in here.'

Maura was already at the door, carrying the box.

'There we are – thank you, Maura.' He smiled at her and she left the room, closing the door behind her. He placed it on the table.

'I have no idea where she kept the key,' said Shelagh, and for answer he put a hand into an inside pocket of his jacket; he held out his palm, and on it rested the heavy iron key.

'She gave it to me for safekeeping,' he said.

'Why on earth couldn't she have given it to *me*?' she asked in bewildered resentment.

'I'll try to explain, Shelagh. Would you like to unlock it?'

'No, *you* unlock it – you've seen it all before, anyway, when you came round here that afternoon, behind my back.' Her face was flushed, and angry tears stood in her eyes. 'Just because you visited her when she was in hospital, and amused her with your nonsense – made her laugh and take a liking to you, and then took advantage of that!' Her voice rose higher.

'Ssh, my dear, you'll upset Maura if she hears you. When you're ready, perhaps you'll take a look at these certificates, but you must stay calm.' He had opened the box, and took out three certificates which he laid on the table. 'There's her birth certificate, you see, and yours. Yours gives the date and place of birth, your mother's name and occupation as schoolteacher, and your father's as James Hammond, able seaman.'

'Yes, he was away at sea when I was born. So what are you saying?'

'There's no marriage certificate, Shelagh. Bridget was never married,' he said quietly.

'*What?* What are you talking about? Of course my mother was married to my father, how dare you say otherwise!'

He drew a deep breath. 'Stay calm, my dear, let me try to explain, as she explained to me that afternoon. This is just the sort of reaction that she so much dreaded – and why she never told you, poor woman.'

She stared at him wildly. 'But it's not true, it can't be! Her name was Bridget Hammond, and his was James Hammond. What nonsense are you trying to tell me?'

'For heaven's sake, Shelagh, just *listen*, will you? Yes, your father was James Hammond, but they were never married. Bridget was a courageous woman, and when he never returned to her, she left Ireland and came to Liverpool where she changed her name to Hammond by deed poll. There's the certificate of deed poll to prove the legality of the name change, and you were born in Liverpool. She never went back to Ireland, and none of your relatives knew that she never married, not even Maura – and you're not to tell her, Shelagh. I promised Bridget on my word of honour that her family will never know, but there was no way that I could keep it from *you*.'

'Oh, my God,' she whispered. 'Oh, my God – my poor mother.'

'Yes, Shelagh, your mother sacrificed her whole life to you. There's nothing for you to be ashamed of on her behalf. She was a very brave woman, and only feared one thing – that you'd condemn her if you ever found out. Remember that she grew up in an Irish backwater where unmarried mothers just weren't accepted, it was such a disgrace. Think of it, Shelagh – she was a quiet, respectable girl, the eldest daughter of a strict Catholic family. And then she fell in love.'

Shelagh covered her face with her hands. 'Was he really a sailor, then?' she asked shakily.

'Yes, he was, and after he rejoined his ship, she found that she was pregnant and tried to contact him, but without success. She told her family that she was going to meet him in Liverpool, and in due course she wrote to tell them that she was married, and later that she'd got a daughter, but was widowed – she said her husband had been drowned at sea. Oh, Shelagh, what that girl must have gone through during the months before you were born! A most remarkable lady, a mother to be proud of. I know I would be.'

She could not reply, but leant on the table, her head between her hands, utterly confused – sorrow, regret and anger hopelessly mixed. Leigh McDowall had considered offering to drive her to the registrar's office in the Town Hall, to support her there, but in her present state it was impossible. He tentatively laid a hand on her right shoulder, but her only response was a shuddering sob.

'Shelagh,' he said, afraid to put an arm around her in case it would be unwelcome. He stood silently beside her as the minutes ticked by, and they heard the telephone ringing; Maura went to answer it, exchanged a few words with the caller, and came to knock on the parlour door.

'Come in, Maura,' said Leigh. Maura stared in concern at her niece's bowed head, and he added, 'Don't worry, my dear, she'll be all right in a while. Who's on the phone?'

'It's himself, doctor, the other one – Dr Sykes. He says he wants to speak to her, and he's comin' round this afternoon, he says.'

Shelagh raised her head. 'Oh, no, Auntie, I can't see him, I *can't*, not yet,' she begged, her voice rising.

'All right, Shelagh, you don't have to – don't worry, Maura, I'll come and speak to him.' So saying, Leigh strode out of the room, towards the receiver lying on the hall table.

'Sykes?

'Er, yes, Paul Sykes, wanting to speak to Dr Hammond if possible. It's quite urgent.'

'McDowall here, and I'm ordering you to keep away from Dr Hammond. She's suffered enough, with her mother dying while you were putting on that ridiculous exhibition yesterday evening.'

'But look here, McDowall, I want to tell her that—'

'I'm warning you, Sykes, if you come round here pestering Dr Hammond before she's ready to see you, you'll regret it – is that clear? Stay away.' He replaced the receiver, and returned to the parlour, where Maura was comforting her niece.

'I'm going now, Shelagh – Maura – but I'll be back if you need me, and maybe tomorrow if you feel up to it, Shelagh, I'll drive you to the registrar's office, OK?'

'He's a good man,' said Maura as he closed the front door behind him. 'And ye mustn't grieve too much for your dear mother, Shelagh. She's at peace now.'

'Oh, but what she must have gone through, Auntie – and I never knew,' wept Shelagh.

Maura drew her closer. 'Is it what Dr Leigh told ye, dear?'

'Yes, but – I can't tell you, Auntie, you don't know it all – oh, my poor mother!'

'Who says I don't know, Shelagh? I've been close to me sister all these weeks, and I've got eyes and ears. And when she sent for Dr Leigh that afternoon – well, I couldn't help but guess, ye see. She was a good woman, and wanted to spare ye till after she'd gone.'

'Aunt Maura! You knew all the time, then!' said Shelagh, lifting her head and looking straight into her aunt's eyes. 'You *knew*!'

'Not all the time, dear, nobody told me, it just came into me mind. And I never told her that I knew, because it would've troubled her, after keeping a secret all these years. As if I would've blamed her!'

'And as if *I* would have blamed her! When I think of what she suffered, going through the pregnancy alone, betrayed by that damned sailor. The thought of an illegal operation would never have crossed her mind; did she think about adoption? Perhaps she did, until she saw her baby in her arms – *me*! All that she had left of – oh, Auntie, when she was coming round from the anaesthetic, she asked me to forgive her, and I didn't know why – dearest Mother, there was nothing to forgive!'

'Maybe she knows that now, dear – her troubles are over, God rest her soul.'

Miss Gladwell was doing an evening visit, so as to meet the husband as well as the wife. Such a nice couple, she thought, so deserving, it would be a pleasure to bring them good news. So often in her job as a social worker, she had to bring disappointment, of mothers who changed their minds, of medical reports that dashed the hopes of eager couples; this time, Miss Gladwell thought, there would be no reservations, no obstacles to be overcome.

They were waiting for her as she drew up outside their semi on the new estate to the north of Everham. They saw her from the window, and the wife opened the door before she reached it.

'Miss Gladwell, good evening, nice to see you, do come in. Would you like a cup of tea?' Jenny hoped that she was not babbling, but could not control her emotion.

'No thank you, Mrs Gifford, I'd rather get down to business, as I'm sure you would. Good evening, Mr Gifford,' she nodded to Tim who was smiling nervously.

They showed her into the living room, and sat down. Miss Gladwell had her briefcase on her lap, and opened it; the couple stared at it as if it held news that would change their lives, as indeed it did.

'As you know, you impressed the adoption panel, and are considered eligible as adoptive parents,' said Miss Gladwell, taking a document from the briefcase. 'And I've now come to tell you that there is an available child.'

'Oh, Miss Gladwell!' Jenny sat upright on the edge of her chair, her hands tightly clasped together. Tim smiled at her, and held up a forefinger to advise her to listen.

'Go on, Miss Gladwell,' he said. 'We are all ears.'

'Right. Well, I've got a photograph here of a little boy born just before Christmas, which means he's now around five and a half months old. He's at present with a foster mother who has had him since he was hardly a week old. His medical report is entirely satisfactory, he can sit up and smiles a lot, as you can see. He's been fed on formula milk, and has started taking solids—'

'Oh, let me see, let me see!' cried Jenny, getting up and taking the photograph, which she showed to her husband. They both exclaimed in delight.

'Did you ever see such a dear little fellow, Tim? Look at that smile! How soon will we be able to have him, Miss Gladwell?'

'First you must meet him at his foster home to

see how you all react, yourselves and the boy. We'll arrange an appointment, shall we?'

'Yes, please, as soon as possible,' said Jenny, looking at her husband with tears of anticipation.

'That'll mean travelling quite a distance, then,' said Tim.

'No, the foster mother lives at South Camp, a bus journey away. I have the address, and I'll meet you there.'

'So he must have come a long way,' said Tim. 'We know you don't place children too near to the birth mother.'

'He was born here, at Everham Park Hospital, actually,' replied Miss Gladwell.

'Oh, no! We'll be *much* too near,' said Jenny in dismay. 'The mother might come round here trying to see him, or some other relative might decide to snoop!'

'Not in this case,' said Miss Gladwell gravely. 'His mother was a single girl of just seventeen who died of kidney failure a few weeks after he was born by caesarean section. The girl's mother is an alcoholic who won't be interested. His mother named him Donovan, but of course you can change that if you like when you legally adopt him.'

'How very sad for the girl,' said Tim, shaking his head.

'But how lucky for *us*, to be able to take him and bring him up as our son!' cried Jenny happily. 'Wait till I tell my mother! Donovan! It's a good name – shall we keep to it, Tim, and let him be called by the name his mother chose for him?'

So Donovan he remained, and his future was assured.

'Mr Kydd says to stay off work until after the funeral,' said Shelagh, 'though to be honest I'll be very glad to be back at work.'

'Yes, he'll have to rely on his junior houseman while you're away,' said Leigh with a grin.

They were returning from the registrar's office three days after Bridget's death.

'So that's over, and I can only thank you again for your kindness and support, Leigh,' she said, clicking the safety belt as he took the driver's seat and switched on the ignition.

'I've been meaning to ask you – have you heard any more from our friend Sykes?' he ventured.

'Yes, he has sent me a letter and a sympathy card. I hear you gave him short shrift on the phone,' she answered. 'He says he won't come to my home while you're in charge!' She did not tell him that Sykes had asked to take her out to dinner.

'Is Aunt Maura going to stay on with you?' he asked.

'Until after the funeral, then she'll go home, she's needed there. I'll miss her a lot.'

'I'm sure you will. A very special lady, like her sister.'

She switched the conversation to Denise North and her twins. 'They must be every bit of thirty-six weeks now.'

'Yes, and her toxaemia is worsening by the day,' he said. 'What's the betting that Harry Kydd will intervene and get them out by caesarean?'

'Every day they can stay inside her puts on another ounce,' she answered. 'But yes, he probably will.'

Outside the little terraced house, he got out and opened the passenger door for her.

'I won't come in, Shelagh, if you don't mind, I'd better get back. Give my love to Maura.'

'Thanks again for everything, Leigh. Remember me to Tanya and Laurie.'

'Will do. See you soon, then, dear. Bye for now!'

CHAPTER ELEVEN

The hearing at Winchester Magistrates' Court took only ten minutes. The Reverend Derek Bolt and Mrs Bolt took their places with solicitor Mr Jamieson; a woman clerk recorded the proceedings, and a reporter from the *Everham News* sat in the otherwise empty public gallery. Miss Beryl Johnson was a lonely figure in a plain navy costume and matching hat, and her answers to the questions put to her by the magistrate were so low that she was told to speak up, and then a microphone was brought to her, so that her voice could be heard in court. Mr Bolt's sworn statement and letters produced by Mr Jamieson, together with Miss Johnson's admission that she had written them, were considered sufficient evidence to uphold Mr Bolt's claim of harassment, and a restraining order was placed on Miss Johnson, banning her from contacting the Revd Bolt in any way for twelve months; if she breached the order, the magistrate warned her that she would have to appear in the Crown Court, and could face a prison sentence.

A photographer was waiting for Miss Johnson when she emerged white-faced from the court, and Mr and Mrs Bolt were also photographed. All three parties declined to comment.

The report on the court case broke in Everham the following day, and all newsagents reported that copies of the *Everham News* had sold out by mid-morning. The whole town was in a turmoil of mixed opinions, and pity for Miss Johnson's humiliation outweighed support for Mr Bolt, especially among the women. On the following day, a national newspaper carried the story, which became a talking point, with increased sympathy for Miss Johnson; the vicar was considered to have been harsh, not to say cruel, to a lonely woman who had committed no crime, and it was whispered that his wife had put him up to it, and he must therefore be under her thumb – a wimp, not a recommendation for a man of the cloth.

'One thing about all this, Derek old chap, you've gone way ahead of me in the gossip stakes,' commented Jeremy North wryly. 'We're both bastards as far as the women are concerned.' They were in the vestry, divesting themselves of cassock and surplice. Derek Bolt pulled off the green-and-gold embroidered stole he had worn at the morning service, and threw it over a chair.

'Yeah, and I'm a hypocrite into the bargain, preaching a gospel of love while treating a parishioner with calculated cruelty. Daphne hasn't come out of it well, either. At least your wife gets all the sympathy.'

'My Iris doesn't,' replied Jeremy with a grimace. 'Bloody hell.'

'Same here. I suppose that eventually it'll blow over.'

But the following Monday brought a sequel to the harassment case. Unable to obtain admission to Miss Johnson's house, a Mrs Mary Whittaker had informed the police who had forced an entry. Miss Johnson was found unconscious in her bed, clasping a framed photograph of the Revd Derek Bolt. A half-empty bottle of paracetamol tablets and a half-bottle of gin were on the bedside table. An ambulance was summoned, and Miss Johnson was rushed to Everham Park Hospital, where a stomach washout was performed, too late to prevent the absorption of the drugs into the bloodstream, but as a casualty officer listened for a heartbeat, her eyelids began to flutter, and a moan issued from her throat. She had lapsed into unconsciousness after taking only half the dose she had intended with half the gin, and was now starting to recover, waking to find herself not in heaven but in hospital, the women's medical ward, having blood samples taken to assess liver damage, if any. A psychiatric report had also been requested.

But ill news travels fast, and not always accurately. When the ambulance was seen departing from Angel Close carrying Miss Johnson on a stretcher, a rumour quickly spread in Everham that she was dead. Mrs Pearce from the bakery lost no time in conveying this to the vicarage, though she was startled by the effect it had on the vicar, who groaned aloud and wrung his hands.

'I'm finished – my life as a priest is finished!' he said brokenly, and when his wife tried to remonstrate with him, he shouted at her to leave him alone and get out of his sight. It was Mrs Whittaker, who had accompanied Miss Johnson to hospital, who later called at the vicarage with the news of her recovery, whereupon Derek shut himself in his study and fell on his knees in a wild ecstasy of thanksgiving.

One scandal followed another. Two days later the media gleefully disclosed the confession by the government minister John Profumo of his illicit affair with the young model, Christine Keeler, made ten times worse by his having lied to the Commons three months earlier, insisting upon his innocence. Grave pronouncements were made in the editorials of *The Times* and the *Daily Telegraph*, and by senior churchmen, while The Volunteer and other such bastions of public opinion echoed with guffaws at bawdy jokes about the scandal. And there were men who kept their opinions to themselves, silently thanking their lucky stars that there but for the grace of God . . .

It was time for the dinner engagement with Paul Sykes, and Shelagh dressed carefully. A silk-jersey dress with a bold flowered print, fashion sandals and a white leather handbag seemed to fit the bill, but then she rejected the sandals for high-heeled red leather shoes, and a handbag to match. A crystal necklace with matching drop earrings and a silvery chiffon shawl completed her image, and she nodded her approval at the mirror: no sad-eyed lady needing to be comforted, but a – what had Leigh McDowall said? *A beautiful, intelligent woman like Dr Hammond . . .*

She noticed Paul's start of surprise when she opened the door.

'Good God, Shelagh, you look stunning.'

'Thank you. It's a lovely evening,' she said with a smile, following him to the car. 'Where are we going?'

'I'd thought of somewhere quiet and off the beaten track, like the Badger's Nest – have you ever been there? We can eat outside in the garden if you like, it's ideal for a quiet chat.'

She settled herself in the passenger seat, wondering what he had to say that was so important. An apology, perhaps? An explanation? A quiet chat at the Badger's Nest would no doubt reveal all, and she was resolved to keep an open mind.

Arriving at the pretty cottage that had a kitchen attached at the back, he ordered a bottle of white wine, and took their glasses to an outdoor table.

'So poor old Profumo got his comeuppance, didn't he?' said Paul. 'Silly chump. He should know that illicit affairs are out for men in high places.'

'Yes, it must be agony for him and his wife,' Shelagh replied, remembering their own liaison which her mother had never known about.

'Agreed. Now, Shelagh, we have to talk. I'll admit I was furious at the way McDowall spoke to me on the phone, but now I see that he had good reason, and I'm happy for you both.'

Shelagh took a sip of wine and waited for him to continue.

'It's become clear to me that you and McDowall have grown much closer – more so than I realised, and he was there to console you after your – your mother's death, and I'm very sorry about that.'

'Thank you.'

'I'd have come over straight away, but – er – decided to lie low as long as he was around. And to have a good, quiet talk with you, like now.'

'So what are we quietly talking about, Paul?' she asked, taking another sip of wine.

'Oh, Shelagh, you're so sweet and understanding, and I quite envy McDowall. But in fact it's worked out very well. The truth is, you see, that – well, I've fallen for Diane in a big way, and she with me, incredible as that sounds.' He watched her face closely as she sipped her wine, her face impassive.

'So, Shelagh, you must be feeling that I—' He broke off, hardly knowing how to continue. She put down her glass, and faced him squarely.

'It's no surprise, Paul. I think I've known it all along. Ever since the day of the accident when you first met her.'

'Really? Oh, my gosh, you were ahead of me, then. Shelagh, I'm so truly glad that you've found a better option in McDowall.'

'You clearly don't realise, Paul, that Dr McDowall is closely involved with Sister Dickenson. They may be unofficially engaged for all I know. It wasn't for my sake that he came to the house several times, it was for my mother. She and he had become friends.'

'Oh – oh, I see,' he said awkwardly. 'So you and he aren't – er – together—'

'It's all right, Paul, I'm really pleased for you and Diane.'

'That's so sweet of you, Shelagh, you make me feel less of a – the fact is, I've never met anyone quite like her – and I can't believe she feels the same way about me. We hope to announce our engagement soon.'

'Congratulations, Paul.'

From then on his talk was all in praise of the divine Diane; she thought he sounded like an eighteen-year-old boy in love for the first time.

'Our marriage will be somewhat dependent on

when she can resume work. There's a film contract in the offing, with a location in Scotland as soon as she's fully mobile,' he went on eagerly. Not a word about his Fellowship of the Royal College of Surgeons, she noted.

'Tell me, Paul, if I may ask a personal question: is she younger than me?'

'The answer will surprise you, Shelagh, because in fact she's a few years older. It's her natural vitality that keeps her looking so young.'

About ten years older, then, and five years older than you, Shelagh silently calculated. And the roots of the red hair must need redoing at least every three weeks.

Their meal arrived, and she let him carry on enthusing while they ate it, wondering how long the lovely Diane's infatuation would last when she was back in the world of studios and actors. Would she make him happy, this man who had been her own first and only lover?

'Of course, she'll still be known as Diane Devlin rather than Sykes,' he went on. 'Our marriage won't exactly be conventional.'

You bet it won't, thought Shelagh.

'And the caravan at Netheredge up for sale – I'll see that you get your half share, of course – I can't quite see Diane roughing it at Netheredge in her present state, can you?'

Nor in any other state, thought Shelagh, and

suddenly laughed out loud, so that other diners turned to look at them.

'Oh, my God, Paul, you're so funny!'

'And you're so incredibly sweet, Shelagh,' he said, placing a hand over hers on the table. 'We must always stay friends – you and Diane would get along fine, I know.'

Some hopes, she thought. There did not seem to be much more to say, and after the sun had sunk in the west, the air grew chilly.

'It's been a wonderful evening, Shelagh. We've got such lot of things sorted, haven't we? I don't like to bring it to an end, but—'

'I'm quite ready to go,' she said, and he took her arm as they walked back to the car. A strange uneasiness had come over her, though she could not pinpoint the cause of it.

The countryside was silvery and mysterious by the light of a full moon, but she looked eagerly ahead for the lights of Everham. When she saw the hospital, its lights dimmed except in the theatre and Delivery Unit, she found herself longing to be within its walls.

'Just drop me here, Paul.'

'What, *here*? Don't you want to go home? You're still on compassionate leave, aren't you?'

'Yes, but I've just remembered something. I'll get out here, Paul – thanks for a great evening, most enlightening – bye!'

She scrambled out of the car, and headed for the

lower corridor with urgent footsteps, her high heels tip-tapping on its stone floor. She broke into a run, and flew up the stairs without waiting to call a lift. She reached the maternity department, hurried along the corridor, past the office, kitchen and utility room, until she reached the theatre annexe and Delivery Room Four: she burst through the double door and faced the scene before her.

On the delivery bed lay Denise North, her legs raised up in lithotomy stirrups. Seated on a stool facing her was Leigh McDowall, gowned and gloved for action. Staff Midwife Marie Burns stood close to him, with the delivery trolley, and Elsie the auxiliary watched, ready to be called upon to fetch and carry. Dr Fisher the paediatrician waited beside two heated cots and a cylinder of oxygen, holding between his lips the thin rubber tube of a mucus extractor to clear the air passages of the newborn.

Leigh McDowall turned his head to see her standing inside the door, wearing a glamorous dress and high-heeled shoes. Her crystal earrings flashed in the shadowless overhead light.

'Shelagh,' he said, 'you've come. We're delivering the North twins, as you can see. Mr Kydd went on holiday yesterday to the Algarve, and David Rowan has been involved in some sort of road accident.'

'OK, carry on,' she said. 'Can you see the vertex?'

'It's a breech.'

'Ah. Well, carry on. Foetal hearts OK?'

'About a hundred and forty a minute, doctor,' said Marie Burns.

'Good. Is the cervix fully dilated? Mustn't let her push down on a breech otherwise.'

'I can't feel a rim. Ah, here we go, I can see a little bottom, and it's a boy!'

Shelagh stood watching approvingly as he hooked one little ankle down, then the other. The body soon emerged, the cord attached and pulsating.

'Better do an episiotomy for the head,' advised Shelagh.

'This is where I let it hang, right?' he asked.

'Yes, if the cord's pulsating – and keep him warm. Marie, hand Leigh a towel.'

'Ah, another contraction. All right, Denise, we're nearly there.'

With firm and steady hands Leigh kept the head flexed, and within a minute the first twin's head slid smoothly over the perineum, a small baby but who soon gasped in air and began to make sounds in his throat. Dr Fisher stepped forward and took him from McDowall, to transfer him to a cot with a card labelled North Twin I.

Shelagh nodded approval, but then there was a gush of blood from the vagina.

'We can't give ergometrine, not while the other's still in there. Foetal heart, Nurse Burns?'

'I can hear it, but I can't count it, doctor.'

Another gush of blood, and a groan from Denise. 'We could do with having a drip put up, but right now we have to get the other baby out,' said Shelagh, and asked McDowall to confirm the presenting part, a head or a breech.

As he was about to put a questing finger into the vagina, Denise gave a groan and a push. 'Well done, it's coming,' he muttered, and then, 'Oh, hell, *no!*'

To their surprise and dismay, the bulge that now appeared was not the head of the second twin, but the placenta of the first. Leigh caught it in a dish hastily grabbed from the delivery trolley. Another brisk loss of blood followed it.

'Didn't know it was possible for that thing to come out before the second twin,' he muttered in the low tone used by delivery staff who had to remember that the patient was conscious.

'It can do when it's low-lying,' whispered Shelagh who was now faced with a life or death decision. 'Now we have *no time at all* to play with. That placental site will bleed like fury.'

'Could you do a caesar, Shelagh, if I helped?' he asked bluntly, wiping the sweat from his forehead with the back of his green sleeve.

'No time, we must get it out *now*,' she murmured, adding silently, if it isn't too late. She liberally coated her gloved right hand with antiseptic cream, and thrust two fingers into the vagina. Her worst fears were confirmed.

'It's lying in the transverse diameter,' she said, and he reflected the shock in her eyes.

They knew that delivery of a live baby in the transverse position was impossible, even with a small, premature baby; either the head or the breech had to descend. This baby's chances of survival dwindled with every second that it remained inside the uterus, now filling with blood.

'Get me a gown and a fresh pair of gloves, size six and a half,' Shelagh rapped out. 'I'm going to attempt an internal version.'

'Ever done one before?' asked Leigh with a sympathetic grimace.

'No, it's caesarean these days. And we shall need to put Denise to sleep for this.'

'I'll ring for the anaesthetist on call,' said Elsie.

'No time. Go into the theatre and fetch the Boyle's trolley, Elsie. And Marie, you take an ampoule of pentothal out of the cupboard and check it with Dr McDowall. And Leigh, you're going to have to be gas man.'

Her low, rapid orders were immediately obeyed. Staff Midwife Burns handed the ampoule to Leigh who snapped it open and drew up the colourless liquid into a ten-millilitre syringe which he injected into a vein on the back of Denise's hand. Her eyelids fluttered, her whole body relaxed, and she passed into unconsciousness. Elsie dragged in the heavy Boyle's anaesthetic trolley with its cylinders of gas.

Leigh grabbed an airway which he fixed between the girl's teeth, placed a rubber mask attached to a long, wide flexible tube over her nose and mouth and turned on the nitrous oxide gas mixed with oxygen. It was a simple, basic anaesthetic, and Leigh trusted that it would last until the procedure was completed.

Shelagh whispered a short, silent prayer as she sat on the vacated stool. Her eyes met Leigh's, and she nodded to him above her face mask.

'I'm putting my hand up through the cervix now,' she said quietly. 'I've got hold of a limb – a hand? No, a foot, it's got a heel. I'm going to pull it down now.' Speaking helped her to concentrate and make decisions.

'Now, here it comes – and there it is,' she said as her hand appeared externally, holding a tiny ankle between her thumb and forefinger. Leigh nodded silently. And Dr Fisher was clearly holding his breath: would he be handed a live child or – luckily Dr Hammond's hands were small, he thought, as were the babies.

The delivery room was silent apart from the squeaks of North Twin I, now lying in the heated cot. Shelagh continued with her low commentary.

'I'm pulling on the leg – and there are the buttocks coming down, and it's a girl. Right, now I think I can hook out the other leg – oh, it's come down on its own.'

The baby's body now hung downwards, and Marie

stepped forward to wrap the body in a warm towel. 'Now to bring down a loop of cord,' said Shelagh.

'Is it pulsating?' Leigh hardly dared to ask, as he supported the mother's chin with his hand.

'I think so – yes. Now for the anterior shoulder.' She hooked a finger in the bend of the child's elbow, and the arm appeared. The body rotated until the posterior shoulder came uppermost, and the other arm was free. Everybody in the closely knit team hung on her every word and action as she concentrated on the next crucial stage of a breech delivery, the birth of the head. The child was so tiny that she was able to support the body across her forearm, and then gently raised it to allow the face to appear; the episiotomy allowed the head to slide down over the perineum in a controlled, unhurried movement, and the limp, lifeless body of North Twin II was born. Dr Fisher leant over to clear the air passages while Shelagh clamped and cut the umbilical cord, then received the tiny girl into his hands and placed her in the second heated cot. Shelagh was thankful that the paediatric consultant was at hand to perform the necessary procedures to resuscitate her if it were possible, while the second placenta was expelled almost immediately, and McDowall gave an intravenous injection of ergometrine to make the uterus contract. Even so, the blood loss was considerable.

'Bring her round now, Leigh, and give oxygen,' Shelagh nodded to McDowall, 'and she'll need a drip up and a couple of pints of blood cross-matched.'

They hardly dared to look at Dr Fisher who had sucked out a quantity of mucus, blood and meconium (black discharge from the baby's rectum), from her nose and mouth, then had placed a tiny mask over her face to send a stream of pure oxygen into her lungs, at the same time pressing two fingers rhythmically on her chest to stimulate the heartbeat. One minute passed, and another.

'There's a heartbeat, just,' muttered Fisher, and laying the baby along his forearm, he raised the lower part of the body and let the head hang down; with the mucus extractor between his lips, he sucked more fluid from the air passages. There was a faint bubbling from the mouth, followed by a choking sound, and he upended the body again. Suddenly the baby gave a short, convulsive gasp, and the body twitched; another gasp, and the deathly white skin colour began to turn pink. All the onlookers exchanged glances of hope, just as Denise began to stir and moan.

'You're all right, Denise,' said Leigh in a low, reassuring voice close to the girl's ear. 'You've got two little babies, a boy and a girl. It's all right, my dear.'

The last sentence was uttered with a glance towards Shelagh. Because it was indeed all right; thanks to smooth and dedicated teamwork, the mother and two small premature babies had survived a difficult and dangerous birth.

Dr Fisher removed the two cots to the 'warm

nursery', a small annexe to the main nursery, and Leigh put up an intravenous saline drip on Denise, after cross-matching a blood sample which Elsie took to the laboratory. He sutured the episiotomy, and Marie made out a quarter-hourly pulse and blood-pressure chart for Denise, now ready to be transferred to the postnatal ward to rest and recover.

Suddenly the door opened to admit a white-faced Dr Rowan. 'My God, what the—'

'The North twins – Dr Fisher's taken them down to the warm nursery,' said McDowall. 'Boy and girl, about thirty-six weeks, hardly eight pounds between them. First was a breech, second transverse, Shelagh did an internal version and delivered as a breech. At least two pints of blood lost. We were lucky that Dr Fisher was around, that second twin looked like a goner.'

'God! I'm sorry I wasn't here – thank heaven you sent for Shelagh,' muttered Rowan, eyeing her dress and crystal jewellery. 'And thanks for coming, Shelagh, from wherever you were. It's been quite a night all round. We skidded on a wet road and ran into a tree on our way back from North Camp. Eve was badly shaken, and started to bleed, so I brought her into Gynae, but she's losing our baby at about ten weeks.'

He received their condolences with a sigh. 'But you're still on compassionate leave, aren't you, Shelagh – where were you when you were called?'

'I'd been out to dinner,' she said.

'Well, I'll never be able to thank you two enough. How did you get here, Shelagh?'

She hesitated, and McDowall answered. 'I prayed, Rowan, for once in my life I prayed, and Providence sent an angel. And never was there a more welcome sight.'

Rowan began to praise Shelagh, but she cut him short, smiled sympathetically and sent him to Gynae to comfort his wife.

By now it was midnight. Shelagh sat in the office writing up the case notes of the twin delivery, her crystal earrings flashing and her elegant dress bloodstained. She did not see Leigh McDowall enter. He stood for several moments regarding the back of her head, the untidy dark hair falling forward over the desk as she wrote, the crystal earrings flashing a rainbow of colours. There were smears of blood on her dress, and she had kicked off the high-heeled shoes. When she finished writing, she sat back in the chair and rubbed her eyes. And saw him.

'Thank you, Shelagh.'

'It was lucky that Dr Fisher was around,' she said. 'I didn't have much hope for the girl.'

'You saved her life,' he said simply. 'Suppose you hadn't come, Shelagh, and she'd had to rely on me as an obstetrician? That second twin would have been dead or brain-damaged, and I'd have had to live with the fact.'

'We don't know that, Leigh. It's futile to speculate on what might have happened. It was the smallness of the babies that made the internal podalic version possible. There are still fatalities with second twins, and probably always will be.'

Elsie the auxiliary came in with a tray of tea, and set it down on the desk. 'I reckon you've both earned a cuppa,' she said as she left, closing the door behind her.

'Where were you, Shelagh? And who sent for you, really?'

'I'd been out to dinner at the Badger's Nest. And nobody sent for me. I just got this overwhelming urge to get back here and up to the Delivery Unit. I didn't know that Denise had gone into labour, nor that Rowan and Eve were in trouble. All I knew was that I had to be here.'

'That's interesting, because I meant what I said to Rowan in there. No angel could have been more welcome than you in that room tonight. You took over, and got that second twin out – it was nothing short of miraculous.'

He leant towards her as he spoke, and she remembered how intently he had listened to every word of her 'commentary' during those suspenseful minutes. Was it possible that the sheer intensity of his need had summoned her to the Delivery Unit in that mysterious way?

She shook her head as she gratefully drank the tea. 'Who took you out to dinner, Shelagh, if I may ask?'

'You may. Paul Sykes.'

'What, *him*? Are you still seeing – after all that nonsense with the actress? Oh, Shelagh, Shelagh, how could you?'

'He asked me,' she replied. 'He said he had something to tell me, and so I went.'

'And you put on this stunning dress and crystal necklace and earrings just for *him*? He's got a nerve! So when's this overdue announcement of an engagement to be made?'

She got up. 'I must ask switchboard to ring for a taxi. I'm tired.'

'You must be. But – when is it to be announced, Shelagh?' he asked urgently.

Suddenly her eyes filled with tears. 'Soon. Everybody will hear about it, Diane Devlin's engagement to the young surgeon who saved her life.'

'*What*? Do you really mean that, Shelagh? Oh, what marvellous news! Congratulations!' And he drew her into his arms, holding her close and kissing the top of her head. 'Don't cry, Shelagh my dear, you've had a lucky escape, an incredible stroke of luck! If you'd married that bastard, I think I'd have throttled him.'

'But we'd been lovers, Leigh – we've spent weekends together—'

'Yes, and that's what drove me berserk, to see how you let yourself be used. And your dear mum never knew, did she?'

'No. She and Aunt Maura always thought it ought to be—' She broke off in confusion, the tears still wet on her cheeks.

He gently released her and rang the switchboard to order a taxi, then escorted her down to the lower corridor and the front entrance. When the taxi arrived, he helped her into the back seat.

'Good night, Shelagh my angel. I'll come and see you as soon as I can.'

As the door closed and the taxi moved off, Shelagh tried to organise her thoughts, the words he had used, the feel of his arms around her. So had Paul Sykes been right, then? Or had this amazing evening been a dream? She looked down at a bloodstain on her dress and a ladder in her tights: no, this had been no dream!

Staff Midwife Burns met McDowall on his return to the unit. 'Sorry, Dr McDowall, no peace for the wicked – there's an Italian lady on her way in with ruptured membranes at thirty-six weeks, and she can't speak English. So you'd better not go to your bed yet!'

'That's all right, Marie,' he said cheerfully. 'Let half a dozen Italian ladies come in, and I'll teach them English. *O sole mio!*'

Marie Burns stared at him. Had Elsie put anything into that that tea?

He caught her glance and winked. Dr Leigh McDowall was walking on air!

* * *

'Yes, it was a very difficult birth, so Shelagh Hammond said,' Iris told Jeremy the following day. 'It was touch and go with the second twin, and Shelagh came in specially to deliver it, though she's still on compassionate leave after losing her mother. Everybody's praising her to the skies, except for, er, your wife. She was livid because she hadn't been informed when Denise went into labour, and came in today to visit them all – the girl twin's in an incubator.'

'And I didn't even know,' said Jeremy gloomily. 'Fiona hasn't sent a word to me.'

'Ah, I've spoken to Dr McDowall who says you can go in to visit your daughter out of visiting hours, and likewise the twins, only make it short, he says, ten minutes at most. We can't have any – er—'

'Encounters, bust-ups, arguments, untoward scenes between visitors,' he finished for her. 'Not that Denise will want to see her erring father. But thanks to your Dr McDowall, I'll just pop in and see the tiny tots – a boy and a girl, you said? – poor little bastards, at least they won't sit up in their cots and order me out!'

'Oh, Jeremy my love, don't be too bitter,' Iris pleaded, touching his shoulder and kissing him on the cheek. 'You've been chucked out of the house, and that awful woman would chuck you out again if you went round there and offered any help.'

'I dare say she would, but Denise is never going to

cope with premature twins, and there's Peter-poppet to think about, poor little chap. I'll have to send more money.'

'Oh, yes, she'll have no objections to your money,' said Iris with a bitterness she prided herself on not showing. Damn and blast that useless lot, she thought silently. She knew that Fiona would take all the money he offered, and still demand more, leaving very little over for himself. Iris had no objection to being the breadwinner for them both, and not charging him rent. Just so long as he doesn't leave me, she thought – I'm his only happiness, and whatever that madwoman says, he's staying here with me, come what may.

'What would I do without you, darling Iris?' he asked, and she tightened her arms around him.

'You don't have to, dearest,' she said.

Jeremy's own thoughts were of a more practical nature. Fiona could look after the twins and Peter, while Denise got a job to earn some money for herself and her three children. Catherine would have to get a job, and Roy's destiny was in his own hands. When the divorce eventually took place, he intended to apply for access to his innocent little grandson.

After only one week's absence, the Reverend Derek Bolt was back in harness as vicar of St Matthew's, and Beryl Johnson had not reappeared. Mrs Whittaker informed him that Miss Johnson wished to attend church as she had always done with her mother, and for the past two Sundays had attended St Peter's at North Camp, four miles away, and had cycled there and back, though Mary would have offered her a lift.

'I honestly don't think she's likely to do anything like *that* again, Derek,' Mary had told the vicar. 'She's been prescribed tranquillisers by the psychiatrist she saw while in hospital, and she doesn't want to go and live near her brother in Canada, as some have suggested. She says that she misses her friends here at St Matthew's, but she knows she mustn't breach the injunction, and I've told her she'll make new friends at St Peter's after a while, won't she?'

Derek was still deeply troubled about Beryl Johnson, and had prayed for and about her since the near-tragedy. And then one morning he woke up with the answer to his prayers: *He* must leave St Matthew's, not poor Miss Johnson. He lost no time in telephoning Bishop Grieve to ask for a change of parish, and knowing of the Bishop's sympathy, thought that his request would be granted.

As indeed it was. To Daphne's dismay and resentment, Derek was transferred to a parish in a built-up area where greater London had spread into Surrey, and where the present incumbent was taking early retirement. St Christopher's was a relatively new red-brick church, and had fold-up seats as in a cinema. The vicarage was one of two dozen new houses on an adjacent estate where drugs and knife crimes were a constant problem.

'It will be a challenge to you, Derek,' said the Bishop, 'and I don't expect that Mrs Bolt will be too impressed, but—'

'It'll be fine, George, and I'm deeply grateful. Just so long as Miss Johnson can worship here as she has always done, without embarrassment, I'll gladly take up the challenge.'

And Daphne can like it or she can lump it, he thought silently.

CHAPTER TWELVE

Sister Iris Oates was unusually thoughtful. The North twins, Daisy and Danny, were progressing well and putting on weight, Jeremy had told her. He'd had no say in choosing names for them, which he only knew from their cot cards.

'It's a strange sensation, Iris, looking down on two new human beings, knowing that they're of your blood and wondering what in God's name lies ahead for them. No father that we know of, an absentee grandfather and a drunken uncle, a scatterbrained aunt and a nice little half-brother. They'll be brought up by their mother and grandmother, not much of a prospect.'

'You had no say whatsoever in their conception, Jeremy, so don't look on them as your responsibility.'

Iris spoke forcibly, unable to suppress her irritation at his constant concern for these babies. 'Let's face it, Jeremy, you were thrown out of that house, she physically attacked you, and if you went back there, you'd be thrown out again. You came to me that night because you had nowhere else to go – those were your own words, and I was so happy to be here for you – oh, Jeremy my love, *this* is your home!'

'I know, Iris, I know, I know,' he soothed, holding her in his arms and kissing her cheek. 'I don't know how I'd manage without you.'

Nor I without you, she thought silently. For Iris had a secret, a suspicion she would keep to herself for the time being, in case she was mistaken; but if it materialised, everything would be changed. Everything. She had missed her May period, and was waiting to see what June would bring or not bring. She would have to wait until she was absolutely certain before telling Jeremy of his latest responsibility, and to miss two periods would be confirmation enough. Now, if her suspicion was correct, he would be bound to her – and their child. O Lord, let it be!

When the doorbell rang, Shelagh's heart leapt, and she was suddenly breathless. Could it possibly be—?

It was. Leigh McDowall stood there on the doorstep, smiling at her. 'Shelagh.'

'Oh – Leigh! Are you coming in?' She held the door open, but he made no move.

'I – I'll be returning to work tomorrow,' she said, unable to think of what to say.

'I know, that's why I need to see you first.' She sensed there was something different about him; could it be hesitation, or even shyness? Surely not, a man as laid-back as McDowall. He went on, 'There's something I have to ask you, Shelagh.'

Her heart was thudding as she held on to the door handle. 'Aren't you coming in?' she repeated.

'Not until you give me an answer.'

'An answer to what?'

'Will you marry me, Shelagh?'

She drew a quick intake of breath. Was he serious or joking? She could not organise her thoughts, and the words that came out were, 'It's what my mother and aunt wanted.'

'Well, there you are, then – we can't go against their wishes, can we?'

'If you're serious, Leigh, then yes – oh, yes!' She held the door wide open, and he stepped across the threshold.

'Shelagh, my angel, my love.' She was enfolded in his arms, and all doubts, all misgivings were swept aside on an overwhelming tide of happiness. Her only surprise was that it had taken her so long to know her own heart.

'But Leigh, what about Tanya Dickenson?' she asked, drawing back a little.

'I've had a word with her, Shelagh – though she

was beginning to have her suspicions. There was never any engagement, or talk of one. I know I was wrong to act as if we were a couple, but that was because I was half crazy at the way Sykes took you for granted, and you let him. I suppose I wanted to show that I didn't care – talk about self-deception!'

'And I was so slow to realise that you were – that it was *you* I'd gradually begun to – to love over all these months. Oh, Leigh, how ashamed I was when you had to cover for me at New Year when I was back late, and the way you looked at me, despising me for it!'

'All in the past now, my angel, don't look back. Actually that actress has done me a favour, and let's hope she isn't too disappointed with her wonderful doctor! I've an idea that those two deserve each other, but that needn't worry us, my love, my angel who came to me just when I – and Denise North and her babies – most needed you.'

For the next few minutes there were no words but tender, joyful, astonished kisses, until he exclaimed, 'I must get to the office of the *Everham News* to put in this notice in time for tomorrow!'

'Notice? What notice?' she asked blankly.

'The notice of our engagement, of course – we want them all to read about it tomorrow, don't we?'

A shower of good wishes greeted Shelagh when she re-entered the maternity department the next day. Smiles, handshakes, kisses and a few naughty jokes expressed the delight of all, and Tanya Dickenson managed a smile and a nod that showed her goodwill. Laurie Moffatt was delighted, and the Rowans sent an engagement congratulations card.

In the staff canteen at lunchtime the ward sister of Women's Medical approached Shelagh with a certain diffidence.

'I hear that congratulations are in order, Dr Hammond,' she said. 'And I believe you're a friend of Sister Oates.'

'We sometimes work together in Outpatients,' said Shelagh warily, not willing to be drawn into any gossip about Iris.

'I wonder if she knows that Mrs Fiona North has been admitted to my ward with a severe cerebral haemorrhage. She's deeply unconscious, and the outlook isn't good. She may or may not come out of the coma, and even if she does it could leave her with a degree of hemiplegia and aphasia, unable to walk or speak. Terrible for the family, of course, the daughter's just had premature twins, and the husband walked out a few weeks ago. I wonder if you could let Sister Oates know if she doesn't know already?'

'Yes, I'll be seeing her this afternoon in the antenatal clinic,' said Shelagh, 'and I'll have a word. Thanks very much for telling me, Sister.'

In clinic that afternoon Sister Oates appeared much the same as usual, calm and quietly efficient; when the last patient had left the clinic, Shelagh suggested that they get a cup of tea from the Women's Royal Voluntary Service counter, and sit down for a talk. Surprised, Iris agreed, looking apprehensive.

'I take it that you've heard the latest news, Iris.'

'What latest news?' Iris was at once on the alert. 'Is it to do with those twins you delivered? I hear they're doing well.'

'No, m'dear, it's not the twins, it's their grandmother, Mrs North. She's had a stroke, and is in Women's Medical in a coma. She's—'

'What? *What* are you saying? Oh, Christ, what will he do? Is this true? Are you *sure?*'

Poor Iris Oates had no time for politeness, and leapt from the chair Shelagh had drawn up for her. Taken aback by this reaction, Shelagh too rose quickly, and tried to advise calmness, but Iris was in no mood to be soothed.

'I'm sorry, but I must go.' And still in uniform, she hurried from the outpatients hall.

'Jenny, he's *beautiful*,' said Phyllis Maynard in wonder, holding the baby on her lap and smiling down at him, receiving a cheeky, toothless smile in return. 'Yes, little fellow, I'm your granny, and we're going to see a lot of each other, aren't we? You know, Jenny I'm sure he knows who I am!'

'Whether he knows or not, Mum, he's certainly taken a fancy to you!' said Jenny, holding out a blue plastic rattle and watching Donovan stretching out chubby fingers for it.

'Ba-ba-ba-ba!' he said, and Jenny laughed.

'Look, he's blowing bubbles – who's a clever boy, then?'

Phyllis could not remember when she had last felt such happiness. If only Ben had lived to see this third grandchild, and yet she felt his presence in the room with her, and believed he shared her joy.

'We want Marion to be his godmother at the christening, and Tim's friend to be godfather – you know, he was best man at our wedding,' said Jenny.

'It'll have to be soon, before Derek Bolt leaves the parish,' said Phyllis. 'Isn't it a pity, so sudden and unexpected – I've heard his wife's furious.'

'Surely it can't be because of poor Miss Johnson, can it?' asked Jenny. 'I'm sure nobody blames him for what happened.'

'I'm afraid that a lot of his parishioners *do* think it was cruel and unnecessary to take her to court over it, and I'm sure he blames himself. Mary Whittaker thinks he's doing the right thing.'

'We must ask Mary to the christening,' said Jenny, 'because it was thanks to her handing us that cutting from the *Daily Mail* that set us off on the road to adoption – and to Donovan.'

'How do Tim's parents feel about it now?' asked Phyllis.

'Oh, they can't help loving him, can they? You

know Tim's father said he'd never be able to love a child that wasn't Tim's – and told us we didn't know what we were getting. Tim told him that *no* parents know what they're getting, I mean, just look at the way that awful North family has turned out! Anyway, now that they've seen Donovan, his Gifford granny and granddad think the world of him.'

Phyllis looked thoughtful. 'To be quite honest, I have to admit that I've felt sorry for Jeremy North, even though on the face of it he's a neglectful father and has taken advantage of Iris Oates – it's cut her off from taking the Sacrament in church, and makes her share in his—I wonder, does he ever consider the effect on her?' She sighed, but Donovan claimed her attention.

'Oh, look, Jenny, he's smacking his lips, and any minute now he's going to holler for his tea! You'd better take him and see if he needs changing, and I'll go to the kitchen and get him a drink and a rusk!'

Mother and daughter exchanged proprietary smiles over the adored baby who had come into their lives. I already love him as much as Marion's two, perhaps more, thought Phyllis in gratitude for this answer to her fervent prayers.

Jeremy North believed that his life had changed forever on the day he had left his family and gone to live with Iris Oates in her pleasant flat, her welcoming bed. He knew that he was breaking a commandment and causing her too to commit adultery, but such was the relief he found with her, the unreserved love that was like bread to a starving man, he could not in his heart believe that God condemned them. He felt no guilt, except in the case of Peter, his three-year-old grandson, soon to be four, the only family member whom he truly loved, and who loved him in return. He had approached Fiona by letter and by telephone, to request contact with the boy – to take him out occasionally, but had met with total refusal; Peter was to have no contact with that wicked woman, that slut he had chosen in preference to his duty to his own family. He told himself that when he was finally divorced from Fiona – and to date there had been no move on either side to commence proceedings – he would apply for legal access to his grandson, so that Iris could build up a relationship with the little boy.

Such had been his plan, such was his dream. Then had come the telephone call from the hospital to the school, and another frantic call from Denise; Mrs Whittaker had also telephoned, to make sure that he knew. Now as he stood beside the bed of his wife in a single room on Women's Medical, he realised that his life would have to change again. Fiona was deeply unconscious, and might not recover; without her presence in the home, how would his adult children cope, especially when the premature twins were discharged home with all their needs and necessities? Jeremy North's conscience could no longer be dismissed, and the way ahead now appeared frighteningly bleak.

And what about Iris? Sweet, adoring Iris who had withdrawn from the Sacrament because of him, as well as her place in the church choir; he trembled at the prospect of the pain he would have to inflict, and tried to pray for courage as he got into the car and headed for Number One Elm Grove.

He found that she already knew, and was home when he arrived, her face pale and anxious.

'Iris, my love.' It was all he could say at first, enfolding her in his arms. 'How did you hear?'

'Via the hospital grapevine – news travels fast. Jeremy, what are you going to do?'

'I've just come from seeing her, Iris. I went there straight from school. She's in a coma, and being fed through a tube down into her stomach. It doesn't look good, they say she's got a less than fifty-fifty chance of recovering, and even if she does, she's going to need a lot of care. She won't be able to carry the family around under her arm, as she has been doing, and it will be chaos.' He gave a groan.

'But they're *adults*, Jeremy, and they'll have to learn to stand on their own two feet!' protested Iris. 'And if you go back to those – those good-for-nothings, they'll expect you to take her place and hold their hands for evermore. Don't let them, Jeremy – you belong *here* now, with me!'

'I know, dearest, I know, but for the time being I'll

have to go back to see what's best to be done. Don't worry, I'll read them the riot act and won't stay a day longer than necessary.'

'How long?' He heard the note of urgency in her voice.

'I'll be back when things are sorted out – no, Iris, don't get into a state, you'll have to back me up and help me to do the right thing. We're both going to have to be brave, dearest.'

'I'll try – but you must promise me on your word of honour that you will come back to me. That's all I ask.'

'Thank you, my love, I promise. Only I'll have to go there straight away, you must see that.'

'Do you mean *now*? Can't you stay for supper – it's salmon salad and yoghurt.'

'I'll have to go, my love, to see how things are. And there's Peter-poppet.'

Yes, thought Iris, Peter-poppet. I've known that all along. 'Can't you bring him back with you? I can take unpaid leave to look after him till you break up for the summer holidays.'

'No, you've already done so much, Iris.' He straightened his back and spoke firmly. 'I have to go and see how things are. I'll phone as soon as I can.' He kissed her, and left her standing at the door as he got into his car and drove to his former home. Several people saw him, and noted that his car remained in the drive overnight. The word went round that

Jeremy North had come to his senses and was facing up to his responsibilities.

And Iris, because he had promised to return, and because she could not yet be one hundred per cent sure until three months from the date of her last period, kept her secret. She spent a restless night, imagining that he was being attacked and thrown out of the house again by his wife, miraculously recovered from her stroke; in the morning she felt nauseated, and could not eat any breakfast.

It was coffee time in Maternity, and the antenatal ward was quiet. Laurie Moffatt was full of the news that Roger Stedman had passed on to her.

'What do you think, girls, Diane Devlin's thirty-eight if she's a day!'

'How does he know that?' asked Tanya Dickenson, who with Staff Midwife Marie Burns listened eagerly.

'She was married to a policeman, and has got a son who's now eighteen!'

'Never!'

'It's the truth. They were divorced, and he's married again. The son lives with his father and stepmother who've had another couple of children. Diane has no contact with her son. It all came out when a national newspaper ran the story of her accident and engagement to the young surgeon who saved her life – or at least her leg! So the tabloids got busy digging up the details of her past!'

'Hm. Bit of a blow for Sykes, then,' said Marie. 'Did you hear that, Dr Hammond?' she asked Shelagh who had just entered the office.

'Hear what?'

They took great pleasure in repeating the news, and Shelagh raised her eyebrows. She could well believe it to be true, and wondered whether Diane had told Paul before the press caught up with her.

'What will Leigh McDowall say when he hears it?' asked Marie, glancing at Shelagh.

'Laugh like a drain, I should think,' said Elsie the auxiliary, coming in with the coffee tray, at which everybody chuckled, except for Dr Hammond who could not help reflecting on the man who had been her lover. Leigh had been talking about their future.

'We've both done our stint on obs and gynae now, my love, and I've been looking at general practices,' he had said. 'There are a few vacancies, including one in Essex, which sounds interesting. I've written off to ask for a few more details, and if they ask me for an interview, would you care to come along?'

'Anywhere in the world, Leigh, you know that.'

'Yes, but there's a bit of a problem, you see.'

'How do you mean?'

He deliberately put on a worried expression. 'Well, they'd want me to start as soon as possible, which means we would have to get married in a hurry.' Shelagh laughed.

'In that case, I suppose I'll have to make the best

of it and marry you, as long as you don't mind all the mental arithmetic, how many weeks, and so on.'

'Oh, bless you, Shelagh, my angel – oh, come here and let me—' There was no further need for words.

As soon as Jeremy North turned the key in the lock and entered the house, he was greeted by Peter-poppet, who cried and clung to his grandfather's leg.

'G'andad come home! Stay here, G'andad!'

Jeremy picked him up, and the little boy put his arms around his neck. In that moment Jeremy's future was sealed.

Denise and Catherine, their eyes red from crying, were making half-hearted attempts to tidy the house. There were unwashed dishes in the sink, the beds needed clean sheets and the soiled linen basket was filled to overflowing. Roy had come to visit his mother in hospital, and had looked in on his sisters hoping to be offered supper.

Still holding Peter, Jeremy spoke to the three of them. He did not raise his voice.

'Roy, have you still got that garage job, and are you still sharing a flat with your drinking companion?' When his son tentatively nodded, Jeremy continued, 'Then you can go straight back there, because I don't intend to keep you. Off you go.'

Roy did not argue, but obeyed with a grimace. Jeremy faced his daughters.

'Denise, you're to look after the home properly, and

care for your son. Daisy and Danny will be discharged from hospital at some point, and they'll be your responsibility round the clock. You either take care of them or they will be fostered out and put up for adoption. Catherine, you've got to get a job, any job, and stick to it, because you're going to have to earn your keep. I shall pay the bills and make an allowance for food and household requirements, nothing more.'

They stared at him, wide-eyed, and Catherine asked tearfully, 'What about Mum?'

'We don't know yet whether your mother will recover from the stroke, probably caused by slogging day after day for you lot, but if she does, she'll need a lot of care. Time will show. It's not going to be easy, and I shall expect you both to pull together and make a home fit for children to grow up in. *You* are going to have to grow up!'

There were tears and protests, but his words had sunk in. He ordered Denise to get supper ready; there were sausages in the fridge and potatoes in the vegetable rack – 'so we'll have bangers and mash this evening, and tomorrow you'll have to get out and do some sensible shopping, Denise.'

That was all. He had said his piece, and turned to Peter, who was smiling broadly.

'You heard what G'andad said, didn't you, Peter-poppet? No more tears, you'll be all right. G'andad's back with you again.'

* * *

It had to be by telephone.

'Iris, my love, I'm going to have to stay here for a while, until I get things straight. It's a mess, and—'

'How long will it take?' she asked.

'It could be a while. I've read them the riot act, but we'll have to see how things work out when Danny and Daisy are discharged. And we don't know yet about Fiona, whether it's the end or – Iris? Are you still there?'

'I'm here, Jeremy.'

'Did you hear what I've just been saying, dear?'

'Yes.' Her voice was flat.

'And you understand? You do see the position I'm in – my responsibilities – oh, Iris, I'm so sorry, so *sorry*.'

There was no answer, and he wondered again if she was still on the line, and then she spoke in the same flat monotone. 'It's Peter-poppet, isn't it?'

'I can't leave him here as things are, Iris. He needs me.'

'And I don't?'

'Iris, you'll have to be brave, and so must I. Look, I'll come over on Saturday morning to pick up a few things, clothes and stuff. If you'd prefer to be out while I'm there—'

'No, I'll be in while you're here.'

'All right, then. I'll drop in at about ten, if that's all right.'

'Nothing's all right, Jeremy, it's all wrong. But I'll be here.'

* * *

278

On Saturday morning he arrived at Number One Elm Grove at ten o'clock. She thought how strained he looked, his eyes shadowed by anxiety. He thought how pale she was.

'Iris, you're not taking proper care of yourself. I shall worry about you as well as all my other worries.'

'I have something to tell you, Jeremy.'

'Go on. What is it?'

She could have said that she was about ten weeks pregnant, but she chose a more old-fashioned way of telling him that message. 'I'm carrying your child.'

'What? *What?* But you can't be! I always used condoms, you know that!'

'Except for that first night, Jeremy, when you came to me because you had nowhere else to go. Those were your exact words. So, I lost my virginity and conceived a child at the same time.'

'Good God, Iris, what can I say, what can I do – oh, God, what a – you're absolutely sure?' he asked distractedly.

'Absolutely. It's due about the end of January.'

He clenched his fists and punched his head between them. 'Oh, you poor love, and all because of my carelessness. There must be something we can do – let me think – I know a doctor who runs a clinic in London. We were at university together, and I can look him up again. I'll get in touch straight away, and make an appointment. He – he'll attend to it, and I'll pay, of course.'

The look in her eyes was one that he did not recognise. 'I – I'll see to it, Iris,' he repeated, patting her shoulder reassuringly.

She drew back a little, and when she spoke, her voice was quiet and firm. 'If you think that I'm prepared to kill my child – the only child I'm ever likely to have, you can think again, Jeremy. I'm thirty-three, no beauty, and I've only had one lover – you. This baby may not be as precious to you as Peter, but it's all I've got left. I'm going to be a *mother*, Jeremy, and I'm determined to manage. I have a little money put by—'

'I'll make you an allowance, Iris, it's the least I can do – oh, my God,' he babbled like a man demented.

'You won't have much money left after all the demands of your family. I can claim six months' maternity leave, and then I'll go back to work to pay for childcare.'

'I'll pay for that,' he said at once. 'Will you – will you stay in Everham?'

'I don't see why not. I have friends here, I have this very nice flat, and I enjoy my work in Outpatients.'

'But there'll be such a scandal, Iris, all the talk—'

'This has been a year for scandals, what with us and Mr Bolt and Mr Profumo – I don't mind in the least about having one more. There was talk enough when you left home and came to me, and there'll be more talk now that you've gone home and left me with a baby. They can talk their heads off, but why should *I* be dismayed?'

* * *

The wedding of Dr Shelagh Hammond to Dr Leigh McDowall was fixed for Saturday, August the seventeenth, to be held at St Matthew's church; Shelagh knew that her mother would have wanted her to be married at the Convent Chapel of Our Lady of Pity six miles away, but being no longer a practising Catholic, she preferred to stay in Everham where most of her friends were. Her aunt Maura Carlin would be the only relative there to see her married, but there were numerous friends to wish her well.

'It'll be a bit awkward, my parents being divorced,' Leigh told her. 'My dad's remarried, and he and his wife will be coming, but so will my mother who lives on her own up in Cheshire. My brother Andrew says he'll bring her down with his wife and young son, but there isn't much love lost between my mother and Dad and his wife. The atmosphere could turn a little frosty.'

'Families!' exclaimed Shelagh. 'It's such a pity, when ex-wives and ex-husbands have to face each other at the weddings of their grown children – but think of all the *friends* who'll be coming, Leigh. *Two* consultants, Mr Kydd and Mr Fielding and their registrars, that will make an impression!'

'Did you by any chance send an invitation to our friend Sykes?' asked Leigh curiously.

'Yes, I did, but he's declined and sent a cheque for twenty-five pounds as a present,' she answered with a slight shrug. 'Things aren't going too well there, I hear. Diane Devlin's filming on location somewhere in the West Country, and her new leading man's got his eye on her, according to Laurie Moffatt. Poor old Paul.'

'Poor old Paul, my foot! It was inevitable that she wouldn't hang around with him once she got back in front of the cameras. And yet – yes, I suppose I *am* a bit sorry for the silly chump, when I think of what he's lost and I've gained!'

'Iris! So glad to find you in. I wasn't sure when you had your half-day, and I've had such an abundance of sweet peas this year, I'm giving them away by the bunch. Here are yours!'

'That's kind of you, Phyllis,' said Iris, guessing the real reason for this visit. 'I'll put them in water – mmmmm, what a delicious scent! Would you like a cup of tea?'

'If you're having a brew, yes, that would be lovely,' said Phyllis Maynard, slightly taken aback by Iris's calmness, having come expecting to offer a shoulder to cry on. When the tea was poured, she spoke of her grandson Donovan and the happiness he had brought to the family. Iris smiled and said she was happy for them all.

It was time for Phyllis to put down her cup and address the real matter in hand.

'Iris, dear, how are you? I've heard the latest

news, of course, we all have, and I just want to know how you're coping.' She looked into Iris's face, half expecting her to start crying, or embarking on a tale of loss and betrayal, perhaps bitterness at Jeremy North's desertion of her. But Iris remained calm.

'Thank you, Phyllis, but you can go back to St Matthew's and tell them that I'm fine.'

'Oh, Iris my dear, I'm so glad to hear that!' exclaimed Phyllis sincerely. 'It's good, of course, that he has, er, gone back, but I'm equally concerned about you. You've got your work at the hospital, and the church—' She broke off, remembering that Iris had not been seen at church since Jeremy's departure. 'You're not planning to move, then?'

'No, why should I?'

'Good. You'll find that people are mostly sympathetic, though we believe that, er, Mr North has done the right thing.'

There was an awkward silence while they drank their tea. Then Iris spoke again.

'I wonder how sympathetic they'll be when they know the consequence of his time spent here with me.'

'What consequence?' asked Phyllis in some bewilderment, and Iris looked down at her body, then raised her head again.

'What do you – oh, my dear, you surely don't mean—'

'Yes, I'm expecting a baby, Phyllis, due early in the New Year. I shall become a mother, and I intend to keep my child, come what may, whatever difficulties there may be.'

Phyllis Maynard was so astonished that she could only stare for a minute, and then found her voice.

'Will your parents help you?'

'I'm not going to ask them for help, Phyllis. They'll be horrified when they eventually find out, because even in this day and age, there's still a stigma attached to illegitimacy.' She gave a half smile. 'This will be yet another scandal, but my mind's completely made up, and I shan't ask Jeremy North for a penny – he's got more immediately pressing responsibilities.'

'Oh, my dear, Iris my *dear*, what a *tragedy*, when you and he were so much happier, and—' Words failed Phyllis Maynard.

'Thank you, Phyllis, I appreciate that. But he's had to go back, and my life will completely change. I feel better each day, so please don't worry about me. As I said to Jeremy, why should *I* be dismayed?'

The August sun shone on the last week of Derek Bolt's ministry at St Matthew's Everham, which was remembered for a popular wedding and a christening. The marriage of two doctors took place on the Saturday, and not only Everham Hospital staff but a fair number of ex-patients, some with their babies, turned out to attend the ceremony and see the bride in her powder-blue dress and jacket and flowery hat; the groom wore a grey suit with a white carnation in his buttonhole, and a tie with rainbow colours. Mr North played the organ accompaniment to the one hymn, 'The King of Love My Shepherd Is', and their happiness radiated out to friends and family, healing the rift between the groom's divorced parents, at least for the day of their son's wedding.

Mrs Maynard and her friend Mrs Whittaker attended the ceremony, but politely declined a general invitation to the buffet set out in the hospital boardroom.

'I thought Mr North looked rather grim,' remarked Phyllis. 'He didn't smile once.'

'Ah, but he's doing his duty, and that's what matters,' replied Mary. 'He's got a big burden to carry, with Fiona in a wheelchair and carers going in each day. Denise has a specially trained health visitor calling to check on the twins, and I've fixed them up with a home help three times a week.'

'What about the son?' asked Phyllis.

'Roy's going to Alcoholics Anonymous, and Jeremy told me that he hopes he'll be reunited with his wife eventually, and their poor little girl.'

'Frankly, my sympathies are more with Iris Oates,' said Phyllis, but Mary did not agree.

'She and Jeremy are both to blame for her pregnancy, but I think it's wrong of her to stay in Everham, announcing her condition to all and sundry when she starts to show.'

'I wish her well,' insisted Phyllis, and their talk

turned to the christening of Phyllis's grandson on the following day at the morning service. It was the Revd Derek Bolt's last duty as vicar at St Matthew's, and his farewell to Everham; a large turnout was expected, and a buffet lunch was prepared in the church hall.

Once again Mr North was at the organ, playing 'All Things Bright and Beautiful', and especially for Donovan Gifford, 'To Be a Pilgrim'. Many handkerchiefs were needed when the little smiling boy was held up in his godmother's arms to be baptised and welcomed into the church.

After the service Jeremy North sought out Derek Bolt, alone in the vestry before joining the congregation in the hall.

'So, time to say farewell, Rev,' he said. 'You'll be missed.'

'On the contrary, most of this lot will be glad to see the back of me,' Derek answered wryly.

'Don't be daft, there's a lot of goodwill towards you. I, on the other hand, have to stay in Everham and face the music, a whole orchestra of it.'

'You're doing the right thing, though, and so am I, that's all that really matters,' said Derek, and added, 'I noticed Iris in church this morning, and looking very well, I thought. Happy. Nice to see her back again.'

Jeremy winced, for seeing Iris and knowing that she would bear his child was the hardest part of his self-imposed duty.

Derek continued, 'Anyway, old chap, God go with you and, er, the family.'

'D'you think he will? Is he there? God, I mean.'

'Oh, he's there all right, he doesn't leave us in peace. He's the voice of conscience who's brought us both to where we are today.'

'Dishing out prizes and kicks up the arse, as appropriate.'

Derek suddenly grinned. 'God bless us *all*, old chap. We're going to need it!' He held out his hand which North clasped warmly.

'Goodbye, then, Jeremy. Be happy.'

'You too. And good luck.'